A LADY OF NOTORIETY

Diane Gaston

Published in Great Britain 2014
by Mills & Boon, an imprint of Harlequin (UK) Limited,
Eton House, 18-24 Paradise Road, Richmond, Surrey, TW9 1SR

© 2014 Diane Perkins

ISBN: 978 0 263 90967 8

Harlequin (UK) Limited's policy is to use papers that are natural, renewable and recyclable products and made from wood grown in sustainable forests. The logging and manufacturing processes conform to the legal environmental regulations of the country of origin.

Printed and bound in Spain
by Blackprint CPI, Barcelona

As a psychiatric social worker, **Diane Gaston** spent years helping others create real-life happy endings. Now Diane crafts fictional ones, writing the kind of historical romance she's always loved to read. The youngest of three daughters of a US Army Colonel, Diane moved frequently during her childhood, even living for a year in Japan. It continues to amaze her that her own son and daughter grew up in one house in Northern Virginia. Diane still lives in that house, with her husband and three very ordinary housecats. Visit Diane's website at http://dianegaston.com

AUTHOR NOTE

Beauty and redemption. Two subjects that continue to fascinate me.

Can people truly change or are their characters fixed for life?

I believe in change. I believe any of us can overcome past mistakes, past weaknesses, past faults, and strive to become better people.

Beautiful people, though, may have a more difficult path than the more ordinary of us. Prized, cosseted, celebrated for their appearance alone... I believe beautiful people have fewer opportunities to face their imperfections. I suspect it is more difficult for them to learn and grow into better people.

In my previous *The Masquerade Club* book, A MARRIAGE OF NOTORIETY, a beautiful lady tries to wreck the marriage of a man she's long desired. As a result she creates a destruction that might be devastating. Can such a woman learn from that experience? Can she redeem herself? And can any man truly believe in her redemption and love the woman she strives to be inside?

Read on and see.

Dedication

To Catherine, a beautiful friend in all ways.

Chapter One

~~~~~~~~~~

Ramsgate, Kent—April 1821

'My lady! My lady! Wake up! Fire!'

Daphne, Lady Faville, jolted awake at her maid's cries. Smoke filled her nostrils and stung her eyes. Shouts and pounding on doors sounded in the hallway of the Ramsgate inn.

'Fire! Get out,' a man's voice boomed.

Fire. Her biggest fear.

Daphne leaped out of bed and shoved her feet into slippers. Her maid began gathering their belongings, stuffing them into a portmanteau.

'Leave them, Monette.' Daphne seized her coin purse and threw her cloak around her shoulders. Her heart raced. 'We must go now!'

She reached for the door latch, but her maid pulled her arm away.

'Wait! The hall may be on fire.' The maid pressed her hand against the door. 'It is not hot. It is safe.' She opened the door.

It was not safe.

The hallway was filled with smoke, and tongues of flame licked the walls here and there, as if sneaking up from below. In a moment the wallpaper would curl and burn. The fire would grow. It could engulf them.

Daphne saw a vision of another time, another fire. Her heart pounded. Was she to die in flames after all?

'Keep your skirts away from the fire,' she cried to Monette.

They moved blindly ahead, down the long hallway, through its fiery gauntlet.

'Hurry, Monette.' She took the maid's hand and lamented asking the innkeeper for rooms that were as private as possible.

Their rooms were far from the stairway.

'Someone is in the hallway. At the end,' a man's voice cried.

Through the grey smoke he emerged, an apparition rushing towards them. He grabbed them both and half-carried them through the hallway past other men who were knocking on doors, and other residents emerging in nightclothes.

They reached the stairway and he pushed Monette forwards. The girl ran down the stairs. Daphne shrank back. The flames below were larger, more dangerous.

'I'll get you through.' The man gathered her up in his arms and carried her down the three flights of stairs. She buried her face in his chest, too afraid to see the fire so close.

Suddenly the air cooled and she could breathe again. They were outside. He set her down and her maid ran to her, hugging her in relief. They were alive! Daphne swung back to thank the man who rescued them.

He was already running back into the fire.

Her footman appeared. 'You are safe, m'lady. Come away from the building.'

He brought them to where a group of people in various stages of undress huddled together.

'I must go back to the buckets.' He looked apologetic.

'Yes, Carter. Yes,' Daphne agreed. 'Help all you can.'

He ran to the brigade passing buckets of water to the fire. Other men led horses out of the stables and rolled coaches away from the burning building.

Daphne's eyes riveted on the doorway, willing their rescuer to reappear. Other men carried people out, but she did not see him. She'd not seen his face, but she knew she would recognise him. Tall, dark haired and strong. He wore the dark coat and fawn pantaloons of a gentleman.

Finally he appeared, two children tucked under his arms and a frantic mother following behind.

Daphne took a step forwards, eager to speak to him, to thank him. To her shock, he ran towards the door again. One of the other men seized his arm, apparently trying to stop him, but the man shrugged him off and rushed back inside.

Daphne's hand flew over her mouth. *Please, God, let him come out again.*

An older gentleman approached her. 'Lady Faville?'

She wanted to watch for her rescuer, not engage in conversation.

'Do you remember me?' he asked.

She presumed he was someone she'd met in London. 'I am sorry. I do not—'

He looked disappointed. 'I am Lord Sanvers. We met several times at the Masquerade Club.'

The Masquerade Club?

It was a place she wanted to forget, the London gambling house where players could gamble in masks to protect their identity. It was also the place she almost destroyed.

By fire.

'It is two years since I attended there,' she answered him. 'There were so many gentlemen I met.'

It was inadequate as an apology. Surely he—and everyone—knew that she'd been obsessed by only one man, a man who would never love her. She'd fled to the Continent and eventually to Switzerland and Fahr Abbey. The abbey had become her retreat and her salvation, chosen by whim because its name was similar to her husband's title name and the name of the village where she'd once felt secure. At Fahr Abbey, though, she'd come face-to-face with her failings.

But could she change?

Could she be as selfless as her brave rescuer?

Minutes seemed like hours, but he finally emerged again, leading two more people to safety. The fire intensified, roaring now like a wild beast. Were there more people inside? Would he risk his life again?

He ran back to the fire and was silhouetted inside the doorway when a huge rush of glowing embers fell from the ceiling. The building groaned, as if in the throes of death. Timbers fell from the roof and the man's arms rose in front of his face. Daphne watched in horror as one large flaming timber knocked him to the floor.

'No!' Without thinking, she ran towards him.

Other men reached him first, pulling him by his clothing until he was in the yard. The building collapsed entirely.

Daphne knelt down next to him as they brushed away glowing cinders from his coat and patted out smoking cloth.

'Is he alive?' she cried.

They rolled him on his back, and one man put a finger to the pulse in his neck. 'He's alive for now.'

Daphne gasped. 'I know him!'

Though his face was dark with soot and pink

with burns, she recognised him. He was Hugh Westleigh, younger brother of the new Earl of Westleigh. He was also the brother of the lady she'd so terribly wronged at the Masquerade Club.

Had he arrived on the packet from Calais, as she had? Or was he bound there? Either way, she suspected he would not have liked seeing her after all the trouble she'd caused.

He was not conscious, and that alarmed her.

'We'd better carry him to the surgeon,' one of the men said.

They lifted him. Daphne followed them.

Her maid and footman caught up to her. Monette's eyes were wide. 'My lady?'

'I know this man,' she explained. 'I must see he receives care. Wait for me here.'

They carried him to what looked like a nearby shopfront. Inside several people sat on benches while one man, the surgeon apparently, bandaged burns.

'We have a bad one here, Mr Trask.'

The surgeon waved a man off the chair where he'd been tending to him and gestured for the men to sit Westleigh in it. He was still limp.

Daphne wrung her hands. 'Will he live?'

'I do not know, ma'am,' the surgeon said.

'He was hit on the head,' she said. 'I saw it.'

The man checked Westleigh's head. 'Appears to be so.'

Westleigh groaned and Daphne released a pent-up breath.

The surgeon lifted his head. 'Wake up, sir.' He turned to Daphne. 'What is his name?'

'Mr Westleigh,' she said. 'He is the younger brother of the Earl of Westleigh.'

'Is he?' One of the men who had carried him in raised his brows. 'Who would have expected it of the Quality? The man has pluck.'

'Westleigh!' The surgeon raised his voice. 'Wake up.'

He groaned again.

'Open your eyes.'

Westleigh tried to comply, straining. He winced and tried to rub his eyes. 'I cannot…'

Thank God he could speak.

The surgeon pulled his hands away. 'Do not do that. Let me look.' He examined Westleigh's eyes and turned to Daphne. 'His eyes are cloudy. Damaged from the fire.' He tilted Westleigh's head back and rinsed his eyes with clear water from a nearby pitcher. 'His eyes must stay bandaged for two weeks or he will lose his sight.' He shrugged. 'He may lose his sight no matter what, but sometimes the eyes heal remarkably well. I'm more concerned about his head. He is certainly concussed. He needs to be cared for.'

'In what way?' Daphne asked.

'He needs rest and quiet. No excitement at all. For at least a week.' He looked into Westleigh's mouth and in his nose. 'No bleeding. That is good.'

'Head hurts,' Westleigh mumbled.

The surgeon folded bandages over Westleigh's eyes and wrapped his head to keep them in place. No sooner had he finished than another victim of the fire was brought in, covered with burns. The surgeon's attention immediately went to his new patient. 'I must see this man.' He waved Daphne away. 'Keep his eyes bandaged and keep him quiet. No travelling. He must stay quiet.'

Daphne dropped some coins from her purse on the table. The surgeon deserved payment.

The man who had carried Westleigh to the surgeon got him to his feet. 'Come along, sir.' He turned to Daphne. 'Follow me.'

He must think she was in Westleigh's party.

They walked out of the building into a day just beginning to turn light.

Carter, her footman, ran up to her. 'M'lady, John Coachman found a stable for the horses. He and your maid are waiting with the carriage, which was left near the inn.'

The man assisting Westleigh strained with the effort to keep him upright. 'Give us a hand, would you?' he asked her footman. Carter rushed to help him, but the man handed off his burden entirely. 'I must see to my own family, ma'am.' He pulled on his forelock and hurried away.

Westleigh moaned.

'What do I do with him?' Carter shifted to get a better hold on Westleigh.

Daphne's mind was spinning. 'Take him to the carriage, I suppose. We must find someone to care for him.'

Men were still busy at the inn, extinguishing embers, salvaging undamaged items, of which there were very few. Daphne's and her maid's trunks had been with the carriage, so they had lost only what had been in their portmanteaux.

Carter and John Coachman helped Westleigh into the carriage.

'Is he coming with us?' Monette asked.

'Oh, no,' Daphne replied. 'He would detest that. He must have been travelling with someone. We should find out who.' She turned to Carter. 'Can you ask, please? His name is Hugh Westleigh, Lord Westleigh's brother.'

Westleigh stirred and tried to pull at the bandages covering his eyes.

'No, Westleigh!' Daphne climbed inside the carriage and pulled his hands away. 'You must not touch your bandages.' She arranged the pillows and rugs to make him more comfortable.

'Thirsty,' Westleigh mumbled.

How thoughtless of her. He must have a raging thirst after all his exertion.

'Monette, find him some ale and something nourishing.' What ought an injured man eat? She had no idea, but dug into her purse again and

handed both her maid and footman some coins.
'Both of you buy something for yourselves to
eat and drink and bring something back for John
Coachman, as well.'

Monette returned within a quarter-hour with
food and drink from a nearby alehouse for
Westleigh and the coachman.

'They have a room where we might change
clothes,' she told Daphne. 'I paid for it and for a
meal, so that we can eat privately.'

It was better than eating in the carriage on the
street with the smell of ashes still in the air.

'I'll tend to the gentleman, m'lady,' John
Coachman said. 'I must watch the carriage in
any event. He'll be comfortable enough inside,
with your pillows and all.'

Monette climbed on top of the carriage and
retrieved clothing from the trunks, rolling them
into a bundle. She led Daphne to the alehouse,
about two streets away.

The place was crowded with people in various
stages of dress and from various walks of life,
who had all apparently escaped the fire. Daphne
followed Monette through the throng. The smell
of sweat, smoke and ale made Daphne's empty
stomach roil.

Surely a lady of her stature should not be required to endure this sort of place.

She placed her hand over her mouth.

The words of the abbess at Fahr came back to her. *You must practise compassion for all people, my lady. We are all God's children.*

The dear abbess. The nuns at Fahr had told her the abbess was very old, but to Daphne she'd seemed ageless. For some unfathomable reason the abbess had bestowed her love and attention on Daphne.

Her eyes filled with tears. The woman's death had been a terrible blow, worse than her own mother's death, worse than her husband's. She could not bear to stay at Fahr after such a loss.

At least the abbess's words remained with her. Sometimes, when Daphne needed her words, it was almost as if the woman were at her side, whispering in her ear.

Daphne glanced around once more and tried to see the people in the alehouse through the abbess's eyes. Most looked exhausted. Some appeared close to despair. Others wore bandages on their arms or hands.

Daphne ached for them.

More truthfully, a part of her felt sorrow for their suffering; another part was very grateful to have been spared their troubles.

As they reached the door to the private room, a gentleman rose from a booth where he'd sat alone. He was the gentleman who had spoken to her before, who remembered her from the Masquerade Club. What was his name?

Lord Sanvers.

'My good lady. There you are. I was concerned about you.' His silver hair was neatly combed and he appeared to have changed into fresh linen. Compared to the others he was pristine.

'I am unharmed, sir.'

He blocked her way. 'May I assist you in any way? I am at your disposal.'

He could take charge of Westleigh! Would that not be a better situation for everyone?

She glanced at the booth Lord Sanvers had all to himself and to the numbers of people who did not even have a chair.

Would he have extended his offer of help if she had not been the beautiful, wealthy widow of a viscount?

She curtsied to him. 'My servants have seen to everything, sir, but I thank you.'

She walked past him and through the open door where Monette waited.

Once inside the room, Daphne collapsed onto a chair in relief.

And guilt.

Why should she have this private room and so many others so much less? Was she just as selfish as Lord Sanvers?

She hurriedly changed out of her nightclothes and into the dress Monette had pulled from her trunk. Monette did the same. After quickly eating a breakfast, she handed the innkeeper money and asked him to give the room and some food to those most in need. She and Monette did not stay to see if he honoured her request.

They left the alehouse and returned to the carriage.

Carter waited there with the coachman.

'Did you find Mr Westleigh's travelling companions?' Daphne peeked in the carriage, but saw Westleigh lying against the pillows.

'I found the innkeeper, m'lady,' Carter told her. 'He said that Mr Westleigh travelled alone. Not even with a manservant.'

Who would care for him, then?

'How is he?' she asked her coachman.

'Sleeping,' he answered. 'Talking a bit and restless, but sleeping. He did drink the ale, though.'

Daphne glanced around. 'We must find someone to care for him.'

Carter shook his head. 'I believe that cannot be done. There were many people injured in the fire and many others displaced. It would be difficult to even find him a room. Or rooms for ourselves.'

'We should leave today, then, m'lady,' John Coachman said. 'If we start soon we can find lodgings on the road and still reach Faville the day after tomorrow.'

It would take three days for them to reach her property in Vadley near Basingstoke. Her husband had left her the unentailed country house and estate instead of consigning her to the dower house in Faville. She'd spent very little time in Vadley, though, only a few weeks past her days of mourning. Now she planned to return and live a retired life. Whether by doing so she could atone for her days of vanity and thoughtlessness, she was not certain.

'We cannot take him with us,' she said.

But she could hear the abbess, clucking her tongue. *You must find grace to help in time of need.*

'The surgeon said he cannot travel,' she protested.

'We don't have a choice, m'lady,' Carter said in a low voice.

'I say we start out and ask at every posting inn until we find someone to care for him,' her coachman added. 'It will be a more practicable task once we are out of Ramsgate.'

'We cannot leave him.' Monette's eyes pleaded.

These servants were prepared to take care of a stranger, but she was merely trying to think of a way to abandon him, just because she knew he would hate being cared for by a lady who'd wronged his sister.

Or was she merely thinking of her own discomfort?

You must find grace to help in time of need.

'Very well.' She nodded decisively. 'But let us head towards London. I am certain his family will be in town. When we find a place for his recuperation, we can send for them and they will not have far to travel. Or if we fail to find him care, we will take him the whole way.' It would mean not even two full days of travel.

By late afternoon they'd not found any suitable place for Westleigh, nor had they found anyone willing to take responsibility for his care. Worse, it became clear he could not travel another day to reach London.

The ride had been a nightmare. The coach jostled him and he cried out in pain. He woke often, but was feverish and disoriented and difficult to calm.

They managed to reach Thurnfield, a small village on the road to Maidstone. Its one inn could not accommodate them, but the innkeeper knew of a cottage to let nearby. Daphne signed the papers and paid the rent. Before they set out the short distance to the cottage, she spoke to Carter, John Coachman and Monette.

'I told the leasing agent that I am Mrs Asher, not Lady Faville. I think Mr Westleigh will be more comfortable if he does not know it is me seeing to his care. He only knows me as Lady Faville, you see, and—and his family has reason to dislike me. He would be quite displeased if he knew Lady Faville was caring for him.' She took a breath and rubbed her forehead. 'Asher was my maiden name, so we would not really be lying to anyone....'

Who was she fooling? She was lying to herself as well as lying about her true identity.

Had not the abbess said she must break herself of telling falsehoods as a means of avoiding unpleasantness? Even if the lies were little ones.

She would do so, she vowed.

Next time.

She swallowed more guilt. 'Try to remember to call me Mrs Asher and don't call me m'lady, if you can help it.'

The three servants nodded agreeably.

Was she wrong to make them go along with her lie? Of course she was.

'It will be as you wish it, m'lady,' Carter said. 'I mean, ma'am.'

'Let us go, then.' She allowed Carter to assist her into the carriage. Monette climbed in after her and Carter sat with John Coachman.

They drove the short distance to a white stucco cottage with well-tended shrubbery and a small stable for the horses.

Carter opened the carriage door and put down the step. Daphne and Monette climbed out as the housekeeper and caretaker walked out to greet them.

'We are Mr and Mrs Pitts, ma'am,' the caretaker said. 'At your service.'

'I am Mrs Asher,' Daphne shook their hands,

feeling only a twinge of guilt. She introduced the others. 'We have an injured man with us. Mr Westleigh. He will need to be taken to a bed-chamber as quickly as possible.'

The housekeeper gestured to the door. 'Come in, then, Mrs Asher, and tell us which room shall be the gentleman's.'

Leaving Monette to watch over Westleigh, and Carter and Mr Pitts to unload the trunks, Daphne followed the housekeeper inside. The decor was modest, but luxurious if she compared it to Fahr Abbey. They should do very nicely there. It would only be for a day or two, until Westleigh's family could come.

'Let us look at the bedchambers.' Mrs Pitts started up the stairs. 'You may pick which one should go to the gentleman.'

Carter and Mr Pitts entered.

'We have Mr Westleigh's trunk,' Carter said.

'Follow us.' Daphne walked up the stairs.

She chose the nicest of the bedchambers for Westleigh. It was a corner room with windows on both sides to let in lots of light and fresh air.

'Does the bed have fresh linens?' she asked.

'Indeed,' responded Mrs Pitts. 'We readied the rooms when the agent sent a message that you were to arrive right away.'

That was what a good housekeeper should do, Daphne thought. She'd learned, though, that even servants liked to be thanked.

'How very good of you.' She smiled at Mrs Pitts and turned towards Carter. 'Bring him here.'

He and Mr Pitts set down the trunk and left the room.

'Do you wish to see the rest of the house now?' Mrs Pitts asked Daphne.

'I will see the gentleman settled first,' she replied.

'Let me see to the meal, then, ma'am.'

Mrs Pitts left and a few moments later, the men helped Westleigh to the bed.

'Where am I?' Westleigh asked, tense and confused. 'Where have you taken me?'

Daphne came to his side and touched his hand. 'You are in a cottage on the road to Maidstone.' She used her most soothing voice.

'Not going to Maidstone. Going to London.' He tried to stand.

Daphne put a hand on his shoulder and he sat again. 'You are too ill to travel to London.' She had been making explanations like this for the past two hours—every time he woke and did not know where he was. 'You were in a fire and you injured your eyes and your head. You need to rest in this bed here and we will care for you until you are better. Then you will go to London.'

'Rest?' He relaxed. 'Then London.'

Carter spoke. 'You should leave the room, m'l—Mrs Asher, while I undress him.'

She turned to the housekeeper's husband.

'Would you bring him water? Soap and towels, too, if possible, so Carter can bathe him a little? I am certain he will be more comfortable when clean again. Be gentle with his face, though.'

'Water, soap and towels are already here, ma'am.' The man pointed to a chest of drawers upon which sat a pitcher and basin and folded towels. He left the room.

Carter spoke. 'I'll clean him up, ma'am. Leave him to me.'

Daphne moved her hand, planning to step away, but Westleigh groped for it and seized it, pulling her back. 'Do not leave,' he rasped. 'Do not leave me alone.'

His firm grip and his intensity shook her. She did not know how to calm him.

She stroked his hair—what little hair was not covered by bandages. 'Shh, now,' she said, trying to sound like the abbess who'd soothed her when she'd become overwrought. 'You are not alone. Carter is here.'

'I am here, sir,' Carter said.

Daphne continued. 'Now remain still and Carter will take off your boots. Will that not feel more comfortable?'

'I'll give you a little wash and put you in clean bedclothes,' Carter added.

Daphne felt Westleigh's muscles relax.

'Do not wear bedclothes,' he murmured.

Chapter Two

The dragon pursued him, its fiery breath scorching his skin. Stinging his eyes.

Hugh pushed himself to run faster, to escape.

The way out was ahead, a pinpoint of light that seemed to become more distant the harder he pumped his legs to reach it. The flames roared, as if the dragon laughed at him. The blaze encircled him, bound him. Devoured him.

He jolted awake.

To darkness.

He sat up and his hands groped for his eyes. 'I can't see! Why can't I see?' His eyes were covered in cloth.

Then he remembered. The fire had not been a dream. It had burned his eyes, all brightness and pain. Was he blind?

'The bandages. Take them off!' He pulled at them.

There was a rustle of fabric and the scent of roses filled his nostrils. Cool hands clasped his.

'Your eyes are injured.' The voice was feminine and soothing, but not familiar. 'The bandages need to stay on for you to heal.'

'Who are you?' He swallowed. His throat hurt when he spoke.

'I—I am Mrs Asher. You carried me out of the fire—'

He remembered only one woman he'd carried out of the fire, down the flame-filled stairway, all the way to the cool night outside.

'Where am I?' he rasped.

'You—you are in my cottage in—in Thurnfield.'

Thurnfield?

The village on the road to London? He'd passed through it many times.

She went on. 'You cannot travel, so we brought you here.'

That made no sense. 'I was in Ramsgate. If I cannot travel, how is it I came to Thurnfield?'

Her voice turned cautious. 'We could not find a place for you in Ramsgate. Not one where you could receive care.'

She was caring for him? Who was this woman? He wanted to see her. Look her in the eye. Figure out the reason for the uneasiness in her voice.

But that was impossible.

He cleared his throat. 'You said *we.*'

'My maid and footman and me.'

She had a maid and a footman. A woman of some means, then. Of wealth? Were there more servants, perhaps? 'A maid and footman. Who else is here?'

'A housekeeper and her husband.' She paused. 'That is all.'

Modest means, then, but she was holding back something, he would bet on it. 'Where is Mr Asher?'

'I am a widow.' Her voice turned low, and that provoked a whole new set of emotions.

He suddenly recalled that the woman he'd carried had weighed hardly more than a whisper. She'd curled trustingly against his chest, hiding her face from the fire.

He cursed the bandages covering his eyes. He wanted to see her. Face her like a man.

'My name is Westleigh.' He extended his hand, which seemed to float in empty space.

She grasped it.

Her hand felt soft, like the hand of a gently bred woman.

'I know who you are,' she said, her voice turning tight again. 'We learned at the inn that you are Mr Hugh Westleigh. We have your trunk. Like ours, it was with the carriages and spared from the fire.'

Had she also learned he was the younger brother of the Earl of Westleigh? Was this a factor in bringing him here?

If only he could look into her eyes—he could read her character.

If only he could see.

He pressed the bandages covering his eyes. The pain grew sharper.

A soft, cool hand drew his fingers away as it had done before. 'Please do not disturb your bandages. The surgeon said your eyes are to remain bandaged for two weeks. That is how long they will take to heal.'

'Will they heal, then?' he demanded. 'Or am I to be blind?'

She did not answer right away. 'The surgeon said they must stay bandaged or they will not heal. That much is certain. He said they could heal, though.'

Hugh laughed drily. '*Could* heal. That is not very reassuring.'

Her voice turned low again. 'I am only repeating what he told me.'

He caught himself. She obviously had taken on the task of caring for him. He need not be churlish in return.

He lifted his throbbing head again and turned in the direction of her voice. 'Forgive me. I do not customarily succumb to self-pity.'

'Of course you do not.' Now she sounded like his old governess. 'Are you thirsty?'

Good of her to change the subject.

He was thirsty, by God. Parched.

He nodded.

He heard a swirl of her skirts again and the

sound of pouring liquid. She lifted his hand and placed a glass in it. He took a sip.

It was water, flavoured with a touch of mint. Who took such trouble for a stranger?

He gulped it down. 'Is there more?'

He held out the empty glass, again into nothingness. He waited for her to grasp it.

She took it and poured more, then again put it in his hand.

He drank and handed the glass back to her. 'I detest feeling so helpless.'

'Certainly you do,' the *governess* responded. 'But you must rest. You not only burned your eyes, you also suffered a blow to the head. The surgeon said you need rest to recover.'

He lay back against some pillows. The mere exertion of waking in strange surroundings and drinking two glasses of water had fatigued him. How annoying. How weak. He hated weakness.

'Shall I bring you breakfast?' she asked. 'Or would you like to sleep some more?'

His stomach clenched at the mention of food.

He forced his raspy voice to remain calm. 'Breakfast, if you would be so good.'

Again her skirts rustled. 'I will be right back.'

Without his eyes, he must depend on this woman for food, for everything. How much more helpless could he be?

Her footsteps receded and a door opened.

When he heard it close again, it was as if the room turned cold and menacing.

He'd never been afraid of darkness as a child. He'd never been afraid of anything, but this was a living nightmare. Had he traded the fiery dragon of his dream for darkness?

Blindness?

Carefully he felt his bandages. They were thick over his eyes and wound firmly around his head. He tried to open his eyelids, but they hardly moved, the bandages were so snug. The effort shot daggers through his eyeballs and he dared not try again lest he injure them even more.

Was his fate to be blind and helpless?

He pounded a fist on the mattress, but wished he could put his hands on something he could smash into a thousand pieces.

He didn't fear darkness. He didn't fear danger, but the idea of being helpless was too abhorrent for words. And he was, indeed, helpless. Helpless and confined.

He patted his arms and legs and torso—someone had put him in a shirt and drawers, he realised. He lifted the fabric of the shirt to his nose. Clean clothes. Not a hint of smoke. Someone had bathed and clothed him.

Had she undressed him and clad him in a clean shirt? In drawers?

He strained to remember. He recalled leading people out of the fire. Of fire blasting his face. He vaguely remembered being jostled in a carriage, but those memories were mere flashes, with no coherence at all.

His head throbbed and he pressed his temples. How injured was he? He stretched his arms, flexed his legs. The rest of him seemed in one piece. He felt the sting of burns here and there on his skin, but nothing of significance.

He could still walk, could he not? If so, he'd be damned if he remained bedridden.

He slipped off the bed. His legs held him, so he felt his way around the bed's edge before stepping away. He hated not knowing what lay in his path. Waving his hands in front of him, he took tentative steps. Was this life without sight? Caught in emptiness? Unsure of every step?

A door opened.

'Mr Westleigh!' It was Mrs Asher's voice. 'You should not be out of bed!'

He heard the clatter of dishes—and smelled porridge. He felt her come near. Caught the scent of roses.

She took his arm. 'Let me help you back to bed.'

He pulled away. 'I will not be an invalid.'

She tugged at him. 'No, but you must rest or you risk being that very thing.'

He still did not wish to comply. 'Did you bring food?'

'Yes,' she replied. 'And a tray. See? You will be able to eat nicely in bed.'

He jerked away. 'I cannot see.'

She stepped back and left him in the emptiness again.

Let her abandon him! He'd find his own way back, if necessary.

He turned to where he thought she stood. 'Is there a table and chair in this room?'

She did not answer right away. 'Yes.'

'Then I will sit and eat like a man.'

'Very well.' She sighed. 'Stay where you are.' He heard furniture being moved. She took his arm again. 'Come here.'

She led him to a chair. He sat and heard the table being moved towards him. A moment later he smelled the food and heard the sound of a tray being placed in front of him.

She took his hand and placed a spoon in it, and showed him the bowl. 'It is porridge. And tea.'

He was suddenly famished, but he paused, trying again to face her, wherever she might be. 'Mrs Asher?'

'Yes?' Her voice was petulant, as it should be after his abominable behaviour.

'Do forgive me.' He'd behaved badly towards her again. 'I should be thanking you, nothing else.'

It took several seconds for her to speak. 'Your apology is accepted, Mr Westleigh.' Her voice softened. 'But do eat. You need to eat to gain strength.'

'I am grateful for the food. I am quite hungry.' He dipped the spoon, but missed the bowl. 'Blast.' He'd forgotten where the bowl was located.

She directed him on his next try. This time he scooped up a spoonful of porridge and lifted it. He missed and hit the corner of his mouth.

She wiped it with a napkin. 'Let me help you.' Putting her hand on his, she guided the spoon to his mouth.

The first taste made him ravenous, but he could not bear being fed like a helpless infant. 'I think I can manage it.' He groped for the bowl and picked it up in one hand and held it close to his mouth. With his other hand he scooped the porridge with the spoon and shovelled it into his mouth.

No doubt his manners were appalling.

He scraped the bowl clean and felt for a space on the table to put it down. With his fingers, he carefully explored what else was there.

A tea cup, warm to the touch. How was he to manage lifting a tea cup without spilling it?

'How do you take your tea?' she asked. 'I will fix it for you.'

'Milk and one lump of sugar.' He listened to the clink of the spoon as she stirred.

When the clinking stopped, she again guided his hand to the cup. He grasped it in both hands and carefully brought it to his mouth, aware of the aroma before attempting to take a sip. He sipped slowly, not because he savoured the taste, but because he did not wish to spill it.

When he finished, he managed to place the cup into its saucer. 'Thank you, Mrs Asher. You have been very kind.'

'You should rest now,' she responded. 'The surgeon said—'

'I will give you no further argument.' He felt for the napkin and wiped his mouth.

She came close again and touched his arm.

'I want to try to manage by myself.' He pushed the chair back and stood, getting reoriented to where the bed was. He groped his way back to it and climbed under the covers, aware that she must be watching his every awkward move. In his underclothes.

'Shall I write to your family and tell them where you are and what has happened to you?' she asked.

His family? Good God, no.

After this trip he intended to throw off the shackles of family responsibility for a time. He'd been at the family's beck and call ever since leaving the army.

'Do not write to my family.' He raised his voice. 'They must know nothing about this.'

She did not speak.

He shook his head, realising how he must

have sounded. 'I apologise again.' He spoke in a milder tone. 'My family would be the very worst of caretakers.' They were not expecting him, so they would not worry. He'd not written that he'd left Brussels. Better to not give them any time to find a new task he might perform for them. 'I beg you would find another solution. I realise I am imposing, but I can well pay for my care. I must not be put in the hands of my family. On that I must insist.'

'Very well. I will not contact your family.' He heard the sounds of her picking up the tray from the table. 'But you must rest now. Someone will check on you later.' He heard her footsteps walking towards the door. It opened and she spoke once more. 'Mr Westleigh?'

'Yes?' He stiffened, expecting a rebuke.

'You are not imposing.'

The door closed.

He was alone again. In the dark.

Mrs Asher's presence was a comfort, an anchor. Alone it was as if he floated in a void. He listened and thought he heard a bird singing outside, a dog's bark at some distance, footsteps outside the room.

He stilled, waiting to hear if the door would open.

The footsteps faded.

His head ached, his throat ached, his eyes

ached, but he was determined to remain awake. If he remained awake, he was not totally helpless.

To keep awake, he recalled the details of the fire.

He'd been leaving the inn's tavern, returning to his room, when shouts of 'fire!' reached his ears. He'd jumped into action, knocking on doors, getting people out. The fire had started in a room on the ground floor. He and others had cleared that floor and worked their way up to the higher floors while the fire kept growing and the task grew more dangerous.

The excitement of it had spurred him on. People had needed saving and someone had to brave the threat to save them, a perfect role for Hugh. He always did what needed to be done. If there was risk involved, so much the better.

He'd fought in the war because England needed him and, if truth be told, he'd loved the adventure of it, the risk to one's life, the chance to test his mettle. The army in peacetime was not for him, though. He'd sold his commission and prepared to discover his next adventure. He'd travel, he thought. To Africa. Or the Colonies. Or Chile— no, not Chile. With his luck he'd get embroiled in their War of Independence. It was one thing to risk one's life for one's own country, quite another to act as a mercenary. Besides, it was his own independence he yearned to indulge.

Instead, a family crisis had snared him. First

his father had nearly impoverished the family by gambling and philandering away its fortunes, then he had tried to cheat the man who'd come to their rescue, his own natural son, John Rhysdale.

After that, Hugh, his brother Ned and Rhysdale had forced their father to move to Brussels and turn over the finances and all his affairs to Ned. Hugh was charged with making certain their father held to the bargain, which meant repeated trips to the Continent. At least this last trip had been the final one. Hugh had been summoned back to Brussels because his father had dropped dead after a night of carousing and drinking.

Hugh suffered no grief over his father's death—the man hadn't cared a whit about him or any of the family. His father's death freed him at last.

Now Hugh's independence was again threatened when nearly in his grasp. Only this time it might not be family obligation holding him back.

This time it might be blindness.

Daphne strode immediately from Westleigh's bedchamber through the cottage and out into the garden where beds of red tulips and yellow narcissus ought to have given her cheer.

How could she be calm? She'd counted on Westleigh's family coming to care for him. Who would not want family to nurse them back to health? She'd planned on leaving as soon as a family member arrived. They would never see the elusive Mrs Asher. A mere note would be all they knew of her.

The Westleighs would detest knowing the despised Lady Faville had cared for a family member. Hugh Westleigh would detest it, as well. She'd once tried to steal away Phillipa Westleigh's new husband after all.

And, because her vanity had been injured, she'd heaved a lighted oil lamp against the Masquerade Club's wall. It had shattered, just as her illusions had shattered in that moment. In a flash, though, the curtains and her own skirts had caught fire.

Her hands flew to her burning cheeks. She'd been so afraid. And ashamed! What sort of person does such a thing?

Yes, the Westleighs would hate her, indeed.

She'd been a coward that day, running away after Phillipa had saved her from her burning skirts. She was a coward still. She should simply tell Hugh Westleigh her identity—she should have told him from the beginning—

What would the abbess have said? *Do what is right, my child. You shall never err if you follow the guide of your own conscience. Do always what is right.*

But what happens if one does not know what is right? What is one supposed to do in that event?

Was it right to tell him the truth or better to hide the truth and not upset him?

Daphne paced back and forth. It would only be two weeks until his bandages came off and he'd be on his way. She stopped and placed her hands on her cheeks.

Unless he was blind.

Please, dear God. Let him not be blind!

She shook her head. Who was she to pray?

She, Carter and Monette simply must take the best care of him. Not upset him. Give him the best chance to heal.

Perhaps the dear abbess would intercede with God for him on Daphne's behalf. And perhaps the abbess would forgive her if she did not tell the truth this time. No real harm in him thinking she was merely Mrs Asher for such a little while. Feeling only slightly guilty, Daphne strolled around to the front of the cottage.

Two young women approached from the road and quickened their pace when they saw her.

'Beg pardon, ma'am. Are you Mrs Asher?' They looked no more than fifteen years, each of them.

'I am Mrs Asher,' she responded.

'We've come looking for work, ma'am,' one said. 'Mr Brill, the agent, told us you might be needing some help in the cottage—'

'We can do whatever you need,' the other broke in. 'We're strong girls. Mr Brill will vouch for us.'

Both were simply dressed and their clothing looked very old and worn. In fact, their gowns hung on them.

'We need work very bad, ma'am,' the first girl said. 'We'll do anything.'

'I am not sure…' Daphne bit her lip. Would it be right to hire maids to work in a house where she would stay for only two weeks?

'Please, Mrs Asher,' the second girl said. 'We can show you how good we work. Give us a chance.'

What difference did it make to her? She had plenty of money to pay them. It was the easiest thing in the world to say yes. Besides, the abbess would say she'd done a good thing.

'Very well, girls,' she said. 'Follow me. If Mrs Pitts approves, you may become our new maids of all work.'

They could deliver the meals to Mr Westleigh. Daphne would be able to avoid him altogether. Then it would not matter who he thought she was.

Chapter Three

Hugh lost his battle to stay awake. He had no idea how long he slept, but he woke again to darkness.

Cursed eyes!

Was it day or night? Was he alone or was someone in the room?

Was *she* here?

He remained still and strained to hear the sounds of someone moving, someone breathing.

It was so quiet.

The hiss of the fireplace; otherwise, silence. Was anyone near? Would they hear him if he called out for help?

Although he'd be damned if he'd call out for help.

Or for water.

His throat was parched with thirst. There must be water somewhere in the room. She must have left some for him.

He climbed out of bed, not as steady on his

feet as he might wish. The carpet on the floor was soft and cool on his bare feet. Carefully, he started from right next to the bed, groping—and finding—a side table. He ran his hand over the table's surface. No water. Merely a candlestick—certainly an item for which he had no need.

He groped past the table and bumped into a wooden chair. He backed away and knocked the table onto the floor. The carpet muffled the sound. No one would be roused by the noise.

Crouching, he felt around for the table, found it and righted it. The candlestick must have rolled away. Useless to search for it anyway.

Moving cautiously again, he made his way past the chair. With the wall as his guide, he inched his way towards the fireplace, feeling the fire's heat grow stronger as he neared. His hand found the mantel. His toes smashed against the hearth.

He backed away and found more chairs and another table upon which there was a book. Another item for which he had no use.

Continuing, he discovered a door. It was a dressing room, smelling of dust, its shelves empty. He closed the door and his fingers felt along the wall until he came to another door. The door to the hallway. He turned the latch and opened the door and felt the change in temperature. But the hallway was silent.

He closed the door again and groped his way back to the bed. On the other side was another table. On the table he found a drinking glass and the water pitcher. He could never pour the water into the glass. He lifted the entire pitcher to his lips and took several gulps of the cool, minty liquid.

Placing the pitcher back on the table, he felt his way back to the bed, but halted. Lying abed like an invalid held no appeal.

He might as well continue his haphazard search of the room.

He found his trunk in one corner, his boots, smelling of bootblack, next to it. He found a rocking chair and a window.

A window! Fresh air. Hugh found the sash, opened the window and felt a cool breeze against his face. On the breeze was the scent of green grass, rich soil and flowers. He stuck his hand out the window and tried to sense whether it was day or night.

Without eyes, he could not tell.

He felt for the rocking chair and turned it towards the window. She must have sat in this rocking chair while in the room; her scent, very faint, clung to it. He lowered himself into it and rocked. The rhythm soothed him. The breeze cooled his skin. And banished the memory of the fire's infernal heat.

He must have dozed. For how long this time? Half awake, half asleep, he became aware of a knock at the door. The door opened. He knew instantly it was not she.

'Sir! You are not abed.' A male voice.

Hugh shook himself awake. 'Who are you?'

'I am Carter, sir. La—Mrs Asher's footman.' The voice did not come closer, so Carter must have remained by the door. 'I came to attend you.'

'I am grateful.' She'd said her footman would come. 'Can you tell me what time it is?'

'Seven, sir,' Carter replied.

'Morning or evening?' Did they not see he could not tell?

'Morning, sir.'

'What day?' Hugh tried not to let his impatience show.

'Oh! You must not realise—' Carter's voice deepened. 'Forgive me—I will explain—it is Friday. We arrived here Wednesday. The day after the fire. You slept most of yesterday. It is Friday morning now.'

He'd lost two days.

'I will assist you, sir. Shave you and whatever else you might require.'

Shave? Hugh scraped his hand against the stubble on his chin. He must have appeared like a ruffian to her.

Carter's voice came closer. 'Unless you would like me to help you back into bed.'

'No.' Hugh forced himself not to snap at the man. It was not Carter's fault he needed the as-

sistance. 'I will not return to bed. Shave me and
help me dress, if you would be so good.'

Gentlemen of Hugh's rank customarily em-
ployed a valet, but Hugh never did. He had no
qualms about borrowing the services of someone else's valet when absolutely necessary, but
what he could do for himself, he preferred doing.
It made him free to come and go as he wished
without having to consider anyone else's needs.

Now, though, he was not free. He was as dependent as a suckling babe.

He submitted to Carter's ministrations with
as good grace as he could muster, even though
Carter needed to help him with his most basic
of needs. He'd do them all without help as soon
as he could, he promised himself. After he was
shaved, bathed, toileted and dressed, he found
his way back to the rocking chair, more fatigued
than he would ever admit.

'Thank you, Carter,' he said. 'What of breakfast?' His hunger had returned. 'Will you help
me to the breakfast room?'

He sensed Carter backing away. 'I—I believe
Mrs Asher preferred you eat here, sir. Your health
is fragile, I'm given to understand.'

Hugh refused to be fragile. 'Very well, but tell
Mrs Asher I wish to speak with her as soon as it
is convenient.'

'Very good, sir.' Carter moved towards the
door.

'In fact—' Hugh raised his voice '—tell Mrs

Asher that I would like to see the village doctor. I am well able to pay for his services, so let there be no worry over that. I wish to see him today.' And find out, if possible, if he was to be blind or not.

'As you wish, sir.' He imagined Carter bowing. 'Breakfast as well, sir.'

The door closed and the footman's steps receded.

Hugh rose again. It felt better to be dressed, even if he was merely in shirt, trousers and stockings. At least when Mrs Asher returned, he would look more like a gentleman and less like an invalid.

If one could ignore the bandages covering his eyes.

He made his way around the bed. If his memory served him, the table on the other side of the bed, the table he'd knocked down during the night, was where he had eaten the porridge. He found the table again, bumped into the wooden chair again and kicked the lost candlestick with his toe, sending it skittering away.

Nonetheless, he managed to arrange the table and chair for eating. It was a minor matter, but a victory all the same. He was not entirely helpless.

Even so, a lifetime like this would be unbearable.

Daphne had left the two prospective maids in the company of Mrs Pitt after finally sorting out the matter. She'd thought she could simply hand them off to the housekeeper and be done with it, but the woman was shockingly dependent upon Daphne to make even the smallest of decisions, like what their duties should be, whether they should live in the house—yes, they should. Why have maids if they were not around when you needed them? Mrs Pitt also would have offered the girls a pittance for what would be very hard work, tending to the fires, cleaning the house and otherwise seeing to her needs. It was also very clear that they needed new clothes.

And that they were hungry. They both kept eyeing the bread Mrs Pitt had taken from the oven, and neither could pay attention to the discussion. So Daphne told Mrs Pitt to feed them, which led to a long discussion of what to feed them and what to feed Mr Westleigh and how was she—Mrs Pitt—to cook all that food, now that there were two more mouths to feed and two more workers to supervise.

By the time they'd finished, Daphne had given Mrs Pitt permission to hire a cook, a kitchen maid, another footman and two stable boys to help John Coachman. Mr Pitt was sent into the village to speak with some people he and Mrs Pitt thought would be perfect for the jobs, and Monette was getting her cloak and bonnet so she could accompany the girls to the local draper for fabric to make new dresses and aprons.

What fuss. Her husband would have been appalled at her being so bothered by such trivial matters. Even at the convent at Fahr, someone else saw to the food, the clothing, the cleaning.

As tedious as it all was, Daphne walked through the hall with a sense of pride. Her decisions were good ones after all. And she could well afford to pay all the servants even if she stayed here a year instead of two weeks.

As she crossed the hall, Carter descended the stairs.

She smiled up at him. 'How is Mr Westleigh this morning, Carter?'

He reached the final step. 'Much improved, ma'am. He wishes to speak with you.'

Oh, dear. And she wanted to avoid him.

'What about, do you know?' Perhaps he'd changed his mind about contacting his family.

Carter frowned. 'He wants to see a local doctor. I believe he is most unhappy about being bandaged and confined. He wants to see a doctor immediately.'

It was a reasonable request. He'd been nearly insensible when the surgeon at Ramsgate examined him. If only she'd known a few minutes earlier, she could have asked Mr Pitt to fetch the doctor.

'Could you go to the village and locate the doctor? Or find Mr Pitt and give him the errand? He left for the village a few minutes ago.'

Carter's brows knit. 'Shall I take Mr West-leigh his breakfast first, ma'am? I told him it was coming.'

The poor man must be famished. He'd only eaten a bowl of porridge since they'd arrived here.

She sighed. 'No. I will take him his breakfast. Perhaps there was something else he wanted to say to me.'

Carter came with her to the kitchen where Mrs Pitt gave him the doctor's direction and fixed the tray for Mr Westleigh.

Daphne carried the tray up the stairs and knocked upon Westleigh's bedchamber door.

'Come in, Carter.' His voice sounded stronger than the day before.

She opened the door and entered the room, kicking the door closed behind her.

He was seated at the table and chair where he'd eaten the porridge, and was dressed in a clean white shirt and dark brown trousers that showed off his broad shoulders and lean hips. She swal-lowed, suddenly remembering his strong arms carrying her in the inn.

'I can smell the bread from here.' He gestured with his hand. 'I will eat at the table.'

She crossed the room. 'It is Mrs Asher, not Carter.'

He tensed, as if he'd not liked mistaking her identity, and stood as a gentleman does when a lady enters the room. 'Good morning,' he said stiffly.

'Please sit,' she responded. 'Carter said you wished to see me, so it is I who brings you breakfast.'

He lowered himself back in the chair. 'I appreciate you coming so quickly.'

She placed the tray of food in front of him. 'I sent Carter to fetch a doctor and we did not wish you to wait. Are you hungry?'

'Ravenous.' He carefully ran his hands over the food.

She'd instructed Mrs Pitts to serve foods he could eat with his hands and spare him the struggle of manoeuvring utensils. They'd settled on warm bread sliced open with melting butter inside, two cooked eggs, cubes of cheese and a pot of tea.

He hesitated.

It made her uncertain. 'I will pour your tea,' she said. 'I remember how you take it, but do, please, eat. You must be very hungry.'

'I hope my manners will not offend.'

Oh, he was merely being polite. 'Have no fear. I am not easily offended.'

How odd of her to say such a thing. At a formal dinner party, she once would have had much to say about poor manners, and she'd often shaken her head at the way some of the lower classes consumed their food. Perhaps she was develop-

ing some tolerance, like the abbess had often encouraged her to do.

'I am surprised to see you dressed,' she went
on in a conversational tone. 'I thought you would
still be in bed.'

'No more bed.' His voice was firm. 'I am well
enough to be up.'

She pursed her lips. 'Are you certain? The surgeon in Ramsgate said you would need time to
recuperate. I think he meant you should remain
in bed.'

'I think him wrong,' he said stiffly. 'I feel re-
cuperated. Perhaps the village doctor will say I
may have my bandages removed and be on my
way.' He paused. 'I told Carter I am well able to
pay whatever the expense. I intend to compensate you, as well.'

'Money does not concern me. I certainly need
no compensation.' She waved a dismissive hand.
'I—I do not know if Carter can produce a doctor
this very day, though.'

The village did have a surgeon, Mrs Pitts had
said, but he was kept very busy.

Westleigh took a bite of bread, chewed and
swallowed it. She could not help but notice the
muscles in his neck move with the effort. She
touched her own neck.

'Let us hope he can come today,' he said.

He must be as eager to be on his way as she
was for him to leave, but should she trust his care

to a village doctor? Perhaps she should send for a London physician. She would love to send for the physician her husband had used when he was in town, but that man knew her.

Of course she could simply tell Westleigh now who she was.

She opened her mouth.

But he spoke first. 'Might I have a clock?' he asked. 'A way to keep track of time. I cannot even tell if it is day or night.'

How awful! All sorts of things must be difficult if one was not able to see. How much worse if one would never see again.

She vowed she would leave a large coin in the cup of the next blind beggar she came upon.

'I am so sorry,' she cried. 'I should have thought to provide you a clock. Perhaps I can purchase a watch that chimes. I have seen such watches. You could keep it next to you.'

Although, now that she thought of it, would a small village have such a watch? She'd only seen them in London shops.

'A clock will be sufficient,' he responded. 'And I am well able to pay for it, if there is not a spare one in the house.'

'We'll find you one, do not fear.' There was one on the mantel in the library. She'd have it brought to him immediately.

Or she would have to bring it herself, since

she'd sent everyone else away besides Mrs Pitts, who would be much too busy.

'Wait here a moment,' she said, which was a silly thing to say. Where could he go without sight?

She hurried out of the room and ran down the stairs to the library. Carefully she took the clock from the mantel and carried it back to his room.

'I've brought you a clock!' she said as she entered. 'I'll place it on the mantel and we'll make sure Carter winds it for you.'

'I did not mean for you to bring it so quickly, but I am very grateful.' He had finished the food and was feeling for the tea cup.

She walked over and guided his hand to it.

He stilled and his face tilted towards hers.

She wished she could see him, see all his face. She had seen him a few times at the Masquerade Club and had been introduced to him once. It was the only time she could remember speaking to him, and she'd paid little attention.

'Is there anything else?' she murmured. 'Anything else I can do for you?'

He continued to seem as if he was facing her. 'I want to leave this room,' he said. 'To come and go as I wish. Surely there must be a drawing room or a library or someplace I could sit without disturbing anyone.'

'But how can you? You can't see,' she cried.

He scowled. 'I can walk.'

She feared he would injure himself even more. What would she do then?

'The surgeon at Ramsgate said—' She cut herself off. 'Let us at least wait until another doctor examines you. I would hate to risk your recovery.'

He gulped down the cup of tea.

She leaned closer to pick up the tray.

'Roses,' he said softly.

'I beg your pardon?'

'You smell like roses,' he explained.

She felt her cheeks flush. It delighted her that he'd noticed. It was her favourite scent. She always rinsed herself with rosewater and any perfume she purchased must smell like roses.

'I—I should leave now, unless there is something else I can do—' She bit her lip.

'Nothing.' His voice dipped low. 'I am grateful for the breakfast and the clock. And for sending for the doctor.'

She cleared her throat. 'Let us hope he comes soon.'

Balancing the tray, she exited the room and only then did she realise she'd again not told him who she really was. Maybe when the doctor came, he would indeed say Westleigh was recovered. Maybe he would remove Westleigh's bandages and his eyes would work perfectly and she could have her coachman take him to London this very day.

* * *

It was late afternoon before the doctor called at the cottage.

Carter announced him to Daphne as she sat in the drawing room, writing a letter to her man of business, informing him of her arrival in England and her stay at Thurnfield.

She, of course, did not explain *why* she remained at Thurnfield.

She rose at the doctor's entrance. 'Mr Wynne, how good of you to come.'

He was a man of perhaps fifty years, with a rough but kindly appearance. When he saw her, his face lit with surprise, then appreciation. 'Mrs Asher! My word. May—may I welcome you to Thurnfield. You are a very delightful addition, if I may be so bold as to say.'

'Thank you, sir.' Daphne's response was well practised. Men who saw her for the first time often reacted so. In this instance, however, she did not want her beauty to distract the doctor from why he was here. 'I do believe Mr Westleigh is anxious for you to examine him. Carter can take you up to him directly.'

He tapped his lips. 'In a moment. I understand from Mr Carter that you witnessed the injury and the examination by the other surgeon. I think it best I should speak with you first.'

She sat again and gestured to a chair. 'Do sit.'

He lowered himself into the chair and leaned

towards her, all ears. And eyes. 'Now. Tell me what happened.'

She relayed the information as succinctly as she could, but he asked several questions about the injury and other surgeon's examination, forcing her to repeat herself.

It was a good thing she had not ordered tea, or the man would never make it up to Westleigh's room.

Her patience frayed. 'I do think you should see Mr Westleigh now, sir. He has been waiting a very long time.'

'Indeed. Indeed.' Mr Wynne took his time rising from his seat. 'You will accompany me? I may need information only you will have.'

She'd just given him all the information she possessed. Several times.

But it seemed expedient to do as he requested, merely to get him to actually see Westleigh, who had waited all day for the man. She rose. 'Come with me.'

Daphne heard the clock in Westleigh's room chime the quarter-hour as she raised her hand to knock.

'Please, come in.' Westleigh sounded impatient.

'Mr Westleigh, it is Mrs Asher,' she said as she opened the door. 'I have brought Mr Wynne, the surgeon, to see you.'

Hugh had been seated in the rocking chair next

to the window, which was open to the afternoon breeze. He stood and extended his hand almost in the surgeon's direction. 'Mr Wynne. I have been eager for your arrival.'

Wynne clasped his hand. 'Westleigh. Pleased to meet you. Mrs Asher has told me of your injuries.'

'She has?' His posture stiffened. 'Perhaps you would be so kind as to tell me what she said.'

'I told him you were in a fire,' Daphne responded. 'And that you were hit on the head and your eyes burned. I told him the other surgeon said you were concussed and that your eyes needed to remain bandaged for two weeks.'

'I could have told him that,' Westleigh remarked.

'I agree.' She had not wished to be this involved. Should she tell him the surgeon preferred her company to the duties that called him here?

'A nasty business, eh?' Wynne finally turned his attention to the patient. 'Please do sit and I will bring a chair closer to you.'

Westleigh lowered himself back into the rocking chair and Wynne brought the wooden chair over to him. Daphne stood near to the door.

'Now,' Wynne said, 'tell me—do you have any difficulty breathing?'

Westleigh took a breath. 'No.'

Wynne nodded, but from his bag pulled out a cylindrical tube. 'Best to check, in any event.' He placed one end of the tube on Westleigh's chest, the other against his own ear. 'Breathe deeply for me.'

Westleigh did as requested and the surgeon moved the tube to various locations on his chest.

'Your lungs are clear,' Wynne said. 'Have you experienced any dizziness?'

'None now,' Westleigh answered. 'Not even if I walk. I am quite steady on my feet.'

'Any pain?' the man asked.

Westleigh shrugged. 'My throat feels a bit rough. My head aches still, but not excessively. It is my eyes—my eyes concern me the most. They ache with a dull sort of pain. Again, not excessive. If I try to move my eyelids, however, the pain sharpens a great deal.'

'Best you not move your eyelids.' Wynne chuckled.

Westleigh frowned.

This was not a joking matter to him, Daphne wanted to say.

Wynne leaned forwards. 'Let me have a look at you.'

He placed his fingers on Hugh's head. His fingers looked stubby, but his touch seemed sure.

'It is most remarkable you were not more burned.' Wynne moved his fingers around his head and looked closely at the exposed parts of his face. 'The eyes can get the worst of it even if your skin's damage is superficial. Your hair is singed in places and I cannot see under the bandage, but I suspect you are fairly unscathed.'

Daphne had seen his eyes, though. His eyes had been alarmingly cloudy.

Wynne leaned back. 'I would like to examine under your bandages, but you must promise me something.'

'What is that?' Westleigh asked.

'Keep your eyes closed.' Wynne emphasised each word. 'If you do not keep your eyes closed, you risk further injury and blindness. Do you understand me?'

'I understand.' Westleigh answered in a low voice.

Wynne turned to Daphne. 'Mrs Asher, may we close the window and draw the curtains?'

'Certainly.' She hurried to do as he asked.

Westleigh remained still as Mr Wynne unwound his bandages. He was like a taut string vibrating with tension. The bandages seemed endless, but finally Wynne came down to the two round pieces of cloth that were pressed against Westleigh's eyelids.

'Remember, keep your eyes closed,' he warned.

He removed the last and moved even closer to peer at Westleigh's eyelids. He touched one very gently with his thumb.

Westleigh winced.

'Does that pain you?' Wynne asked.

'Some,' Westleigh responded tightly.

Wynne held the lids closed, but turned to Daphne. 'Will you bring me a lighted candle?'

She took the candlestick from the bedside table and lit it with a taper from the fireplace.

Wynne brought the candle close to Westleigh's face.

Westleigh's eyelids were still red and a yellow-ish crust clung to his eyelashes. If he did open his eyes now and could see, he'd know instantly who she was, but Daphne thrust that thought aside. He was more important this moment than her pride...and shame.

Westleigh remained like a statue.

'Are you able to see the light?' Wynne asked.

'Yes!' His voice filled with excitement. His eyelids twitched.

'Keep them closed,' Wynne warned again.

'Does that mean I will be able to see?' Westleigh asked.

'I wish I could make that promise.' Wynne leaned back and pulled out more bandages from his leather bag. 'Your eyes need more time for us to be certain. Two weeks, like the other surgeon said. If you want a chance to heal completely, wait the two weeks. There is no infection now, but to open your eyes now—well, I cannot stress how urgent it is that you wait the two weeks. It is your only chance.'

Westleigh's chin set and his head remained erect.

Chapter Four

Hugh was through with confinement. He was through giving in to his fears. He would see again. He must. He would not sit in one room for two weeks waiting. He'd move around, act as if he could see, no matter how many pieces of furniture he bumped into, no matter what came crashing to the floor. He'd pay for the damages.

But he would not be confined.

Mr Wynne did not require him to remain in bed. The only admonition the surgeon had made was that he was not to remove the bandages over his eyes. Wynne said he'd return in a few days to check him and change the bandages, if necessary. In the meantime, Hugh intended to leave this room.

Wynne also said he could travel, if he wished. He could be in London in one day's coach ride and straight into the suffocating confines of his mother's care.

He'd rather impose on Mrs Asher. Was that ungentlemanly of him? He suspected so, but an unwanted invalid would receive the least fussing and he had no wish to be fussed over. It might cause the lady some annoyance if he did not remain in his room, but he'd go mad otherwise.

Carter knocked and entered the room. 'Do you require anything, sir?'

'Nothing at the moment,' Hugh replied.

'Very good, sir.'

The door sounded as if it was closing and Hugh raised his voice. 'Carter?'

It opened again. 'Yes, sir?'

'What time is dinner to be served?'

'Whenever you desire, sir,' Carter responded.

'I do not wish to cause undue inconvenience,' Hugh countered. 'When is Mrs Asher served dinner? I can wait until she is served, certainly.'

'M'l—' Carter faltered. 'Mrs Asher dines at eight o'clock.'

'Eight o'clock. Splendid. I can be served after she dines.'

'Very good, sir,' Carter said again. The door closed.

Hugh listened for the next chiming of the clock.

Six chimes. Plenty of time for him to prepare.

He groped his way to the corner of the room where he'd discovered his trunk. Opening it, he dug through until he felt smooth, thick fabric, a lapel and buttons.

As he'd hoped. One of his coats, and beneath it, a waistcoat.

He felt around more until his fingers touched the starched linen of a neckcloth. He could tie it blindfolded, could he not? How many neckcloths had he tied himself over the years?

He wrapped the cloth around his neck and created a simple mail-coach knot. Or hoped he had. Next he donned his waistcoat and coat and carried his boots over to the rocking chair. Seated on the chair, he pulled on his boots.

For the first time since the fire, Hugh was fully dressed. Already he felt more like a man.

He made his way confidently to the door.

But missed, touching the wall instead. He ran his hand along the wall until it touched the door. Excitement rushed through him. Would a man released from prison feel this way? Free, but wary, because he did not know what was on the other side.

He took a step out into the hallway and paused again, trying to listen for sounds, searching for the staircase.

This time he could hear sounds coming from below. He must be near the stairs. He stepped forwards carefully and reached the wall. Good. The wall could be his guide. He inched his way along it until he found the banister. His excitement soared.

Hugh laughed. You'd think he'd discovered a breach in the enemy's defences.

He carefully descended the stairs, holding on to the banister. Amazing how uncertain he felt. He'd crept around buildings and other terrains in the dark before without this much apprehension.

Although he could at least see shadows then. Now he could see nothing.

He reached the last step and still kept one hand on the banister. Chances were that the front door to the house was ahead of him, facing the stairway, which meant that the rooms would be to the right, left or behind. Which would be the dining room?

It would have helped if he'd once seen this house, even from the outside.

He took a breath and began walking straight ahead until he, indeed, found the front door. Then, following his strategy for the bedroom, he started to feel himself along the wall.

'What are you doing, sir?' A woman's voice. A village accent. The housekeeper of whom Mrs Asher spoke?

'Are you Mrs Pitts?' he asked.

'Goodness, no, sir,' the voice replied. 'I am Mary, one of the housemaids, sir.'

Mrs Asher had not mentioned housemaids.

'But what are you doing here, sir?' she went on. 'You should be upstairs, should you not? You are recuperating, is that not the way it is?'

'I came downstairs for dinner.' He spoke with a confidence a maid would not question. 'I realise I am early, but if you direct me to the dining room, I would be grateful.'

'It is early for dinner, sir,' she said. 'Would you like to wait in the drawing room? Mrs Asher said we are to announce dinner to her in the drawing room.'

'The drawing room it is, then.' Hugh smiled. 'Can you show me where it is?'

'Oh!' The maid sounded as if she'd just figured out a big puzzle. 'You cannot see and you haven't been there yet! I remember Mrs Asher saying you were taken directly upstairs.'

He heard her approach him.

She touched his arm. 'Come with me.' She led him to the right and through the threshold of the drawing room. 'I think Mrs Asher will be here soon. She and Monette are talking about our new dresses, you see, so I expect she will come here after that.'

'I expect so,' he replied.

'Begging your pardon, sir, I should be about my duties.' She said this with a surprising sense of pride.

'Thank you for your help, Mary.' He did

not wish her to leave quite yet. 'I have just one question.'

'Yes, sir?' She sounded very young. And inexperienced. Otherwise she would not talk so much.

'How long have you worked for Mrs Asher?' Because the lady had not informed him of the presence of a housemaid.

'Oh, this is my first day, sir. For me and my sister, Ann. So I must not dawdle.' She paused. 'May I go, sir?'

'By all means.' Were the extra maids hired because of him? 'Thank you again, Mary.'

She gave a nervous little laugh and he heard the door close.

Once again he was in a strange room with no sense of his bearings.

But he was getting used to it. He turned around and listened carefully for the hiss of the fire and the heat of it on his skin. He memorised the location of the fireplace and the location of the doorway. Somewhere in between there would be chairs and other seating. He trod carefully until he found one. When he was still, he also heard the ticking of a clock. Good. He'd keep track of time that way.

The half-hour, then three-quarters chimes sounded.

Shortly after, the door opened and Hugh smelled roses.

'My goodness.' It was Mrs Asher. 'Mr Westleigh, you gave me a start!'

He stood. 'My apologies.'

'What are you doing here?' She did not sound very pleased.

'Carter said dinner was at eight. Since I am not confined to bed, I saw no reason to trouble your servants to wait on me.'

She came closer. 'But Carter did not tell me—'

'I did not consult with him.'

She sounded confused. 'Then how did you get here? From upstairs, I mean.'

He straightened. 'The way of all men, I suppose. I walked.'

'By yourself?'

'Well, I made it to the hall by myself,' he said. 'Mary helped me to the drawing room.'

'Mary?' She sounded confused again. 'Oh. *Mary.* The new maid. That was kind of her.' She paused before saying, 'Do sit, Mr Westleigh.'

He lowered himself back into the chair.

She was a puzzle to him. She'd taken the trouble to bring him into her home to care for him, yet at the same time she seemed displeased at his presence. She was a woman who concealed things, that was certain.

He heard her move about the room.

'Would you like a glass of claret before dinner?' Good manners crept back into her voice.

'I would dearly like a glass of claret.' He missed

wine. He missed brandy even more. He wondered if she would have brandy for after dinner.

He heard her open a cabinet and then heard the sound of pouring liquid. She handed the glass to him.

The scent of the claret was pleasure enough. Fruity and spicy, he savoured the aroma before taking a sip. Drinking from a wine glass proved to be quite easy. And the smooth, earthy flavour was a comfort to his sore throat. He felt like gulping.

He heard her sit. 'I understand you just hired Mary and another maid. If that was because of me, you must permit me to bear the expense.' Might as well speak plainly. She might like to conceal, but he favoured being above board.

'The expense is nothing.' She indeed made it sound as if it was a trifle. 'And I did not hire them because of you, not precisely. They needed the work and I thought it would make it easier on everyone to have more help.'

'I should still like to compensate you for the trouble I am causing you.'

'Please say no more about *money*.' She spoke the word as if it left a bad taste on her tongue. 'I detest talk of money. I have well enough money to be a good hostess, you know. You are here to recuperate and that is what you shall do. The cost of it means nothing to me.'

Why was she so tense?

He tried some humour. 'Are you a wealthy widow, then?'

She was silent for a moment before answering in a serious tone, 'Yes. I am a wealthy widow.'

They drank their claret in such silence Hugh could hear the ticking of the clock and each small rustle of her skirts, but it did not take long for Carter to come to the door to announce dinner.

'Dinner is served, m'l— Oh!' He cut himself off. 'Mr Westleigh! You are here.'

'Mr Westleigh will eat dinner in the dining room with me, Carter.' Mrs Asher made it sound as if nothing was amiss. She must be practised in hiding emotions from servants.

'Very good, ma'am,' Carter said. 'I shall run ahead and set his place.'

Hugh heard Mrs Asher stand, and rose himself, offering her his arm—or hoping he was not merely posturing to the air.

Her fingers curled around his upper arm. 'I'll show you to the dining room.'

He smiled. 'That is a good thing, else I might wander the house bumping into walls.'

'You were very clever making it to the drawing room.' She did not sound annoyed.

Perhaps this was a truce of sorts.

She led him out the door. 'We are crossing the hall. The dining room is on the other side, a mirror to this room. The cottage really has a very simple plan.'

So, coming down the steps, the drawing room was to the left; the dining room to the right. 'What other rooms are on this floor?'

'A library behind the drawing room,' she began.

He cut her off with a laugh. 'I don't suppose I'll make much use of that.'

Her step faltered. 'Behind the dining room is an ante-room with cupboards for dishes and cutlery and such. From that room there are stairs down to the kitchen and housekeeper's rooms.'

He was able to visualise it. It did not seem like a large home for a wealthy widow, though.

They crossed the threshold to the dining room and she walked with him to what must have been the head of the table.

He heard the chair being pulled out. She released his arm and sat.

Carter came to his side. 'Your chair is here, sir.' He helped him to a seat adjacent to hers.

'Our meal will be rather simple, I'm afraid,' Mrs Asher said. 'Some lamb stew and bread.'

It must have been near because Hugh could smell it. 'It will be perfectly adequate for me. My appetite appears to have returned full force. I am very likely to eat whatever you put before me and demand seconds.'

He heard Carter pour some liquid. A glass of wine, Hugh could tell by its fragrance.

'That is a healthy sign, I suppose,' she said.

'Perhaps tomorrow we shall have fancier fare. We shall have a cook tomorrow. And another footman.'

He frowned. 'You are hiring many new servants.'

'Y-yes.' Her voice cracked. 'Well.' She recovered. 'I just came from a lengthy stay abroad, you see.'

'You are rebuilding your staff?'

'Yes,' she agreed. 'That is it.'

He tilted his head. Why did she always sound as if she had something to hide?

He had no desire to challenge her at the moment, though. Not when she briefly seemed at ease with him.

'I was abroad, as well,' he said instead. 'In Brussels. Were you there?'

'No.' She paused as if there were more for her to conceal. 'In Switzerland.'

'Ah, Switzerland. A place I should like to visit.'

Carter placed a dish in front of him and the aroma of the stew filled his nostrils. 'Here is the stew, sir. I will place the bread on the left for you.'

'Thank you, Carter.' He lifted his head in what he hoped was Mrs Asher's direction. 'It smells quite delicious.'

He could hear her being served, as well. She thanked Carter and his footsteps receded.

'Do eat, Mr Westleigh,' she said.

He felt for the fork first. Spearing meat with the fork seemed the easiest means of getting the food into his mouth. It took him several tries, but he finally succeeded. The lamb was flavourful and tender. Next he managed to spear some potato. Eating so little in the past two days had wreaked havoc on his appetite. It indeed felt like he could not get enough.

'Is it to your liking?' she asked.

He laughed. 'You cannot tell? I am certain I am shovelling it in like an ill-mannered peasant.'

'You are allowed some lack of graces due to your injuries.' His blindness, she meant.

He forced himself to slow down, searching for the bread and tearing off a piece. 'What brought you to Switzerland?' he asked.

'A...' She paused. 'A retreat, you might say.'

He'd heard of spa towns on the Continent, places where a wealthy widow might go for a lengthy recuperation.

Or perhaps to have a child out of wedlock. Was that her secret? She seemed sad enough for such a happenstance. It would explain that air of concealment he sensed in her.

A wave of tenderness towards her washed over him. Women always had a more difficult lot in life. Men seduced women and women paid the price. A child out of wedlock—it made perfect sense.

Daphne toyed with her food, her appetite fleeing under his questions and the impact of his appearance, attired in coat and waistcoat. His coat fit beautifully, accenting his broad shoulders and tapering to his lean waist. He made it difficult to ignore that he was more than an invalid, more than a member of the family who despised her. He was a man, and his presence seemed to fill the room.

He'd paused and she feared he could sense she was staring at him. She averted her gaze, now wishing he would ask her about her retreat in Switzerland, even if she did not know how to tell him her retreat was in a Catholic convent.

He tore off another piece of bread. 'My stay in Brussels was anything but a retreat.'

She breathed a sigh of relief. He was like most men. Wishing to talk about himself.

'Is that so?' she responded politely.

'My time was spent disentangling my father's affairs,' he went on. 'He was living there, you see. And he died there several months ago.'

'I am so sorry.' She felt genuinely sympathetic. She'd not known of the earl's death.

She'd heard the Earl of Westleigh had been living on the Continent. Some scandal associated with the Masquerade Club, she recalled, but she could not remember the details. In her nights spent in attendance at the club, she'd not paid much attention to anything but her own interests.

'Do not be sorry,' he countered. 'He was the very worst of fathers. The worst of men. Perhaps you've heard of him? The infamous Earl of Westleigh?' He exaggerated his father's name.

'I have heard of him.' He'd been an acquaintance of her late husband's and only a few years older. 'But only his name, really.' It was true. Her husband had not gossiped with her about the people he knew.

'My brother Ned, the new earl, sent me to deal with whatever trouble our father caused. I am glad this was my last trip.'

She did not know what to say to this, so she offered more food. 'Would you like more stew?'

'I would indeed.' He smiled.

He had a nice smile, she thought.

He was also the first person she'd ever met who admitted to not grieving the loss of a family member. Perhaps she wasn't so strange after all, that the deaths of her parents had left her feeling so little emotion. She'd hardly known them. She had regretted that.

'Did you not like Brussels, then?' she asked, just to make conversation.

'It is a beautiful city.' He averted his head. 'But too full of memories for me. When I walk through its streets, all I can think of is Waterloo.'

'You were in the great battle?' All she knew of the battle was what she read in the newspapers that reached Faville.

'Yes.' His voice turned wooden.

She took a big gulp of wine. 'War and battle are not good topics for dinner conversation, are they?'

'Not at all.' He smiled again. 'Tell me about Switzerland. I've seen the Alps from France, but not the other side. Are they as majestically beautiful?'

The Abbey was in a valley. The craggy stone mountaintops of the Alps were not greatly visible there.

'Oh, yes,' she agreed brightly. 'Quite beautiful. It was a lovely place.'

'I should like to travel there.' He laughed. 'I should like to travel anywhere and everywhere. That is what I will do after I report back to the family in London. Travel.'

But he might be blind. What would happen to his dreams of travel then?

'There are many places to see,' she responded conversationally.

They continued though dinner, talking of various places on the Continent where they had travelled. Daphne had seen only the countries through which she travelled to Switzerland and a little of Italy when her husband had taken her there.

The meal was companionable, more pleasant than any meal Daphne could remember in a long time. She enjoyed it far more than she ought, especially considering her resolve to stay away from him.

* * *

After dinner, they retired to the drawing room. 'I do not have brandy to offer, I am afraid.' She'd send Carter into the village to procure some the next day, however. 'Would you care for tea?'

'Tea will do.'

He'd been so churlish that morning, but now was agreeable and diverting. She could almost forget that she was Lady Faville and he was a man who would certainly despise her, if he knew.

As they finished their tea, she could see his energy was flagging.

'I believe I shall retire for the night,' she said, saving him the need to admit he was tired.

He smiled. 'Will you escort me upstairs? I am uncertain I will be able to find my room again.'

'It will be my pleasure,' she said.

As they climbed the stairs, he asked, 'What time is breakfast served?'

Goodness. She did not care. 'Whenever you wish.'

'Name a time.'

She ought to check with Mrs Pitts before making a decision. The woman had toiled very hard this day. The new maids had caused her more work and the prospect of hiring more workers had created more anxiety in the poor woman.

What thoughts were these? When had she ever considered the feelings of servants?

'I will send Carter in the morning to help you dress. We will have breakfast ready soon after.'

She left him at his doorway. 'Goodnight, Mr Westleigh. Carter will be up to tend to your needs soon.'

His hand slid down her arm to clasp hers. 'Thank you for a very enjoyable evening.'

Her heart fluttered with pleasure. Appreciation from a gentleman had always gratified her, but did not usually excite such emotion. Not from her husband, certainly. From only one man, the man who'd married Westleigh's sister.

It must merely be the novelty, she thought. She'd been secluded from men for a long time when at the convent. Certainly Hugh Westleigh was the last man on earth who should excite her sensibilities.

She crossed the hallway to the bedchamber opposite Westleigh's. It was smaller than the one she'd given Westleigh, but there was another, even smaller room next to it that was perfect for Monette.

Besides, she'd become used to sleeping in a room in the Abbey even smaller than a maid's room. A cot. A side table. A chest for her clothing. It had been all she needed.

Inside the room, Monette was laying out her nightdress.

She looked up at Daphne, her brows raised. 'Was that Mr Westleigh I heard with you? Carter said he came down on his own for dinner.'

'Yes. I walked with him upstairs.'

'Is he to be up and about, then?' Monette asked.

'Yes. He has no wish to spend time in his room.' Unfortunately.

'That makes you unhappy,' Monette guessed.

Monette was not in Daphne's confidence. In fact, Daphne had told the younger woman very little about her life. She was the widow of a viscount, that was it. Daphne had not told anyone, even the abbess, any more than that. While in the convent, she wore her unhappiness as plainly as the sisters wore their habits, but she'd never explained.

She needed to give some answer, though. 'It makes matters more complicated. No matter what he thinks, he cannot get about on his own.'

Monette folded down the coverlet and bed linens. 'It is good, then, that you have hired more help. There are more of us to tend to him.'

Yes, but Westleigh was her guest, and a hostess did not leave a guest to be entertained by the servants.

'That is so,' she said, there being no reason why Monette should know precisely how difficult it would be for her to spend time with Westleigh.

Spending time with him was like a constant reminder of her lie and of what she was most ashamed.

And now she was also too much aware of him as a man.

Chapter Five

As promised, Carter appeared the next morning in time to ready Hugh for breakfast, and, rather than eating alone, Hugh had company. Mrs Asher breakfasted with him, making polite conversation as if seated with a man who could see. The food was easy for him to eat. He suspected she'd made certain of that.

Her chair scraped against the floor. 'If you will excuse me, Mr Westleigh, I must meet with the housekeeper.'

He stood.

'A new cook and kitchen maid are arriving today,' she explained. 'A new footman, as well. Mr and Mrs Pitts need to involve me in the arrangements, for some reason. Carter will attend to you. He is here to assist you when you are finished eating. Do take your time, though.'

The dining room held no further appeal after she left and Hugh did not remain long. Carter walked with him to the drawing room, although what he would do there, he did not know.

He sat in the same chair as the day before. 'How long have you been with Mrs Asher?' he asked Carter.

'Not long,' the servant replied somewhat hesitantly. 'She hired me right before her travel home.'

'You were in Switzerland?' An odd place to find a footman for hire.

'I was, sir,' Carter responded, but did not explain.

Not that Hugh required an explanation from the poor man. It was merely that Hugh had nothing to do but talk.

'I must beg your leave, sir, to complete my other duties,' Carter said. 'I will return to see if you are in need of anything. Say, in an hour or so?'

'Go, Carter. I shall do very well on my own.' What other choice did he have?

He heard Carter walk towards the door.

'Carter?'

'Yes, sir?' the man answered.

'Could you find me a cane?'

'A cane, sir? Forgive me, sir, I had not noticed you walking with any difficulty.' His voice was distressed.

'No difficulty,' Hugh assured him. 'I merely thought that if I had a cane, I could keep myself from bumping into things. I could walk around without assistance.'

'I see, sir.' The man cleared his throat. 'I will look for a cane for you.'

Carter closed the door and Hugh drummed his fingers on his knee. What the devil was he going to do to pass the time?

He rose and explored the room, treading carefully and trying not to tumble over furniture or break priceless ornaments.

It was a modest drawing room. He found at least three separate seating groups and some cabinetry along the walls. One of the cabinets held the claret. He was tempted to pour himself a glass, but feared he would spill the liquid and stain the carpet. He could drink from the carafe, but that seemed too ill mannered. Besides, he'd just consumed breakfast. It was a little early for imbibing.

He continued through the room and along the wall until finding a window. He knew from opening his window before breakfast that the day was a chilly one for April and to open this one would defeat the fire's battle to warm the room, but he could not resist. The fresh air smelled like freedom.

He took in big gulps of air, as hungry for it as he'd been for his first meal here. But he closed the window again. Nothing was more of a nuisance than a guest who took over and changed a household's entire routine. He was just so extremely tired of being closed inside walls.

But that was his lot for the moment. He ought, at least, to bear it without this constant pitying of himself.

He continued his way around the room.

He found a pianoforte in one corner of the room and ran his fingers down the keys. He pressed one. It sounded a note.

And reminded him of his sister.

How was Phillipa faring? he wondered. Was she still spending long hours at the pianoforte, composing those songs of hers? Was her husband still selling her music? Hugh had heard one of the songs played by the orchestra at Vauxhall Gardens, quite an unusual accomplishment for a well-bred young lady.

Phillipa followed her own desires, no matter the pressure from their mother and the neglect of her father and brothers. Look at the result. She'd married Xavier—a man decent enough to put the whole Westleigh family to shame and well able to provide for her. And she'd just become a mother.

Hugh hoped Phillipa still played music, even though she was now a mother. He'd never given her music much thought—if truth be told, he never gave Phillipa enough thought. With her scarred face, she'd always hidden herself away. And she was seven years younger. He'd been at school, then in the army while she grew up.

He admired her now.

Phillipa's scar, her music, the abominable way everyone had treated her, all freed her from any responsibility to the family. Ned, now the earl, was charged with preserving the family property and good name for coming generations. Hugh had been given the task of family workhorse.

Difficulties emerged at the country estate? Send Hugh to fix them. Papa engaging in bad behaviour again? Dispatch Hugh to set him straight.

All that was at an end. Ned must attend to his property now and their father would no longer trouble anyone. Hugh was free.

Or would be, if his sight returned.

He made a fist and struck the keys of the pianoforte again. The sound was as discordant as his emotions. His freedom was dependent upon his eyes. What if they did not heal?

He straightened. Enough self-pity.

He drummed his fingers on the keyboard and made more pleasant music.

For want of anything else to do, he sat at the pianoforte's bench and felt the keys, hearing his sister's endless scales that echoed through their house for so many years. He found middle C and played the simple C scale, which pretty much exhausted his knowledge of playing.

He played the scale again. And again. And again until his fingers moved smoothly from note to note and the novelty wore off. He tried picking out a tune, an exercise in trial and error, but he kept at it.

He picked out the tune for the military bugle call that signalled the end of the day—or the end of battle.

It brought back memories.

'Do you play, Mr Westleigh?' Mrs Asher's voice came from the doorway.

'Not at all.' He turned. 'You may have heard all the skill I possess.' The extent of his pleasure at having company at last shocked him. 'Are your cooks and maids and footmen all hired?'

'They are.'

She said no more. Moved no more. Her wariness towards him persisted and it puzzled him still.

He turned back to the keyboard. 'Tinkering with the pianoforte is at least something I can do without sight. There seems little else.'

He heard her approach from the rustle of her skirts, knew she'd come close by the scent of roses and the warmth of her body. She excited his senses, but he was unsure whether it was due to the loneliness his lack of sight produced or the fact that she was mysterious and female.

Good God. He must watch himself.

Daphne had resolved to stay away from Westleigh as much as possible, but Carter was busy with the new footman and could not attend him.

She should simply ask Westleigh if he needed anything and be on her way, but he'd sounded so...so lonely, it was difficult not to play the hostess.

At least that was what she told herself.

He placed his fingers on the keys. 'See? I can play a scale.'

But he started on the wrong note.

She covered his hand with hers. His hand was large, but with long, strong fingers. She placed one on middle C. 'Try it now.'

He obliged her, then turned and smiled.

She flushed.

It was good he could not see that his smile set her heart to racing. Really, it was nonsensical for her to react so to a man. She'd vowed she would never do so again. Or perhaps she thought she *could* never do so again.

'Do you play?' he asked. 'I am guessing that you do, because you knew how to find C and you have a pianoforte in your drawing room.'

She thought of all the hours of her childhood spent practising scales. 'I learned, of course, but my playing is unexceptional at best.'

Unlike his sister, who had been so skilled Daphne thought she'd played at Covent Garden. Even though her own husband's praise of her skills had been effusive, Daphne had always known he greatly exaggerated.

'What was the tune you played?' she asked,

shaking from her mind the guilt she felt about Faville's devotion.

'"The Last Post",' he responded. 'A bugle call signalling the end of the day.'

'Oh, yes.' She did not know much about bugle calls and military matters. 'I have heard it before, of course.'

He picked out the melody again. 'I believe I hit the right keys this time.' He slid over on the bench. 'Your turn. Come sit and play me something.'

She'd not played since her husband had died, she realised, and she did not wish to play now, but it seemed rude of her to refuse.

'Very well.' She sat next to him, realising for the first time how much larger he was than she.

She played the first piece she could think of, 'The Battle of Prague.'

He laughed.

She lifted her hands, her face burning. 'Was it that dreadful?'

He reached for and found her hand. 'No, that is not it at all. It brought back a memory. My sister played that piece so often, I used to pull out my hair.' He grabbed a fistful of hair and demonstrated.

She pulled her hands away and placed them in her lap. 'Your sister?'

'Lady Phillipa,' he said. 'She loved the pianoforte above all things—until she met her husband, I mean.'

'Oh.' The stab of pain was not nearly what it once might have been. That was not due to Xavier, but her own behaviour; her year at the abbey had done some good.

You will recover, the abbess had assured her. Perhaps she'd made a little progress.

'Please continue playing,' he said.

She wished to flee the room, but her good manners won over. This time she played 'Barbara Allen.'

To her surprise, he began to sing.

'In Scarlet town where I was born,
There was a fair maid dwellin'.
Made every youth cry well-a-day,
Her name was Barb'ra Allen...'

His voice was a pleasing baritone, but anything but smooth. After three stanzas his voice cracked and he stopped. 'Now, I would say *that* was dreadful.'

She had been enjoying it, she realised. 'Is your throat still sore?'

He coughed. 'We shall allow that to be my excuse.'

She'd forgotten her main task. 'Forgive me. I came here to ask if there was anything you needed. Would you perhaps like something to drink?'

'Some water would do nicely.' He coughed again.

'I will see to it.' She rose from the bench and hurried out of the room.

Damn his throat.

Or his attempt to sing. He'd chased her away, he feared. It seemed as if something always chased her away just as soon as some ease developed between them.

It had felt companionable to sit with her as she played, to converse with her a little. It passed the time. It dissipated his isolation.

The tick, tick, tick of the clock seemed to boom in the room. He found a note on the pianoforte and mimicked the sound. How many notes would lead him to the end of this day? The end of this week? The end of two weeks?

No. Shake that thought away. The way to get through this situation was one minute at a time. Sixty notes. Over and over.

He played randomly, keeping time with the clock until, bored, he switched to picking out the melody of 'Barbara Allen'. Or trying to hunt for the right notes.

Eventually she returned. 'Here we are,' she said with what seemed like forced cheerfulness. 'I thought lemonade might be pleasant for you.'

He lifted a finger. 'Listen to this.'

He picked out the notes.

'Barbara Allen?' she asked uncertainly.

'Correct!' He was pleased she could recognise it. 'And thank you. Lemonade will do very nicely.'

He lifted his hand, again aware that he did not know precisely where she or the glass of lemonade was. She placed it in his hand and he drank it thirstily.

She said, 'I ought to have made certain you had something to drink before leaving you at breakfast. I believe your experiences also gave you a great thirst.'

Indeed. His throat seemed perpetually dry and raw. 'Do not chastise yourself. I am capable of asking for what I need.' However, he hated asking.

He'd even hated asking Carter to find him a cane. At least the cane would make him more self-sufficient, though.

'Of course.' Her placating governess voice was back. 'You must tell me, then, what else you might need, before I take my leave.'

Take her leave? He'd been counting on her helping him pass the time. He might despise being needy, but that did not mean he couldn't be selfish. 'I would like your company for a longer period.'

'My company? What for?' There was the faintest tremble of trepidation in her voice.

'I want to go outside.' He waited, but she said nothing. 'I want to stretch my legs and feel the sun on my face.' She still said nothing. 'If you cannot escort me, perhaps you can send a servant to do it.'

'I will accompany you.' She made it sound like an onerous task. 'Please wait here. I will get my hat and shawl.'

He ought to tell her to return to her tasks. That he would amuse himself in some other way, but time passed more quickly in her company. Besides, he needed a challenge, and solving her mystery was the only challenge available to him. Unless he considered blindness a challenge, and that he refused to do. His blindness was nothing more than a temporary annoyance. Temporary.

In less than a fortnight he would see. He must see.

Daphne hurried up to the maids' quarters, where Monette was measuring Mary and Ann for their new dresses. Daphne had promised to help. Her sewing skills were more decorative than useful, confined to embroidery and needlepoint and other showy arts, but she could stitch a seam if necessary.

'There you are, ma'am,' Monette said cheerfully. 'I am almost ready to cut the fabric.'

Monette had made her own dresses without patterns, copying them from the clothes Daphne had brought with her to the convent. While staying at the convent, Daphne had worn a simple tunic similar to the nuns' habits. Pretty clothes had been part of her vanity.

The maids were brimming with excitement. She'd not thought about maids enjoying pretty clothes just as she had done, not until she'd seen Monette's delight in wearing modern fashions.

The abbess had said to her more than once, *God made us all the same.*

In some ways people were the same, Daphne could agree, but she was always treated differently, even at the convent.

Because of her beauty.

'I cannot help you as I thought,' Daphne said, examining the blue floral print Monette had purchased for the gowns. 'I must entertain Mr Westleigh. He has a desire to take a walk outside.'

'Do not fear, ma'am,' Mary said. 'We can sew and still tend to our chores.' She turned to her sister. 'Can we not, Ann?'

'We can. Oh, yes,' the other girl said agreeably.

'I will help later,' Daphne said.

'Ma'am?' Mary spoke. 'You ought not to be sewing our dresses in any event, if I may be so bold to say. We will finish them.' She turned to Monette. 'Ann and I can finish them, can we not? You will show us what you want?'

Sewing a new dress and tending to maid's chores all in the same day seemed a daunting task to Daphne. She wondered how much work she'd created for the maids at Faville House without giving them a single consideration.

'Well, make the dresses your priority today,' she told them. 'You can tend to the cleaning and other chores tomorrow.'

The three women curtsied. 'Thank you, ma'am,' they said in unison.

Daphne hurried off to her bedchamber for her bonnet and shawl, which should do for the cool day. She stopped in Westleigh's room to get his hat.

Carter was there with the footman, who was to trail him all day to learn his duties.

'Carter, I am taking Mr Westleigh for a turn in the garden,' she told him. 'Does he have a hat and gloves?'

Carter's eyes widened. 'No, m'l—ma'am. I did not think of a hat and gloves. He must have lost them.' He turned to the footman. 'Find Mr Pitts and see if he has a cap the gentleman might wear.'

'No.' Daphne stopped him. 'Let me see first if he minds going out without them. Carter, perhaps you or—or—' She could not think of the new footman's name.

'Toller, ma'am,' he said.

'Toller.' She was ashamed of herself for forgetting. 'Perhaps one of you could go into the village and buy the items for him.'

'We'll see to it.' Carter crossed the room. 'I do have something the gentleman asked for.' He lifted a wooden cane.

'A cane?' She was surprised.

'He said it would help him walk.'

She took it from his hand. 'Thank you. I will take it to him.'

She left the room and started down the steps, but slowed her pace.

What happened to her resolve to spend as little time as possible with him? She could have insisted Carter take him for a walk, but then she would have disrupted his instructions to the new footman. And the maids were right. She should not be sewing their clothes for them.

She could not delegate the care of Westleigh to the servants. It was her job as hostess. She could do so without revealing who she was. He still did not need to ever find out who Mrs Asher really was.

Be truthful, especially to yourself, she could hear the abbess say.

Very well. To be truthful, she liked the man's company. No, more than liked his company. All her senses sparked into life when she was near him, in a way she'd never experienced before.

Such a reaction was simply more she must conceal from him. If it was better he never know the truth about who she really was, it was better still that he never know the thrill she felt in his presence.

Chapter Six

'I fear you have no hat or gloves.' Mrs Asher startled Hugh with her entrance. 'Shall I see if you can borrow some?'

'I do not need them.' He'd walk out in nothing but his drawers, if that was the only way.

'We did not even think of them.' She made it sound as if this was important. 'They must have been lost in the fire.'

With his overcoat, some of his money and a change of clothing.

And possibly his sight.

He certainly did not want to dwell on that topic. 'Let us not think of hats and gloves now. I am too eager to stretch my legs and breathe in fresh air.'

'I do have something for you,' she said. 'A cane from Mr Carter.'

She placed it in his hand.

'Good man!' He gripped the handle and tested

it. 'I must thank him. This should help me walk around on my own.' He'd seen blind people using canes to feel their way, waving them in front of their feet to warn of obstacles. He tested it in the room.

'Not seeing must be so difficult.…' Her voice trailed off.

'None of that.' He extended his hand. 'Come. Show me the way.'

She led him out the front door, holding his arm as if they were walking through Hyde Park. 'There is a step down.'

It felt like flagstone beneath his feet, and he was surprised how insecure it felt to walk into a space without knowing what was ahead. He swept the cane in front of him and it swung free. She held on to him as well, but that gratified him in other ways. The air was crisp and cool and it nourished him. This was not a day to be hesitant or gloomy. This was a day to enjoy the scent of flowers, of a stable nearby, of stone and grass. All cheered him.

They descended the step. 'Tell me what I would see in front of me.'

'There is a walkway,' she responded reassuringly. 'Nothing to trip on.'

'Not what is in front of my feet.' He swept his hand across the vista hidden to him. 'What I would see. I smell the stable. It must be in sight.'

'Oh.' She paused. Had he made her feel foolish? 'There is a stable. Off to the left maybe a hundred yards away. The walkway leads to a road and the stable is several feet away on the road. The road leads past some trees and a field and you can see it reaching a bigger road that leads to the village. You can see the village. It is a mile or two away. There is a church tower rising above the other buildings.'

It could have been a description of anywhere, but it helped him feel grounded.

'What does the stable look like?' he asked.

'It is white stucco, like the cottage.' She turned as if double-checking the cottage's appearance. 'Would you like to walk down the path to the road?'

'That will do.' He did not really care as long as he was stretching his legs.

But they could not move at any great pace. He depended on her support more than he thought he would. His feet faltered a couple of times. She and the cane helped him keep his balance. The only words spoken were her warnings. 'Take heed, there is a puddle. There is a rock.' It made him feel like a cursed invalid.

He forced himself to walk with more confidence, even though he did not know what was in his path.

Perhaps she sensed his frustration. She suddenly made an attempt at conversation. 'Tell me about your family, the ones you refused to allow me to contact.'

His family? He'd already told her about his profligate father. She probably wondered what other horrors his family possessed. 'The others are not like my father.'

'Then why not allow them to be contacted?'

He frowned. Why was she asking? 'Because they would all come running to care for me.'

'And you find that objectionable?' she asked.

She must want to rid herself of his care. 'None would be a good caretaker.' He tried to explain. 'My mother would merely consign me to the role of infant and try to do everything for me. She'd drive me insane in the space of an hour.' He need not mention his mother's lover, now constantly at her side. 'My brother Ned, the new earl, carries the bulk of family responsibility. If he came, he would be neglecting something more important. But worse, he married this empty-headed chit who would be utterly infuriating.' He also did not mention Rhys, his bastard brother. He had no right to ask anything of Rhys. 'Then there is my sister—'

'Your sister?' Her voice tensed.

It was puzzling. 'Phillipa would take good care of me, I am certain. I would not ask her, though. She is busy with the baby.'

'A baby?' Her voice grew soft, but none of the tension in it eased.

He'd forgotten. A baby was the likely reason for her long retreat on the Continent.

'She recently gave birth to a girl.' He was sorry he'd brought this up.

'How nice for your sister.' Mrs Asher's voice turned sad.

He put his arm across her back. 'Is this an unhappy topic for you, Mrs Asher?'

He felt her stiffen. 'No. Why should it be?'

He wanted to ask if she had other children. If not, what a heart-wrenching situation. A childless widow having to give up her illegitimate baby.

He asked a different question. 'Where is your family? Your parents? Sisters or brothers? Do you see them?'

'I have no family.' Her tone hardened.

No other children, then.

He held her tighter. 'Forgive me. I did not know you were so alone.'

She shrugged. 'I am used to it. My parents died a long time ago. As did my husband. There is no one else, really.'

'A long time ago? You make yourself sound as old as Methuselah.' In his mind she was young, but was she?

'I am old,' she said with conviction, avoiding his question.

He halted, dropping his arm from his half embrace. 'I do not believe you.'

'I am,' she insisted.

He hooked the cane around his arm and reached up to her face. He explored her face with his fingers. Her skin was smooth, free of wrinkles, free of blemish. She had high cheekbones, large eyes, a pointed chin. He rubbed her lips with his thumb and felt her sharp intake of breath. Her lips were full. Lush. Moist.

A long sigh escaped her lips and her breath warmed his hand.

His body seized with sudden desire. He leaned closer and felt her tremble.

He caught himself and stepped back. 'You are not as old as Methuselah, that much I can tell.'

She took his arm again. 'I am, though,' she insisted, her voice a bit shrill. 'I am two and thirty.'

He frowned. He was a year older. They were neither of them in the bloom of youth, but neither were they what he would call old. On the other hand, he well knew the feeling of being aged. It came from enduring the horrors of life. The losses. She'd certainly endured losses.

'How old were you when your parents died?' he asked.

This was not the sort of conversation a gentleman should have with a lady, but he preferred talking of something substantial over exchanging inanities about the weather or gossip.

Besides, he wanted to learn about her.

She could always refuse to answer, if she liked.

To his surprise, she did answer. 'I was eighteen. Hardly married a year.'

She'd married so young?

'Poor Papa and Mama,' she went on. 'They never had much of a chance to bask in their triumph.'

'Their triumph?'

She did not speak right away. 'My husband was a wealthy man. It was quite a coup for me to marry him.'

'I wonder that I cannot recall ever hearing his name.' Perhaps her husband was not of society. Or perhaps Hugh had been too busy at war to keep track of the members of the *ton*.

'We did not go to town much,' she said. 'He preferred the country.'

'Tell me about him.' He might as well try to satisfy all of his curiosity.

They walked several steps before she answered. 'My husband was very good to me. My happiness was his greatest concern. Anything I wanted, if it was in his power to provide it, he gave to me.'

Except a child.

Rhys's son and Phillipa's daughter seemed to have sent them both over the moon with happiness. Last he heard from Ned, his wife was obsessed with wanting a child. Hugh had never thought about it for himself. It seemed a part of life to anticipate after one settled down. And he had no intention of settling down.

But she did not know that, did she? What could she know of his situation, if he had a wife or children?

'You never asked me if I was married.' He tried to say this without an accusatory tone.

It took several more steps for her to respond. 'I knew you were not married.'

'How did you know?' He asked, too sharply.

Again she hesitated. 'My husband always received the London papers and I continued receiving them. I—I liked reading about society, the parties, the people. The marriage of a son of Lord Westleigh would have been announced.'

A logical explanation. Still, she was holding something back, something she did not want him to know. Good God. Could it be—?

'Did you know my father, Mrs Asher?' He frowned.

If she'd encountered his father—

Daphne's heart raced. He asked too many questions. Was suspicious of her, as well he should be. She was deceiving him after all.

'No, I did not know your father,' she answered him.

That was the truth. She might have met the man once or twice, in those early days when Faville had taken her to town for the Season, but she didn't remember precisely.

He blew out a breath. 'Good. For a moment I feared he might have misused you. He was entirely capable of such behaviour.'

'But I read of him in the newspapers, of course.' The papers never used full names when spreading scandal and gossip, but everyone knew of whom they wrote.

They passed the stable and two other small buildings whose purpose she did not know. The road was lined with shrubbery, bright green with new leaves. Buttercups and heartsease dotted the lawn beyond. Should she describe them to him? Or would it make it worse to know that spring bloomed all around and he could not see it?

He spoke. 'You never said how long ago your husband died.'

Why must he persist in this interrogation?

She might as well answer. 'A little over three years ago.'

'Three years ago?' His voice rose in surprise. 'I thought you said it was a long time.'

'It seemed like a long time to me.' So much had happened to her since, even if most of it had occurred in her mind and emotions. Her marriage seemed like a dream in comparison.

'How did it happen?' he asked.

'How did what happen?'

He made an exasperated sound. 'Your husband's death.'

'Oh.' Of course. 'He fell from his horse.'

He'd been with her one minute and dead the next. She'd gone through mourning, but had she grieved his loss? She feared not.

What sort of wife did not grieve her husband's death, especially a man who had been good to her?

Faville had always loved her. He'd loved her as a man loved a prized possession or a precious jewel. At the convent she'd realised there had been a man behind all that devotion, a man with his own needs and emotions. He'd given her far more than she'd given him. Instead, she'd filled her head with fantasies of Xavier Campion— husband of this man's sister.

She ought to tell him. Tell him now.

But he would hate her if she did. She could not bear it, knowing a man in her house, under her care, hated her. She hated herself enough.

'Why did you not marry, Mr Westleigh?' she asked brightly. Flirtatiously. Such skills as turning the conversation in the direction she desired were her forte—or had been once.

He answered in a bantering tone. 'I was mostly fighting Napoleon. Not a good time to start a courtship.'

'But the war has been over for years now.'

'I did not sell out until 1818,' he explained.

'Then my brother discovered my father had put our family at the brink of ruin. That certainly did not make me a good marriage prospect.'

She'd had no idea. Gossip about the Westleighs' financial woes had never reached the newspapers. 'The brink of ruin?'

'We were in danger of losing it all. The River Tick was lapping at our toes, you might say. Debt collectors were mere minutes from our door.' He stepped on a rock she'd neglected to warn him about and she had to hold tighter to his arm—his well-muscled arm—so he could catch his balance.

'We should turn around.' They were at the end of the road where it intersected with the road to Thurnfield. When they walked a few steps back towards the house she dropped her flirtatious tone, truly interested now. 'You said you *were* in danger of losing your money. You didn't lose it, then?'

'We were rescued. We scraped together every pound we could get our hands on and convinced our half-brother to run a gaming house for us.' His voice brightened. 'He—Rhysdale—had a brilliant idea. He called the place the Masquerade Club and made it so men and women could gamble there in masks and protect their identity. Ladies are able to attend without risking their reputations.'

Daphne felt the blood drain from her face.

How could she have attended the Masquerade Club all those weeks and not have known its connection to the Westleighs?

'Was—is—the gaming house successful?' It must be. When she'd attended, there had always been a crush of people, all throwing away their money to the roll of the dice or a turn of a card.

'Successful beyond our imagining,' he responded. 'The Westleigh fortune is restored and is growing by the day.'

Daphne had never gambled heavily when she'd attended the Masquerade Club. She'd been too obsessed with making Xavier Campion admit he loved her.

But it had not been she whom Xavier loved.

She'd first seen him in a ballroom when she'd been twenty years old. A beautiful young man, the most beautiful young man she had ever seen, the sort of man who'd inspired the Greeks to make statues. His dark hair and skin had been the perfect counterpoint to her pale, blonde beauty. And even his magnetic blue eyes were the equal of hers. She'd thought that meant they were destined to be together, that they were the perfect lovers, an exquisite pair beautifully matched.

But her husband separated them before they became lovers and Daphne spent years dreaming of a reunion with Xavier. Ten foolish years.

Her head pounded with the memory. Enough of this foolishness. He was nothing but a dream, a fancy. And at the moment she walked beside a very real man, about whom she still knew so little.

'And—and is your half-brother still running this gaming house for you?' she asked to keep him talking.

'Yes, he is.'

She'd heard of Rhysdale, of course. Xavier had been his friend and had managed the gaming house in Rhysdale's absence. Had he known he was a half-brother to the Westleighs?

She glanced at the man beside her, who seemed lost in thought.

Finally he spoke. 'Of all the family, Rhys is the best. Well, he and Phillipa, I suppose.'

Phillipa. Yes. Phillipa. A better woman than Daphne, certainly.

Westleigh went on. 'Rhys was my father's natural son, you see. I grew up despising him, but he saved us when we needed him. He had every reason not to.'

'Do you despise him now?' One could despise a person yet concede his worth at the same time. Was he such a man?

'Not at all,' he responded. 'I hold Rhys in the highest regard. He makes me ashamed of myself.'

They had that in common, then.

'Well, it is what you do today that matters the most,' she said. 'You cannot undo the past, but you can learn from it.' Had not the abbess told her this many times?

'Oh, I have learned from it,' he admitted. 'I don't expect Rhys will change his mind about me, though. We have established a sort of truce, at least, which is more than I deserve.' He smiled ruefully. 'I was horrible to him when we were boys. Taunted him until he'd fight with me. I liked nothing better than a good bout of fisti-cuffs. I was a wild boy, I'm afraid. Still am.'

'Do you still like fisticuffs?' she asked.

'I wouldn't back down from a fight....' He groaned. 'Listen to me ramble on about myself. Soon I will be confessing to you all the mistakes of my youth.'

'I am not certain our walk will be that long.'

He laughed, a deep and resonant laugh that made her insides flutter. 'I might need all of our two weeks, at least.' His smile turned genuine. 'Never fear. I will not burden you, not with all my sins, in any event.'

Her cheeks burned. She was unaccustomed to making people truly laugh.

His cane caught on a thick root and again she held him tightly until he regained his footing. She'd almost forgotten he could not see.

'Now it is your turn,' he said.

'My turn?'

'To confess the sins of your childhood.' He

added, 'Unless you were an obedient, compli-
ant little girl.'

She had certainly not been that. 'I was a trial,
I confess.' More painful memories. 'I was not
quick to learn things.'

'I do not believe it,' he said. 'You do not strike
me as an unintelligent woman.'

They walked on past the out buildings, near-
ing the stable.

'I suppose I was adequate at my lessons, but I
often forgot how to sit properly, how to smile—
things like that.'

He shook his head. 'Are you making another
jest?'

'No.' She'd said nothing foolish.

Her mother had often chastised her, admonish-
ing her to stand up straight, to walk as if gliding,
to smile, to pour tea gracefully, to lean towards
a gentleman so her figure showed to best advantage. Her face would only carry her so far, her
mother insisted. She must be beautiful *and* af-
fect a pleasing manner. So Daphne had practised
being pleasing, over and over, until it had become
second nature. The training had borne fruit, too.
She'd become betrothed to Viscount Faville in her
first Season and married him quickly afterwards.

But she did not want to admit to Westleigh that
attributes a gentleman might think natural were
really only the result of proper training.

She averted her gaze. 'I was not jesting.'

He blew out a breath. 'I dare say a boy's up-bringing differs greatly from a girl's.'

'You should know because of your sister.' Surely Phillipa Westleigh had endured the same training. How much more important it would have been for her.

'I was enough older than my sister to pay little attention,' he said. 'But likely her upbringing was unique. Her face was scarred when she was small. She grew up disfigured.'

Daphne recalled the cruel words she'd spoken to Phillipa at the Masquerade Club and cringed in shame. Now she could only think what it would have been like to have so visible a disfigurement.

'How difficult for her,' she managed.

'I suppose it was.' He pounded the ground ahead of him with the cane. 'In a way it freed her.'

'Freed her?' She did not comprehend.

'She could not be expected to follow the usual course of an earl's daughter. The Marriage Mart and all. Instead, she became an accomplished *pianiste*. Do you know her musical compositions have been performed at Vauxhall and other places?'

What an accomplishment. Phillipa had played beautifully. She'd composed music, as well?

'You sound very proud of your sister.' Daphne envied her. Who had ever been proud of her, except for her marrying well? What had she ever accomplished?

'I am. She does what she wishes to do, no matter what. That is what I will do, as well.' His voice dropped. 'As soon as the bandages are off.'

'You will travel, then. Is that not correct, Mr Westleigh?' They'd spoken of it at dinner.

'Yes.' His voice tightened.

It all depended upon whether or not his eyes healed.

Chapter Seven

After they re-entered the house, Hugh put no further claim on Mrs Asher's time. He asked for the services of the new footman to walk with him around the house. Perhaps if he walked the space enough times, he'd be able to navigate on his own and not disrupt the routine of the servants or Mrs Asher—although if he had his way, he'd commandeer all of her time.

Instead, Toller, the new footman, was placed at his disposal. Toller was a cheerful, chatty young man who seemed perfectly content to walk with Hugh from Hugh's bedchamber, down the stairs, to the drawing room and to the dining room— over and over—all the while telling Hugh about his family, the village, the maids and Mr and Mrs Pitts.

'That Monette is a pretty thing,' Toller went on. 'But I do not suppose I will see much of her,

her being a lady's maid and all. She's probably above my touch, in any event.'

Monette, Toller had told him, was Mrs Asher's lady's maid who had come with her from Switzerland. The footman knew nothing else about her, though, and Hugh had not encountered her here—although he'd done once. In the fire.

'What of Mr Asher?' Hugh might as well turn the man's garrulity to matters of which he was truly curious. 'What was he like?'

'Mr Asher?' Toller sounded puzzled. 'I don't rightly know.'

Bad luck. 'Did you come to Thurnfield after he died?'

'I have lived in Thurnfield my whole life,' Toller responded with pride. 'There is nothing I do not know about it.'

'Then how do you not know of Mr Asher?'

'Can't know of him as he was never in Thurnfield,' Toller said. 'At least he never lived here. He might have passed through. Many folks pass through on their way to London.'

'Mr Asher never lived here?'

'Not in Thurnfield,' the footman insisted.

Had she lived separately from her husband? 'How long has Mrs Asher lived here, then?'

'About three days,' Toller answered.

Three days?

Toller kept talking. 'She drove into town looking for somebody to take care of you or someplace she could stay to care for you. Well, the inn was full of people from Ramsgate. There was a fire there, I was told. Maybe the one where you injured your eyes?' He didn't wait for Hugh to answer. 'Anyway, no one wished to take on the charge of caring for a sick man without knowing if he could pay, and you couldn't travel any farther, so Mrs Asher leased the cottage here. The previous tenants were a navy man and his wife. They left about a month ago. The place has been empty since.'

They reached the stairway again.

Hugh rested a hand on the banister. 'Do you mean Mrs Asher was just passing through? She never meant to live here, then?'

'That I could not say for certain,' Toller replied. 'But Mr Brill, the leasing agent, said she asked for two weeks, but he would not lease for so short a time, so she paid for three months.'

She paid for three months? Why?

And why tell him she lived here?

But did she ever say she lived here? Hugh strained to recall.

He turned his head towards where he thought Toller stood. 'Let us go back upstairs to my room, then I will free you from playing nursemaid.'

'Very well, sir,' Toller said agreeably.

Hugh ascended the stairs with more confidence than when they'd started the practice. He was becoming more accustomed to using the cane. With being unable to see.

At his bedchamber door he thanked the footman. 'This was excellent, Toller. I could not have done it without you. I'm in your debt.'

He'd pay the man a generous vail at the end of his stay. He'd be generous to all the servants, since he was the sole reason they'd been hired, apparently.

Why had Mrs Asher not simply told him she'd taken the house to take care of him? That she'd been required to pay ahead for time she'd not use? Where had she been bound, then? Where was her home?

He was reasonably certain there was no malevolence in her subterfuge, although at first he'd been suspicious of her. She clearly had nothing to gain from assuming his care. All she could gain was his money, but she obviously had money of her own.

Was she simply possessed of a kind heart? Or had she believed she owed it to him because he'd carried her out of the fire? Why, then, not simply order her servants to care for him?

She was a mystery.

She possessed an adept conversational skill that she used to conceal more than she revealed. She swung from the superficial to a hint of deep sadness.

She intrigued him in other ways, as well. Her

musical voice, the scent of roses when she was near, her soft hand. Touching her face had been arousing, more arousing than he liked to admit.

He wanted to *see* her, know her, discover what she needed to so carefully hide. Was that the source of her unhappiness? He could not simply ask her. He wanted to know about her life, about her husband. Had she loved him? Had her husband been good to her? Had there been other men besides him? And what had she been doing, travelling alone on the Continent? Was he correct in his guess that she'd hid herself away to have a baby?

He probably had no right to know such personal matters, but he did deserve to know why she had taken such charge of him and gone to all this trouble and expense as a result. He'd discover that much this night. Or at least confront her with what he knew.

That evening Daphne found Westleigh waiting in the drawing room before dinner. Like the night before, she poured him wine. He seemed preoccupied, disturbed. About his blindness, she guessed.

He responded to her efforts at chitchat with an economy of response, although he did accept a second glass of wine. Her mood darkened. Gone was the ease they'd achieved during their walk. Why? She missed it most dreadfully.

Finally Carter announced that dinner was served.

Westleigh took his cane in one hand and stood. He offered her his arm. 'May I escort you in to dinner?'

What was this? The previous night she'd had to carefully lead him to the room.

It sounded like an order, not an invitation, so she took his arm.

He walked almost directly to the door. She guided him to correct his course, else they might have hit the wall.

'Thank you,' he said, his words clipped. 'Tomorrow I will do better.'

'You are doing very well.' She used a placating voice.

He continued to confidently cross the hall to the dining room, although his manner was a bit determined. He led her to the doorway almost as if he could see and found her chair with equal ease.

He pulled it out for her. 'I commandeered Toller to help me learn how to traverse the house. We walked it a number of times until I could envisage the floor plan and not run into furniture.'

'How very clever of you.'

He glowered. 'You need not do that.'

She did not know what he meant. 'Do what?'

'Speak in your governess voice,' he snapped.

Her heart pounded. 'My what?'

'That governess voice, as if you were talking to a schoolboy. You use it often.'

Speak with your heart, the abbess had repeatedly told her. *It is your true voice.* Daphne still did not know what that meant.

'I—I— That is the way I speak.' She did not know any other way.

Except her tone had changed with her last words. Even she could tell it.

'Not always.' Carter and Toller entered and Westleigh stopped talking.

Toller served the soup under Carter's watchful eye.

When they left again, Westleigh dipped his spoon into the soup and carefully lifted it to his mouth.

Not all of it spilled.

She remained silent, but continued to stare at him. His effort to eat normally was heartbreaking to watch, but he managed to finish most of the soup.

No sooner did he put down his spoon than Carter and Toller re-entered carrying the next course. Toller reached for her soup bowl.

Carter stopped him. 'Are you finished, ma'am?'

She'd forgotten to taste it.

She waved a hand. 'Yes. I had no appetite for soup.'

He placed roasted quail on the table, already carved and cut into pieces for Westleigh.

'Some quail, sir?' Carter asked.

Westleigh nodded.

Carter also served small roasted potatoes and apricot fritters, explaining each to Westleigh.

The two servants left the room again.

Would it be the height of poor manners to ask Westleigh what was troubling him, or a neglect of manners to pretend one did not notice?

She took a deep breath. 'Mr Westleigh, what is distressing you?'

He lifted his head as if to look at her. 'Distressing me?'

She nodded, but realised he could not see. 'Your mood is much altered from earlier today when we took that pleasant walk.'

He pushed his fork around his plate until he speared a piece of meat and lifted it to his mouth. The muscles of his neck flexed as he chewed. Had her husband's muscles moved with such suppressed strength? She'd never noticed.

'I did not mean to make you more uncomfortable,' he finally said.

More uncomfortable?

'I am perfectly comfortable, I assure you.' She kept her voice modulated so the tension shaking her insides did not show.

His mouth twisted with scepticism.

She tightened her grip on the stem of her wine glass.

The door opened again. Carter and Toller stood ready to assist them.

'Later,' Westleigh said, so softly she barely heard.

When the dishes and their plates were removed, Daphne turned to Carter. 'Would you serve Mr Westleigh's brandy and the fruit and biscuits with my tea in the drawing room?'

'Yes, m—ma'am.' He waved Toller off to take care of it.

She stood and Westleigh rose as well, taking his cane in hand and walking over to her to offer his arm again.

'Is the cane helping you?' she asked in the most reasonable voice she could muster, because she needed to say something.

His answer was devoid of expression. 'It is. It gives me confidence, even if it be false confidence.'

'False confidence is at least confidence of some sort.' Agreeing with a gentleman was almost a reflex with her. In this case, what she said was certainly true of her, as well. False confidence was all she seemed to possess lately.

One corner of his mouth rose. 'How very wise of you, Mrs Asher.' It was a good mimic of her voice.

He led her out of the dining room without banging into a wall.

She lowered her head. 'Do I truly sound that way?'

His voice softened. 'I exaggerated.' He waved a hand. 'Do not heed me. It is my mood.'

His foul mood, he must mean.

As they crossed the hall she marvelled again—silently—at how well he managed. The drawing-room door was trickier, but she gently guided him and perhaps this time he did not perceive her help.

Toller was just setting down the tea tray. A decanter of brandy and two glasses were already on the table.

'Thank you, Toller,' she said.

He bowed and left.

'Sit, Westleigh,' she said. 'I'll pour your brandy.'

He found the chair he'd sat in before and lowered himself into it. She handed him the glass and eyed the other one for herself.

Why not have some brandy? She'd seen women drink it at the Masquerade Club. She poured herself a generous amount and took a gulp. With much effort she avoided a paroxysm of coughing. His head rose, but he could not possibly know, could he? She made a clatter of pouring tea, just in case.

But it was the brandy she drank.

He inhaled deeply and released his breath

slowly. 'I have been trying to puzzle out why you should keep me from learning the truth.'

She felt herself go pale. Had he discovered who she was—?

He pressed on. 'Why did you not tell me?'

'I—I do not know what you mean.' At least she did not know precisely what he meant; only what she feared he meant.

'Someone—I will not say who—told me. In all innocence, I might add. This was not a betrayal of your secrets, but someone who did not know the truth was to be withheld from me.'

She took a relieved sip and, this time, savoured the warmth the brandy created in her chest. Only Monette, Carter, and John Coachman knew who she was and if they had told, it would have been a deliberate betrayal of what she'd asked of them.

'Why, Westleigh—' she put on her most charming voice '—I am at a loss. What truth did I withhold?'

He waved an exasperated hand. 'That you leased this cottage for three months because of me. You gave me the impression you lived here.'

'Did I?' The brandy was making this easier. 'If I did so, it was most unintentionally done.'

He took a gulp of his brandy. 'Please, let us speak without pretence. Why have you gone to so much trouble and expense for me? Taking me from Ramsgate. Leasing this cottage for much longer than needed. Hiring servants for me.'

She stared at him, wishing she could see all his face, wishing she could look into his eyes and gauge how much of the truth to tell.

She finished the contents of her glass and gave a little laugh. 'I assure you, I did not plan to take on so much trouble for you. I thought I would find someone in Ramsgate to take care of you and, failing that, I was certain I would find someone on the road. When that also did not happen, events just seemed to pile on each other.' She poured more brandy in her glass. 'Please believe me that the money is a trifle, as I have told you before. And, like you, no one expected me at any particular time.' There was no one to whom her arrival would matter. 'A delay of two weeks was of no consequence.'

'But the hiring of the servants—' he began.

'That was not for your benefit,' she explained. 'I think we could have done well enough with Monette, Carter and me. And Mr and Mrs Pitts. The others—they seemed to need the work.'

'You hired them without needing them?' He sounded surprised.

'Mary and Ann—the maids—they looked… hungry.' She lifted a shoulder, even though he could not see the gesture. 'It—it felt like the right thing to do and very little trouble to me in the doing of it.' More trouble than she'd bargained for, having to organise everything and make certain they had decent dresses and aprons and caps to wear. 'Then Mrs Pitts knew a cook and others to hire. It seemed easiest just to hire them. Our meal was quite good tonight, was it not?'

'Do they know it is for three months?' The surprise had not left his voice.

'Oh…' Telling him about this made her feel foolish. 'I do not know. We talked in terms of yearly wages, so I suppose that is what I will pay them.'

'Mrs Asher—' Now he sounded scolding.

She was certain the abbess would have approved, but she could hardly tell him that. 'It is my money to do with as I wish.'

'Do you have a man of business? Someone to help you manage such matters as bills and servants?'

She sighed. Dear Mr Everard. She'd written to him that she'd returned to England and would stay a time in Thurnfield. 'Yes. I have a very capable man. He was my husband's man of business and he has continued to help me.'

If anyone knew the whole of her folly with Xavier and Phillipa, it was Mr Everard. He'd remained loyal, even so.

Westleigh stood and, using the cane, paced back and forth. 'Mrs Asher, I do not favour anyone paying for my needs. I do not like that you withheld this information from me. It was one thing for me to accept hospitality at your house, but it is another matter for me to allow you to pay a lease and hire servants.'

'My hiring the servants had nothing to do with you,' she protested.

'You would not have been here to hire them if it had not been for me.' He made his way back to his chair, tapping with his cane to find precisely where it was. He sat again and groped for his brandy glass. He drank it empty.

She reached over and poured him some more. 'Here are some biscuits and candied fruit.' She placed a small plate of the treats next to his glass on the table beside him.

He picked up the glass, but did not sample the other. 'I will pay all these expenses. The cottage and the servants.'

Ridiculous! He could not possibly have as much money as she, considering what he'd shared about his family's recent financial woes. She'd wounded his vanity, though, obviously. Perhaps she possessed too much independence, in his opinion. Men did not like women who displayed too much independence, her mother had taught her.

Although the abbess always told her she must think for herself...

She shook her head. 'Very well, Westleigh. You may pay. We'll make an accounting and you may pay.'

He took another drink of the brandy. 'Good.'

She poured herself a little more and sipped it slowly.

After a time he spoke. 'You need not stay, then.'

She looked at him. 'You wish me to bid you goodnight?'

'No, not at all,' he quickly said. 'I meant, you and your servants need not stay with me any longer. You may go on your way. If I am paying—'

'You wish me to leave?' The brandy made her thinking fuzzy and her emotions raw. The idea he wished to send her away unexpectedly wounded her and she fought back tears.

He frowned and paused before going on. 'I have no right to keep you here. It is not as if I could pay you for your assistance.'

Pay her? 'You certainly cannot!'

She'd wanted to do something for somebody, something unselfish. She wanted to do something for *him*. For restitution—and—and because he needed someone so very much. But here it was, the one time she extended herself for another person, *needed* to extend herself, and he was sending her away.

Hugh had made a muddle of this.

She'd been the one acting under false pretences, so why did he feel so rotten? She sounded as if she'd start weeping. How had the situation turned itself around?

He spoke in low tones. 'Why did you do it, then? Why did you assume care of me in the first place? Me, a stranger. You were not the only one I helped to escape the fire. Someone else would have come to my aid.'

'I cannot explain it.' Her voice turned small, sad and defensive. 'I just could not leave you.' She sighed. 'You are correct, though. You can pay Toller, Mary, Ann and the others to take care of you. You do not need me. I will go if you wish it.'

His chest tightened. Wish it? Her leaving was the last thing he wanted. How was he to bear the darkness without her company? His world had shrunk in his sightlessness, but she filled all the space he had left. For her to leave would plunge him into an abyss.

He'd endure what he must, but the two weeks would be deadly without her.

And something was unfinished between them. He did not know what, and if she left him he would never know.

'I do not wish you to go,' he murmured. 'I simply cannot ask you to stay.'

He heard her pouring more brandy into a glass, not his glass. How much was she drinking?

'Why must this be so complicated?' Her voice was strained with unhappiness. 'If we were friends, you would accept my help without question and without all these noble protestations. If we were acquaintances, you would not question my helping you.'

'If we were friends,' he repeated.

'That is what I said.'

He preferred her irritation to her sadness. 'Then let us be friends. Why should we not be? We have a great basis. I helped you escape a fire and you helped me get care for my wounds.'

'We could be friends?' She said this as if she'd never had a friend in the world.

'Certainly.' At least he'd cheered her. 'You can stay and keep me company. As my friend. And you can be my eyes until mine are working again. I confess, I would feel more secure knowing a friend was looking out for me.'

'Yes…' Her voice turned dreamlike. 'I could help you as a friend. Look out for you.' Her tone changed to one more decided. 'Very well, Mr Westleigh. Let us act as friends.'

He relaxed and finished his second glass of brandy. 'How far should we go in being friends?' he asked. 'Should we pretend we've known each other since childhood and use our given names?'

She giggled, a delightful sound. 'If you wish it.'

'Then you shall call me Hugh from now on.' He smiled. 'No more Mr Westleigh. Agreed?'

'Hugh,' she repeated, making his name sound like a gift. 'I am Daphne, then.'

'Daphne,' he whispered.

Chapter Eight

Hugh heard her rise.

'Oh!' she exclaimed. The chinaware rattled. 'Goodness! I am unsteady.'

He grabbed his cane and stood and immediately she seized his arm. She swayed into him.

'Too much brandy, perhaps?' he said.

She threaded her arm through his. 'You knew I drank some brandy?'

He gestured to his bandages. 'Without my sight, I find my other senses vastly improved. I heard you pour the brandy, which sounded nothing like pouring tea, and I smelled its scent.'

She'd poured herself at least three glasses, which seemed out of character for her.

'I—I did not feel like tea,' she explained, sounding defensive. She released him, but fell against him and again took his arm to steady herself. 'Perhaps I should retire. To bed.'

He held on to her. 'Should I call Carter to assist you?'

'I would rather not have Carter know. I'll be fine if I can get to my room.' She tried to pull away again, but he kept hold of her.

'I'll take you then.' He laughed. 'It will be the blind leading the...jug bitten.'

'I am inebriated?' Her voice rose. 'How is that possible? I drink as much wine to no ill effect.'

'Brandy is stronger.' He walked towards where the door should be. 'Did you not know that?'

He felt her shake her head, her curls brushing his shoulder. 'I never drank it before.'

Why tonight, then?

'Move to the left,' she said. 'You are aiming us to the wall.'

'Blast.' He needed more practice in this room, obviously. He moved to the left. 'Are we heading to the door?'

'Yes.'

He did better crossing the hall with her and finding the stairs. He hooked the cane around his arm and gripped the banister. She gripped him. They made slow and somewhat precarious progress. She leaned on him as if in complete trust of his ability to deliver her safely to her bedchamber door, and he'd be damned if he would fail her.

But he had not practised the way to her door.

When they reached the top of the stairs, he stopped. 'Which way?'

'Mmm.' Was she asleep?

He shook her gently. 'Daphne? You must show me the way to your room.'

'Oh.' She started and paused as if getting her bearings. 'This way.'

She took a step and he followed her direction, although definitely not with the complete trust she'd shown him. With his free hand he used the cane to make certain she was not leading him into pieces of furniture.

Finally she stopped. 'Here it is.'

He felt for the door and found the latch. 'I will leave you here, then.'

She still clung to his arm and rested her head against him. 'Feels nice.'

He eased her arm off and now faced her. 'It does indeed feel nice, Daphne.'

'To be friends,' she mumbled. 'It feels nice to be friends.'

The warmth of her body against his, the scent of roses that always clung to her, her low, brandy-soaked voice all intoxicated him as much as the brandy had intoxicated her. At this moment he did not wish friendship from her, but something more. Something between lovers.

He resisted the impulse, but he did not release her. 'I will bid you a friendly goodnight, then.'

He placed his cane against the wall and searched for her face. Touching her cheek and cupping it in the palm of his hand, he leaned down until he felt her breath on his face. He lowered his face to hers and touched his lips to hers, slightly off-kilter. He quickly made the correction and kissed her as a man kisses a woman when desire surges within him.

'Mmm.' She twined her hands around his neck and gave herself totally to the kiss.

He was acutely aware of her every curve touching his body. His hand could not resist sliding up her side and cupping her breast, her full, high breast. He rubbed his fingers against this treasure and she pressed herself against him, her fingers caressing the back of his neck.

He wanted to take her there in the hallway, plunge himself into her against the door to her bedchamber. She would be willing. Never had a woman seemed more willing.

'Daphne,' he whispered.

Some rational part of him heard footsteps on the stairs.

'Someone is coming.' He eased her away from him. 'We had better say goodnight before we do something two friends might regret.'

'I wouldn't regret it, Hugh!' She tried to renew the embrace.

'Not now.' He pushed her away gently.

The footsteps were coming closer, nearly at the top of the stairs, he guessed. He opened her door and picked up his cane.

'Oh, *madame*!' an accented voice said. 'I—I have come to assist you. If—if I do not disturb you.'

'You must be Monette,' Hugh said. 'I have walked Mrs Asher to her room. She is a bit unsteady.'

He heard Monette rush over to her. '*My lady!* Are you ill?'

'Not ill,' Daphne said. 'Feel wonderful. Am dizzy, though.'

'She drank some brandy,' Hugh explained. 'Without realising the effects.'

'*Je comprends*, sir,' Monette said, sounding very French. 'I will take care of her.'

He felt the two women move past him and walk through the doorway. The door closed behind them and Hugh was left to find his own way back to his bedchamber to await Carter's assistance to ready him for bed.

Sleeping would be difficult this night, he feared.

Daphne rose the next morning humming the tune to 'Barbara Allen'. She laughed at herself. Why was she singing a song of death when she felt so happy?

The previous evening was fuzzy to her, but she remembered their quarrel about money and she remembered that she and Westleigh had made a pact to be friends. It felt wonderful to have a friend, even a temporary one. She so rarely had a friend.

She remembered calling Phillipa Westleigh her friend, but, truly, Daphne had simply been trying to use Phillipa to help in her attempted conquest of Xavier. Daphne had been no friend. She wanted to be different with Hugh—she could call him Hugh now. She wanted to be a good friend.

She had a vision of sharing kisses with him, but that was nonsense. A dream, certainly. She'd dreamed of kissing Hugh, like she used to dream of kissing Xavier. One could not help one's dreams.

One thing was certain. Fantasy must never overpower reason in her relationship with Hugh as it had with Xavier. She would be content— overjoyed—that she and Hugh would spend the next ten days as friends.

Monette entered the room to help Daphne dress. Daphne was tempted to ask for the prettiest of the three dresses she had packed with her. It did not matter what she wore, though, because he could not see her. She did not have to look pretty for him. Imagine! He wanted to be her friend without even knowing what she looked like.

Once ready, she hurried from her room. Hugh was leaving his bedchamber at the same time.

'Good morning,' she said, suddenly reticent to

even use his given name. What if he'd changed his mind since the night before?

He smiled and turned in her direction, not quite facing her directly. 'Good morning, Daphne.' His voice was low and deep and warmed her all over. 'Are you bound for breakfast?'

She brightened. 'I am, indeed.'

He offered his arm. 'Would you like to see if I remember how to find the dining room?'

Her fingers wrapped around his muscle. 'It would be my pleasure.'

They descended the stairs together.

'Any ill effects from the brandy?' he asked.

Her head hurt a little, but she was too happy to care. 'None to speak of.'

When they reached the last step, he hesitated. 'Go ahead and lead me. I don't mind floundering on my own, but I would hate to run you into a table or the wall.'

'I will this time,' she responded. 'But you mustn't always act the invalid.'

He smiled again. 'You have surmised it is a role I detest.'

'Oh, yes.' She exaggerated her expression. She did not sound much different than any other time she engaged men in conversation, but inside she felt transformed.

Breakfast was pleasant. It reminded Daphne of those days in her marriage when it seemed as if she made her husband happy.

* * *

After breakfast she suggested they take a walk.

They stepped out of the house into a morning as glorious as her mood.

'Tell me what the day is like,' he said as she led him on the same path as the day before. 'Is it as fine as it seems?'

She did not want to answer right away, too acutely aware of all he missed by being unable to see. 'First tell me why you think it fine.'

'Well…' He paused before they stepped onto the road. 'First the air smells of all the wonderful smells of a spring day, of new leaves forming, fresh grass growing, flowers blooming. The sun feels warm on my face. And the birds are making a great deal of noise.' He covered her hand with his. 'Now tell me what you see.'

It had rained the night before and it was as if the rain had scrubbed the landscape into its most presentable appearance. 'First, there is dew on the grass and it sparkles.' Like tiny jewels, she thought. 'There are spring flowers in bloom, in flower beds around the cottage. The sky is very clear. It is that deep, clear blue one does not see very often.'

How many times had her husband compared the colour of her eyes to such a sky? And her hair to the narcissus blooming in the garden? Men always commented on her beauty. This man could not see her, though, and he liked her anyway.

'We're starting on the road now,' she warned him as they walked on.

They approached the stable where John Coachman stood in the door.

'We're near the stable now,' she said. 'My coachman is there.'

The coachman stepped forwards. 'Good morning, ma'am. Good morning, Mr Westleigh. I'd say you look a sight better than when I saw you last.'

Hugh stopped and extended his hand, but the coachman was too far away to reach it. He strode over to accept Hugh's grip.

'You assisted me,' Hugh said. 'I thank you.'

He coloured. ''Twas nothing, sir.'

'You know my name.' Hugh released his hand. 'What is yours?'

It had not occurred to Daphne to introduce them.

'I go by John Coachman, mostly,' the man replied.

Hugh nodded. 'My father always called our coachmen John Coachman. My mother always knew their Christian names, their wives' names and the names of all of their children. She also knew precisely how they should raise their children and how they should conduct every aspect of their lives.'

Daphne knew none of those things. When she'd sent for John Coachman to meet her in Ramsgate, had she taken him away from his family? She'd certainly never given it a thought.

Her coachman gave Hugh a toothy grin. 'Not married, nor have any children.' He winked. 'That I know of.'

Hugh sobered. 'We'd better not pursue that conversation, not with your employer standing here.'

The coachman darted her an anxious look.

'What is your name?' she asked, feeling ashamed of herself. 'I am sorry I never learned it.'

'Oh, John Coachman does well enough,' he responded. Rather kindly, she thought. 'But, if you would like the real thing, it is Henry Smith.'

'I'll call you Smith from now on, then.' The sounds of voices came from inside the stable. She glanced towards them. 'How are the stable boys working out?'

Smith glanced back, too, a pleased expression on his face. 'They leave me nothing to do. They are good workers, ma'am.'

At least she'd eased his load a bit. 'You must enjoy some leisure, then, Smith. Take some time for yourself.'

His eyes widened. 'Thank you, ma'am.'

She took Hugh's arm again and they continued on their walk.

'I ought to have known his name,' she murmured.

He touched her hand again. 'My mother's style

was always to insinuate herself into everyone's business, whether they were family or servants. Not everyone adopts such a style.'

She knew a little about Monette's life. Monette had been the daughter of English parents who'd lived in Switzerland. She'd also been orphaned at an early age, with no relatives to take her in. The convent had given her a home, but she was never meant for that life. Daphne had given her a different choice.

Of Carter she only knew he had been stranded in Switzerland without employment. Now she wondered about his story, as well.

She thought about the servants at Faville House, about how little she knew of their lives, and of the servants at the estate in Vadley, the house and property her husband had left her and where she had spent so little time. How would the servants feel about her return? she wondered. Would they be dreading it?

His voice broke into her reverie. 'A penny for your thoughts,' he said. 'Or whatever the rate is for a wealthy widow.'

'I was thinking of my servants at home,' she answered honestly. 'Of whether they would welcome my return.'

'How long have you been away?' he asked.

'More than two years.' She'd spent only a few months in the house in Vadley after the new Viscount Faville had taken possession of Faville

House. He was the son of her husband's cousin whose wife had been eager for her to leave.

'You've been two years in Switzerland?'

She guided him around a rut in the road. 'Almost.'

If he was more curious about her stay in Switzerland, he did not say so. The sound of horse's hooves in the distance seemed to distract him.

'Someone riding this way?' Hugh asked.

Daphne turned to see. 'No, one of the stablemen is leading one of the horses. They are going in the opposite direction from us.'

'Which reminds me.' His tone was light. 'Was the hiring of the stable workers more of your charitable efforts?'

'I suppose so.' She furrowed her brow. 'Was I so terribly foolish?'

He pulled her closer to him. 'I think you were terribly generous.'

She felt like weeping at the compliment. At the same time, her senses soared at his closeness. 'You could not see them, but the new maids were so very thin and very eager. How could I say no? And then Mr and Mrs Pitts came up with the idea for hiring the others.' She considered this. 'I wonder if there are many people needing work so urgently.'

'There are many former soldiers out of work, now that the war is over,' he responded. 'And with the Corn Laws there are a lot of hungry people.'

Feed the poor.

One day she had helped the nuns give out bread to needy people. The looks of hunger on their faces had rendered them grotesque. An empty belly was a pain she'd never experienced.

'What is one to do?' she wondered aloud.

'You've done well enough,' he responded.

She jostled him. 'But you are paying, remember? Except I will pay the stable boys. I insist upon it.'

Another stable boy led another horse out of the stable.

'Lord, I miss riding.' His voice turned wistful. 'I do not suppose you have a riding horse in that stable? I'd be tempted to have one of those workers take me out riding.'

'Only the carriage horses.' But Daphne smiled. Surely there were riding horses to procure in the village. Perhaps John Coachman—*Smith*, she meant—would not mind his leisure interrupted to make riding possible for Hugh.

For her friend.

The very next day after breakfast when she and Hugh, complete with new hat and gloves, walked towards the stables, she remarked, 'Oh, there is Smith again.'

'Morning, ma'am. Mr Westleigh,' Smith responded.

'Good morning, Smith,' Hugh greeted cheerfully. He inhaled. 'Do you have a horse with you?'

'I do indeed, sir.' Smith grinned. 'And one of the boys is here, as well. Henry.'

'Hello, Henry,' Hugh said.

Daphne smiled at the young man mounted on a horse and staring open-mouthed at her. Somehow she was glad Hugh could not see the boy's reaction.

'This may sound daft.' A corner of Hugh's mouth lifted in a half smile. 'But may I pet the horse?'

'I'll do you one better, sir.' Smith pulled the horse forwards. 'How about you take a ride with Henry here.'

It was Hugh's turn to be open-mouthed. 'You are jesting.'

'It is no jest.' Daphne pushed him forwards. 'Mr Pitts found us two riding horses. One for you and one for Henry, so he can accompany you.'

Hugh turned back to her, shaking his head, but speechless.

'Enjoy yourself,' she said. 'Smith was told this horse will not dump you in a hedge.'

He laughed. 'That is a good thing.'

Smith brought the horse to him and Hugh patted the animal.

'I'll help you mount, sir.' Smith guided him to the stirrup, but Hugh mounted easily as soon as his foot was in it.

Smith touched his hat and walked back into the stable.

Daphne stood and watched Hugh ride away, straight backed and confident, as if he was free of the bandages.

Her heart soared with joy. Was it always this way when one did something to make another so happy? This was a gift better than any she'd ever received.

Chapter Nine

What were the odds Hugh would find any recuperation enjoyable, especially this one?

For the past four days he'd ridden in the mornings before breakfast, starting the day feeling free and unfettered by the bandages covering his eyes. Afterwards, he shared pleasant breakfasts with Daphne and they spent most of the rest of the days together. Taking walks. Playing the pianoforte. Talking. In the afternoon and evenings she sometimes read the London newspapers to him or books about exotic places, places he intended to visit and see for himself. They shared dinner and afterwards retired to the drawing room where he sipped brandy and she drank tea. That she seemed happy gratified him more than he could say.

She didn't pour herself brandy, though. Did not repeat that release of restraint that had led to the kiss he could not put out of his mind. His senses burned for her; otherwise the time was idyllic.

This morning was no different. He and Daphne walked together to the stable where Henry waited with his horse. Hugh bid Daphne goodbye and he and Henry set off. There was a field nearby where they could give the horses their heads and race at exhilarating speed.

This was Hugh's favourite time, a time he forgot the bandages on his eyes. He merely savoured the wind in his face and the power of the horse beneath him. He'd galloped like this through cannon and musket smoke in the war. This was not so different—except perhaps that no cannon or musket fired at him. He and the horse were familiar with the field now. Hugh knew how long before the horse would slow and they would progress at a milder pace through some brush.

But now he was flying free. Life was good.

The next moment, the horse balked and stumbled back. Hugh pitched forwards, his face hitting the horse's neck and loosening his bandages and pushing them askew. He managed to hold on to the horse, but in his struggle, he did the unthinkable.

He opened his eyes.

He saw nothing but the white of the loosened bandages. A stab of pain lanced both eyes and he immediately shut them again as he found his seat and pulled on the reins to steady the horse. The pain persisted until finally subsiding into an ache reminiscent of the first two days of his injury. He repositioned the bandages as best he could, but he'd injured his eyes again. He was certain of it.

He heard Henry's horse approach. 'Are you hurt, sir? You almost took a tumble.'

'Not hurt,' Hugh said. At least, not hurt in the way Henry meant. 'Merely shaken. Do you know what happened?'

'Something spooked the mare,' Henry said. 'Didn't see what it was.'

'Well.' Hugh's breathing almost returned to normal. 'No harm done. Let's keep on.' He didn't want to turn back. Didn't want to admit to himself that everything he hoped for might be lost.

By the end of the ride Hugh had composed himself. Mr Wynne was due to call this very day. He'd change the bandages and they'd again be tight. Until then Hugh must simply remember to keep his lids closed. Maybe Wynne would tell him he was still on the mend. Maybe he had not done terrible harm.

He managed to act normally during breakfast. Daphne needn't know he might have ruined all her efforts at taking care of him.

'I must go into the village this morning,' Daphne told him. 'Monette asked me to accompany her. I've neglected her of late.'

'You've neglected your lady's maid?' This was indeed an odd statement.

'She is not accustomed to being in England.'

Daphne explained, sounding embarrassed. 'Nor to being around so many people.'

So many people? In a village?

'Besides, I think there is something on her mind,' she went on. 'There is nothing like a nice walk to help loosen tongues.'

He must be careful not to agree to a walk with her today, then.

'I should be back by the time Mr Wynne calls,' she added.

He was due in the afternoon.

'I'll find some way to amuse myself.' Hugh would probably sit in his bedchamber and worry, but she need not know that.

She was gone most of the day, which was just as well. Hugh heard her voice outside as she returned. He left his rocking chair to make his way down the stairs.

'There you are, Hugh!' she said brightly.

Were her cheeks flushed from the exercise and fresh air? he wondered. Would he ever see such a sight?

'Welcome back.' He made himself sound cheerful. 'Are you there as well, Monette?'

'I am, sir,' the maid answered shyly.

'Did you ladies find much to look at in the village?' he asked.

'We had a delightful time,' Daphne answered.

'We had tea in a very nice tea shop and we browsed through all the stores we could find.'

'Browsed? Do not tell me you did not find something to purchase? I do not believe my mother ever merely browsed in a store in her life.'

'We purchased some fabric for Monette and a few other things. Some lovely marzipan from a confectioner. We should have that with tea later.'

Marzipan was typically formed into fancy shapes and colours, to appear like fruits and vegetables. It was a confection that was better to see than to eat.

Would he ever see it? 'That sounds quite nice.'

'I trust Mr Wynne did not call early?' Daphne said.

He could hear the handling of packages wrapped in paper. 'He sent a message that he would arrive late.' More waiting. At least Daphne would be a distraction.

Hugh reached the bottom step.

'Pardon, sir.' Monette passed by him.

He felt Daphne walk near. 'Were you bound for the drawing room? I will join you shortly. I must change. My skirts are full of dirt from the road.'

He nodded, knowing she could see, even if he could not.

It pleased him to hear the sound of pleasure in her voice from a simple walk to village shops. So often he felt sadness around her, even as they were entertaining themselves at the pianoforte or taking a walk or reading. Maybe he was the reason, if spending a day away from him lightened her spirits.

Blast. He was acting gloomy. The least he could do was avoid inflicting his low mood on her.

He made his way to the drawing room and distracted himself at the pianoforte by playing the scales and chords she'd taught him.

It did help to pass the time. It seemed only a few minutes before she came in the room, saying, 'Carter will bring us tea. You can taste the marzipan.' She walked over and stood behind him. 'You are improving very quickly. I am astonished.'

He made himself laugh. 'Not as astonished as I am.'

'Do you wish to keep practising? Do you want another lesson?' Her scent wafted around him.

'No.' He placed his hands in his lap. 'Why don't you read to me a little?'

'Should we continue with *The Annual Register*?' she asked.

'Yes. *The Annual Register*.' They'd found an old Annual Register from 1808. Among the usual topics covered in *The Annual Register*, like politics, finance and notable world and local events, were chronicles of travels, places he'd like to see for himself. *See* for himself—if he could see.

'Banks of the Mississippi from Mr Ashe's *Travels in America*,' she began.

'Mr Ashe?' he interrupted. 'A relation of yours?'

She did not answer for a moment. 'Ashe. Asher. Two different names.' Her voice was stiff.

'Of course.' He'd been trying to make a joke even though he did not feel like joking. 'Proceed.'

She cleared her throat. '"In many respects the Mississippi is far inferior to the Ohio. The Mississippi is one continued scene of terrific grandeur…"'

While she read, Hugh drummed his fingers on the arm of his chair and only half listened. It was Wynne he wanted. Let the man finally show up and get the bad news over with.

Wynne did not arrive until near the dinner hour. 'So sorry to be late,' he said as he bustled into the room. 'Busy day today.' He paused. 'It is delightful seeing you again, Mrs Asher. I hope I find you in good health?'

'I am in excellent health, thank you, sir. I would offer you tea, but Mr Westleigh has been waiting a long time.' Daphne spoke as if she was the hostess of a London ball, but her voice was edged with impatience. The tea was tepid now in any event.

'It would be a pleasure to partake of tea in your company, my dear lady, but alas, I am not at liberty today.' The surgeon sounded mournful. 'I hope you will renew the invitation at a later time. Today, I fear I must not tarry. I have another patient to see before I shall be free to return home to my dinner.'

'I do understand, Mr Wynne,' Daphne responded. 'You must tend to your patients and your family, of course.'

Hugh heard the sound of a strap being unfastened. 'How have you fared, Mr Westleigh?' Had Wynne finally been able to tear his attention away from Daphne so as to tend to his patient? 'You have kept your eyes closed, I trust.'

'I opened them today.' There, it was out. 'I closed them right away, but I did open them.'

'Hugh!' Daphne cried.

'The bandages came loose when I was riding and my eyes opened before I could think about it.' He sounded as if he were making excuses.

'You were riding?' Wynne sounded incredulous.

'Not alone,' Hugh assured him.

'Hmmph.' The surgeon clearly disapproved. 'When you opened your eyes, did you experience pain?'

'A sharp pain, yes.' And the ache persisted. There was more he'd noticed. 'I can feel my eyes move under my lids a great deal when I want to look at something, but they have remained closed except for that one instance.' Now it hurt every time his eyes moved.

'Well—' Wynne sighed as if all was lost '—let us take a look.'

His hand cupped the bandages on Hugh's head and lifted them off rather than unwinding them. Amazing how light-headed Hugh felt with the bandages gone. His lids fluttered.

'Keep them closed.' Wynne briefly touched Hugh's eyelids to still them.

Through his closed lids, Hugh saw nothing.

He felt the warmth of a candle come near. 'Do you see the light?' Wynne asked.

Daphne must have had the candle ready.

'I see light,' Hugh responded, but no better than during that first examination.

The candle moved away, and Wynne's fingers touched his eyelids again. 'Your lids have healed very nicely, Westleigh. I see no signs of infection.' He felt the man back away and heard him rummage in his bag. 'I'm going to apply a salve to your eyes and bandage them up again.'

The salve felt cool and the new bandages clean. Wynne wound the cloth tightly around Hugh's head. 'I dare say you have re-injured the eyes, though. The pain you felt confirms that. We may hope they heal again, but we will not know until another week goes by.'

He rummaged in his bag again and Hugh heard him rebuckle the straps. 'I must take my leave.'

Hugh heard Daphne's skirts and presumed she'd stood, as well. 'I regret not being able to spend more time, my dear,' Wynne said.

'You are a very busy man,' Daphne replied.

He heard them walking to the door. Wynne had told him nothing encouraging. He'd been too busy making himself pleasing to Daphne.

That was unfair. Wynne had examined him equally as carefully as he had the first time. Hugh had not expected good news. He had no choice but to wait.

And hope he kept his eyes closed. And hope he healed.

Daphne saw Mr Wynne to the door and hurried back to the drawing room. 'Hugh!' She rushed over to him. 'Why did you not tell me?'

He shrugged. 'I do not know. I suppose it would have made it seem real.'

She knelt in front of him and took his hands. 'You must be worried.'

'I cannot deny it.'

He leaned towards her and she rested her forehead against his. 'You poor man.'

He inhaled and she leaned back. What was she thinking? Acting so intimately with a man. He was her friend. He was a Westleigh. She must expect nothing of him.

Carter knocked on the door. 'Dinner, ma'am.'

She squeezed Hugh's hand and pulled him to his feet. 'Come. You must be hungry.'

During the meal she tried to cheer him up and she guessed he tried to pretend it was working, but the prospect of his blindness shrouded them.

After dinner, back in the drawing room, she poured him a glass of brandy, and a little for herself, just to warm herself and to calm the emotions she sensed inside him.

'Shall I continue reading from *The Annual Register*?' It was not the book she would have chosen for her own entertainment, but it interested him and might distract him from his worry.

'Certainly, if you like,' he responded without enthusiasm.

She refilled his glass, adding more for herself, as well.

Opening the book, she found the place where she'd left off. 'We were about to begin the part about the price of gold in Abyssinia.'

He made no comment.

'"Price of gold,"' she began. '"Gold at a medium, sells for ten pataka each wakea, or ten derims, salt…"' The words meant little to her but they lulled her as she read about the price of gold, about weights and measures, about servants' wages, about how they made beer and finally about marriage. 'It sometimes happens that the husband and wife mutually, without any cause of ill will, agree to part. In this case the effects

brought by the wife are united with the sum stip-
ulated by the husband, then divided into equal
shares of which the parties take each one, and return to their former places of abode.' She stopped
reading. 'Oh, my.' Had she read correctly? 'What
do you think of that?'

'Of what?'

'Of what I just read.' She scanned the words
again to be certain. 'In Abyssinia, a husband and
wife can end their marriage by mutual agreement.
They divide their agreed-upon settlements and
that is it.' She could not believe this. 'And their
church sanctions it.'

He turned to face in her direction. 'Daphne,
why does this interest you?'

She could not answer him. 'No reason.'

'You have read of all sorts of odd things,' he
pointed out. 'Why did this one interest you?'

'I do not know.' More truthfully she did not
wish to say. 'I suppose it is because it is such a
shameful and difficult thing to get a divorce in
England.'

He lowered his voice. 'Did you wish for a divorce from your husband, Daphne?'

Her stomach flipped. Her response was shrill.
'No. Of course not.' She had not wished that,
had she?

He lifted his glass to his lips. 'Tell me about
your husband, Daphne. About your marriage.'

Tell him? That her husband was good to her,

that he indulged her, but even so, she had never been a good wife to him?

She swivelled towards Hugh. 'I—I—' She twisted her skirt with her hands. How she felt about her marriage did her no credit at all. 'Would you still consider me your friend if I told you I did not wish to talk about this?'

'Of course.' His spine stiffened and he took another sip of brandy.

As did she. 'Please understand, Hugh. I cannot talk about my marriage any more than you can talk about your eyes.'

He stood. 'You are correct. I do not wish to talk about my eyes, although there is not much to talk about. I will either be blind or not.' He searched for and picked up his cane. 'I am going to retire. I'm not very good company for you tonight.'

She rose, too, and put a hand on his arm. 'Please do not be angry with me, Hugh. Please. I want this time between us to be—to be—free of any past. Heedless of any future. I want to enjoy being friends now, while we are here.'

'I am not angry with you, Daphne.' He turned to her, but could not see to face her directly. He placed his hand over hers. 'I hope sometime you will trust me enough to tell me what it is that makes you so sad, but you are correct that tonight is not the night. I need to get myself in order first.'

His fingers, long and strong, wrapped around

hers. The gesture brought tears to her eyes. No one touched her any more. No one held her, not since the abbess had once enfolded her in her arms. Daphne, sobbing like a wounded child, had clung to the old woman as if the abbess had been her last hold on forgiveness. She wished she could be held now. She wished Hugh could hold her and comfort her, but she didn't deserve his embrace, not after wronging his family and deceiving him.

To her surprise, he released her fingers and slid his hands up her arms, to her shoulders, her neck, her face. His palms were warm and gentle against her cheeks, and his touch roused her like no man's touch had ever done before.

His cane fell to the floor and he cupped her face with both hands. 'I wish I could see you,' he murmured.

He'd never touch her if he could see her, she knew. This might be her only chance to receive the comfort for which she yearned. There was no resisting it.

His thumbs stroked the tender skin of her cheeks, and she felt as if the imprint of his touch would remain for ever with her. But she wanted—needed—more. Her body quivered with need. With desire. She wanted something more precious than comfort. She wanted Hugh.

Wrapping her arms around his neck, she rose on tiptoe and urged his head lower. His lips were so near she tasted the brandy on his breath. She trembled with desire, but feared closing the gap between them. Perhaps he meant only to comfort her. Perhaps he did not want her at all.

He held her face more firmly, and the thrill of it radiated throughout her body. He guided her face still closer until his lips took possession of hers with a need all their own.

Her body ignited with passion, passion for this man. She thought she might perish if she could not feel his bare skin against hers, to join her body with his. She wanted him more than she'd ever wanted any man. Even her husband.

Even Xavier.

This was new to her. Irresistible. It would do no harm to make love to him, would it?

He pulled away from her. 'I had best say goodnight.' He lowered himself to search for his cane.

Shaken and bereft, she crouched down to retrieve it for him, her head close to his. 'Hugh?' She touched his arm.

He found her face again for one more caress, even more gentle than before. 'Goodnight, Daphne.'

Tears rolled down her cheeks as he straightened and walked away from her. Why had he stopped? He wanted her as well, did he not?

After he left, she sat a long time, thinking, trying to calm herself, trying to talk herself out of needing him.

Chapter Ten

The clock in Hugh's room chimed the hour. He counted each chime. One…two… Ten…eleven…twelve. Midnight.

Even though Carter had readied him for bed two hours ago, even though the man had left him with a bottle of brandy, Hugh remained awake, drinking and rocking.

At least night evened the odds. In darkness no one could see.

Who was he fooling? He heard the hiss of coal in the grate. The glow from the fireplace would give a person with eyes enough light to make out the furniture in the room. Eyes that worked, that was.

If he wished to be completely honest with himself, he'd admit what was really keeping him awake.

Daphne.

His thoughts were consumed by her. A second kiss with a promise of passion equal to the first had done it. He'd counted how many times she poured herself brandy. Only three times and all had been short, not enough to explain her response to him. No, she'd chosen this kiss with a clear mind.

Had he gone too far? He'd meant only to touch her.

Hadn't he?

His masculine urges were surging, unleashed by that kiss. She was not far, a few steps away. He could find his way. By God, he believed he could find his way without his cane, without feeling for the walls. She drew him so strongly he did not need the glow of coals or a lamp in the hallway.

To bed a widow was not a scandalous matter, but all he could think of was that he would risk creating another child she would need to give up. For all her cool manner to him at first, it was now clear she was a passionate woman whose desires could be easily aroused. The responsibility was his to keep in control of his baser needs. How long could he restrain himself? Even if he decided to behave himself now, could he resist trying for another kiss later? Every moment with her would be one of decision.

To bed her or not.

He burned to feel her bare body beneath him. To fill his palms with her breasts and rub her nipples against his skin. He wanted to bury himself inside her and bring her to pleasure at the same moment of his release.

He took a swig of brandy, not bothering with a glass.

What he ought to do was get himself to London, put himself in the suffocating care of his mother and endure it for a week. Or longer, if his eyes could not heal. If his eyes could not heal, what other choice would he have? It had been unfair of him to impose himself on Daphne, especially since he'd prevented her from proceeding on her way. Wherever that may be.

He drank again and let the liquor burn down his throat into his chest.

Carter could make the arrangements for him. Hire a carriage. It was not even a day's journey.

He heard the door open. Might as well ask the man now before he lost his nerve. 'Carter?'

The scent of roses reached his nostrils. 'It is not Carter.'

He stood. 'Daphne. What are you doing here?' Good God. He wore nothing but his drawers. 'I'm not decent.'

She remained near the door. 'Neither am I.'

'Why, then—?' he began.

She stopped him. 'Don't speak.' He felt her move closer to him, felt the heat of her when she came near. 'I—I felt so unhappy when you left me tonight.'

She was close enough to touch and he wanted

to touch her. 'I had to leave you, Daphne. And you should leave me now.'

'I was thinking,' Her scent, her voice, her nearness, intoxicated him. 'I am a widow and widows have certain licence.'

But she was also a woman and women conceived children.

'We are close, are we not?' she said. 'Why can we not be close in—in a physical way, as well?'

'There are risks, Daphne.'

'No one will know.' Her voice rose. 'Except the servants, of course. Monette and Carter would never gossip, I can assure you, and we'll be leaving the others. They will not care what we do.' She put her hands on his bare shoulders.

His resolve could stand only so much. 'There are other risks, as you well know.'

'I do not care.' Her fingers played in the hair at the nape of his neck. 'Please, Hugh? We have only one week. Can we not spend it truly together?'

One week. Or perhaps one night. Maybe he could risk one night. He could still leave for London in the morning. One chance to love her. Could he turn it down?

Her hands slipped down to his chest. 'After one week you will be off on your travels and I will return to my home.'

'Or I'll be blind,' he said.

She threw her arms around him and pressed herself close to him. 'Do not say you will be blind. You will see. You must see. You must do all those things that make you happy at last. Life cannot be that unfair to you.'

She could not be wearing anything but a night-dress. One thin piece of fabric between them. He was aroused, painfully so.

'I can feel that you want me, Hugh,' she whis-pered. 'Make love to me.'

He could not refuse.

He lifted her into his arms and carried her to the bed. He knew just how many steps it took to reach it. 'Are you certain, Daphne?'

She reached for him, clasping his arm as if she had the strength to pull him onto the bed. 'I am very certain.'

Daphne's heart beat so rapidly she thought her chest would burst. She had brazenly offered se-duction to Xavier more than once, but this was different and she did not know why. She only knew that she'd break into a million shards if she did not soon feel Hugh's hands upon her skin.

He stood at the side of the bed, removing his drawers while she pulled her nightdress over her head. When she tossed it aside, it brushed against his arm.

He caught it and held the fabric in his hand. 'I wish I could see you.'

'I just want you to touch me.' She reached for him, impatient to have him next to her on the bed. On top of her. Inside her. 'Look at me with your hands.'

He climbed on the bed, kneeling over her, her legs between his. His hands touched her lightly, making their way to her head. His fingers ran through her loose hair, like one might run hands through cool water. He combed through the length of it, reaching its ends and exploring the feel of it.

'Your hair is longer than I thought,' he said. 'With some curl. What colour is it?'

She hesitated to say. He could not possibly identify her by hair colour alone, could he? Many women had her hair colour. 'Blonde.' She cleared her throat. 'It is blonde.'

'As I imagined it to be.' He played with her hair, twisting it around his hands, threading it through his fingers, creating sensation that flooded through her.

He explored her face, as he'd done once before, but this time his fingers were reverent, stroking each contour as if he were sculpting her himself out of pliant clay. Could he feel what other men saw with their eyes? Would her face matter to him? She did not want it to matter to him. Or perhaps she did. She wanted him to admire her, did she not?

Tears of confusion sprang to her eyes. Oh, dear! How would she explain tears at such a moment? How could she tell him she did not wish to be beautiful for him, merely loved?

Luckily his hands moved to stroke her neck and trace the contours of her ears. She blinked away the tears and savoured the lovely sensations his fingers created. He slid his hands down farther, reaching her breasts, stroking, tracing around her nipples. Her back arched in response. His hands had been gentle in their exploration, but now she felt their strength as he pressed her flesh more firmly, again taking possession as he'd done with the kiss.

She flared with need. A moan escaped her lips and her body ached for him. Her hands grasped him, kneading his skin, not so much exploring him as urging him to keep touching her, to keep filling her with need.

His hands slid farther, pressing against her rib cage, reaching her waist and spanning it with his fingers as if measuring. Yes, she knew her breasts were full, her waist narrow, and her bottom fleshy enough to please a man. How often had she been told of it?

'Does it matter to you, how I am shaped?' she asked, her voice tinged with both annoyance and gratification.

'Matter?' He swept his hands up and down her torso. 'This is the only way I can see you.'

She did care how he perceived her, she realised. 'Do—do I please you?'

He leaned down and possessed her lips, his kiss long and dizzying. Her muscles melted like butter left too close to the oven.

'You please me very much, Daphne,' he murmured, still touching his lips to hers. 'You have pleased me since the moment I first woke in this room.'

Her spirits soared. He could not have known anything of her appearance then, not even by touch, and still she pleased him. A memory flashed. Of her husband undressing her like a doll and looking at her, admiration glowing in his eyes.

No. She did not want to think of her husband at this moment. She wanted to think only of this night, of this man. Of Hugh. She could seek happiness for a week, could she not? A week with Hugh should be enough to last a lifetime.

He splayed his fingers over her abdomen. She slid hers down his back. Everywhere she touched was firm muscle. How thrilling to think of that masculine power beneath his skin. The light in the room was dim, a mere glow from the fireplace, but it was enough to reveal his magnificence. She could not help but compare him with Xavier, who she'd imagined to be at the peak of masculine perfection. Hugh was not perfection, but there was glory in his rough-edged manliness.

Enough exploring, she wanted to scream. *Take me now.*

She arched her back and pulled one of his hands down to where she ached for him.

Pleasure me, she wanted to say, but she'd never before spoken such wanton words.

She did not have to tell him. His fingers touched her with exquisite intimacy, exciting her even more acutely. Fevered cries escaped her lips, and she writhed in the glory of his touching, stroking, building need and pushing it to the breaking point.

She could keep silent no longer. 'Please, now, Hugh. Now.' She pressed his buttocks and scraped lightly with her fingernails. 'Now, Hugh.'

But first he leaned down and kissed her again, moving his tongue until her mouth opened to him. His tongue was warm and wet and tasted of brandy. When he broke the kiss, he thrust into her and her exhilaration flared. She liked that he was not gentle, not careful. He was assured, skilled. He knew her body was slick and ready for him.

He moved with equal skill and control, just the right cadence to calm her need, but to allow it to rebuild slowly, like an avalanche she'd witnessed once when visiting the mountains in Switzerland. It started slow, building and building until everything in its path was consumed by it and swept along.

She was swept along, almost giddy at the wonder of the journey.

When his control broke, she was enveloped by

the wildness of it, his animal growls, his abandon, until the pleasure burst inside her and he thrust one final, frenzied time. He'd spilled his seed inside her, his gift, the part of him that was now part of her.

He exhaled a long breath, and his weight grew heavy on top of her for a moment before he rolled to her side and nestled her against him. 'Daphne,' he murmured.

Words swirled inside her, words of wonder and thanks and joy, but she could not speak them. She kissed him instead, a long, lingering, tender kiss into which she put all she could not say.

They made love again. And again. Until finally sated and satisfied, she lay next to him, bare skin to bare skin, enjoying the mere fact of his breathing, the soft sound of his heartbeat.

Hugh felt as if his bones had melted like candle wax. Not an essence of tension remained inside him. He was where he most wished to be.

Next to her.

'Daphne, Daphne,' he murmured. 'Nothing could ever be better than that.'

'Mmm,' she said, which he took as agreement.

He knew she'd experienced as much passion as he. He knew she relished it equally as much, but before he could help it, the past crept in. Had it been that magnificent with her husband? If so, what a lucky man. Had it been like that with other men?

She sighed, a contented, satisfied sound. 'I always had the sense there was more.' She snuggled closer to him. 'Now I know for certain.'

Was she reading his thoughts now? 'Do not tell me you have never experienced the like of this with a man before?'

'Like this?' She laughed a soft, near-silent laugh. 'No.'

It made no sense. She'd been created for love-making. How could he believe that no man had ever discovered that before? Had her husband been a fool? The other men, as well?

'My husband was the only other man I've bedded.'

Were their thoughts joined as well as their bodies and souls? Even after making love to her once, Hugh felt a part of her and she, a part of him.

Hugh stroked her glorious hair. The finest silk threads could never feel as luxurious. 'Your husband—?' he began to ask. He'd all but promised he would not ask about her husband again, but he'd also assumed there had been someone else. If she had not gone to Switzerland to wait out a pregnancy and to give up a baby, then why had she gone?

'My husband was older,' she went on. 'Twice my age and more. A vital man, even so. I was very young when he married me. Barely seventeen. It was a very advantageous match for me. He was wealthy and of greater status. His—his lovemaking was—' she paused '—different.'

He frowned. 'Were you unhappy?' Was that the unhappiness he sensed in her?

'Unhappy?' She seemed to consider this. 'No, not unhappy. Just young and foolish and filled with silly ideas.'

He thought her so serious a person. 'Silly ideas? I do not believe you.'

'Oh, yes.' Her tone turned sad. 'I had very foolish notions.'

He rose up on one elbow, wishing he could look down on her. 'What sort of foolish notions?'

She paused again before finally saying, 'I was quite indulged, but I wanted what I could not and should not have. It took me a long while to accept that I should be content with what I have been given.'

There had been another man; he knew it. 'Was it another man, then?'

Again she paused. 'Yes. Once, but not really. I mean, nothing came of it.'

Hugh wanted to know everything. He wanted to put it all right somehow.

'What about children?' he could not help but ask.

'I was not blessed with children.' She sounded sad, but not unduly so. 'Perhaps that was best.'

No children? He'd been wrong, indeed. 'Why best?'

She took a deep breath. 'I would not have made a good mother.'

He lay back down again and hugged her to him. 'Of course you would have made a good mother. Think what a good nurse you have been for me.'

He felt her shrug. 'Well, not then, at least.'

He kissed her temple. 'Tell me about then.' He wanted to understand. To soothe whatever pain she'd endured.

She moved from his grasp and sat up. 'Oh, I do not wish to think of the past. I only want to think about now.'

He reached for her, found her and lifted her on top of him. Straddling him, she leaned down to kiss him, a long impassioned kiss that aroused him once more.

'Well, I am quite pleased with right now,' he told her. 'And I will be more pleased if you consent to make love with me one more time.'

She laughed. He wanted to hear her laugh for ever. 'I shall do as you command.'

'As I ask,' he corrected. 'I do not command.' He positioned her on top of him and slid inside her.

She moved, as perfectly as he could wish, in a rhythm that matched him as if they were created for each other. Only one thing could make the moment better. If he could see her. Gaze upon her, feast his eyes. God knew his eyes were hungry for the sight of her.

She moved faster, more urgently, seeking her own pleasure at the exact moment his need increased. That she became so easily aroused by him aroused him further, until sensation and need overtook him.

She cried out and at the moment of her release, his came, an explosion of sensation equal to the pleasure they'd already shared.

She collapsed on top of him, as he'd done, only her weight was a trifle. He held her there, moving his hands over her skin, enjoying the smooth, slightly damp contours of her body.

'I stand corrected,' he murmured, his lips touching her hair. 'I said nothing could be better than the last time, but this was equal to it. Better, even.' He ran his fingers through her hair. 'Nothing quite matches making love to you, Daphne.'

She released a satisfied breath. 'I thought you would have shared such pleasure with many women.'

It was his turn to laugh. 'Not as many as you would expect. Never as gratifying.'

She nestled by his side again and was silent for so long he thought her asleep. He felt himself drifting towards that state, as well.

'Did you ever think yourself in love, Hugh?' she asked.

'No.' He'd experienced a youthful infatuation or two, but never as a man. 'I was too busy, I suppose. Being an officer and then tending to family matters.' That was the easy answer. He suspected his choices had been affected by his mother's unhappiness and the fact that his father had been a thorough reprobate.

'I dare say many officers found reasons to marry in that period of time.' Her voice turned sad. 'And afterwards you could have married for money.'

It was what she had done, was it not? He could not imagine himself doing the same.

'Enough of this topic.' The last thing he wanted was to make her sad. 'We all do what seems best at the time. Is that not correct?'

'I suppose so,' she said uncertainly.

'I know so.'

He held her beside him and gradually felt her muscles relax and her breathing turn even. What could be more pleasant than this, feeling the warmth of her skin against his?

When she woke in the morning, would she regret this intimacy? Would he? There was no one to be hurt in it, was there? Especially now he knew there had been no child.

Would she ever tell him the true reason she had been in Switzerland? It did not matter. Nothing mattered except loving her. Making love to her had changed everything. He no longer planned on having Carter arrange a carriage ride home for him. He planned on enjoying this week with her. He wanted to spend every week with her in such enjoyment.

The thought surprised him. He did not wish to settle down, to stay in one place, to be beholden to another person, but what better adventure could there be than spending each day with her, forging a life together? Maybe they could travel together. He could think of no travelling companion he could desire more. Even more than travel, though, he wanted merely to be with her. He was certain of it. He'd actually mused that he'd enjoyed his recuperation because of her. When his bandages came off and he became whole again, think how much better being with her could be.

If his eyes healed, that was. That was the larger question. He might end this week blind. Could he really ask her to spend her life with him, if he was permanently impaired and dependent? She would do it, he'd wager. She had gone to all this trouble for him when he was a stranger to her. She would do even more for a lover.

Or a husband.

Hugh tried to imagine living in endless darkness as an invalid. What kind of man, or part man, would blindness make him? He'd have nothing to offer her. He'd merely take, take, take.

In a week, he would know. What was a week to wait? One thing was certain, he would spend

this week loving her and enjoying their time together to the full. If luck would truly be with him,
the bandages would come off and he'd open his
eyes to the sight of her face.

Then his future would be certain. He'd ask
her to share it with him and he was certain she'd
say yes.

Chapter Eleven

The next week proved to be the most beautiful week of Daphne's life, but finally it was at an end. Today was her last day with Hugh. The knowledge that this was her last day with him was like walking around with a dagger in her heart, a dagger she could neither remove nor reveal.

The week had been extraordinarily wonderful and acutely agonising.

Their lovemaking had shredded any barriers between them. She'd never felt as close to anyone in her life as she felt to Hugh. He was a part of her now. He would always be a part of her.

But in a short time she would leave him.

It was all arranged.

Monette, Carter and Smith the coachman were in her confidence, but Carter pursed his lips whenever she mentioned her plan and Monette looked mournful. She'd also told Toller, because she needed his assistance and she wanted someone familiar to Hugh to remain with him when the bandages came off. Toller was also tasked with handing Hugh—or reading to him—her letter of farewell.

She'd arranged for Mr Wynne to call after breakfast, although Hugh thought it would be in the afternoon.

After dressing, Daphne came down to the dining room and waited for Hugh. She stared at the buffet table without appetite. She would have to force food down when Hugh sat with her, or he would notice and wonder why she was not eating.

Why could she simply not tell him who she was, which she should have done in the beginning?

She could not bring herself to do it. Better he think she left for some mysterious reason than that the despised Lady Faville had deceived him the whole time.

The abbess had been correct about lies. They grew worse with time. If at the beginning she had told him she was Lady Faville, not Mrs Asher, he probably would have left for London immediately and this past week would never have happened.

No, she would never regret this week with him. She'd learned so many lessons she could not have learned otherwise. She'd learned that she could love unselfishly, that another person's well-being could mean everything and her well-being nothing. She'd learned that joy came from managing some kind gesture to Hugh. Like helping him to ride. Like reading to him, playing the pianoforte for him. She learned that lovemaking could be glorious when pleasure was mutually shared and when two people loved each other.

Daphne also learned one more thing, perhaps the most important of all. She learned a man could love her for herself and not merely for the beauty of her face or the shape of her figure. She would for ever be grateful to Hugh for that gift.

What had she given him in return? Lies. Deceit. Would she be able to live with herself for it?

She hoped—and prayed—that Hugh would be rewarded for what he'd done for her. She prayed he would open his eyes and see.

Even if he would never see her.

She heard the tapping of his cane as he approached. May this be the last day he would need the cane! She quickly wiped her eyes and blew her nose into a handkerchief and placed a smile on her face, ready to play her part one last time.

Hugh had ridden that morning. He'd galloped over the fields, heedless of the risk he'd open his eyes. What difference would it make now? Today he would either be blind or not.

He could not pretend to be free of anxiety. He wanted so badly to be whole for her, to not have to wrestle with the issue of whether he could stay with her or not.

The whole cottage seemed to have caught his nerves. The very air felt different. Tense with waiting. At breakfast he could tell Daphne was putting on a cheerful front. She spoke with her governess voice, always a sign she was feeling other emotions than she was willing to reveal. After breakfast she excused herself to tend to some servant matter. He retired to the drawing room to practise his scales.

Instead, he played 'The Last Post', which he now could play without hesitation. Its mournful notes seemed foreboding. The other tune he knew by memory was 'Barbara Allen', but it, too, was depressing. He didn't want to think of loss—the potential loss of his sight.

Daphne should have taught him a happy tune.

There was a knock on the door and Toller's voice said, 'Mr Wynne is here, sir.'

'Wynne?' The surgeon was early. 'Find Mrs Asher and ask her to come immediately. I'll see Wynne here.'

'Yes, sir.' Toller sounded tense.

Hugh was touched that even the servants were worried for him.

He moved to his usual chair in the drawing room, where he had been sitting when Wynne had called before.

The surgeon bustled in. 'Good morning,

Westleigh.' He paused. 'Mrs Asher is not here today?'

'I've sent for her,' Hugh said. 'You've come early.'

The surgeon unbuckled the straps of his bag. 'Sometimes I cannot help being late.'

Hugh did not try to make sense of that. 'Did you wish to wait for Mrs Asher?'

'Well…' Wynne sounded tempted. 'I would be delighted to see her, but I cannot stay long.'

'Pardon, sir.' Toller entered the room again. 'I cannot find Mrs Asher.'

'You do not say.' Wynne was obviously disappointed. 'We might as well get started. I imagine you are anxious to know what's what.'

Hugh was disappointed, as well. He had counted on her being with him. 'Yes, proceed.' Perhaps it would be for the best, though. If the removal of the bandages went as he feared, she would not witness his despair.

Hugh sat in a chair and Wynne pulled up another to face him. He rummaged in his bag and Hugh heard the blades of the scissors open and close. Wynne snipped the bandage at the back of his head and started to unwind it.

'Keep your eyes closed, now,' the surgeon cautioned. 'Toller, would you close the curtains? We don't want any bright light.'

Hugh heard Toller attending to the task.

Wynne placed his fingers on the pieces of cloth

covering each of Hugh's eyes and unwound the last of the bandage that held them in place. 'Now keep them closed. I'm going to take these last bandages off and examine your eyes first.'

Hugh kept his eyes closed with difficulty. He could feel his eyes darting behind his lids. Was that a good or a bad sign?

Wynne lifted his lids slightly. 'All good so far.'

Hugh saw light from the slit beneath his eyelids. Seeing light was not the same as having vision, though.

Wynne took a breath. 'Now slowly open your lids. If there is pain,' he added quickly, 'close them again.'

Hugh carefully lifted his eyelids, the first time he'd done so deliberately in a fortnight. There was pain, but not like when he'd opened his eyes before. This pain was more akin to staring into the sun. Everything was blurred. He blinked and tried again. This time he saw shapes. Another blink and the shapes took on a more exact form.

He stared into the weathered face of an older man and laughed. 'I can see. Wynne.' He pointed to him, as if to prove it.

The older man's face creased into a smile. 'Bravo!'

Hugh turned to a tall, skinny young man standing to his right. 'Toller!'

Toller grinned. 'That I am, sir.'

Wynne gathered up the old bandages and set

them aside. He placed the steel scissors in his bag, a worn black leather satchel. 'Mind that you do not strain your eyes, young man. Stay out of strong sunlight for a few days. Don't read too much. Rest your eyes often. Work up to normal use gradually.' He touched Hugh's face. 'You have a few burn marks, but those might fade in time.'

Hugh glanced around the room. The decor was plain and a little worn. The chairs were upholstered in green and the curtains matched them. He knew precisely where to look for the pianoforte, for the cabinet that held the brandy. 'It is just good to see.'

Wynne stood. 'I must go. Give my best to Mrs Asher.'

It had taken no time at all. After hours, days of anticipation.

Hugh walked Wynne out of the room into the hall. The walls of the hall were all oak wainscoting. The front door was oak as well, as was the stairway and the door to the dining room.

Toller handed Wynne his hat and gloves, and Hugh walked him to the door. 'Thank you again, Wynne.' He reached into his pocket and placed coins into the man's hand.

Wynne handed the coins back to him. 'Mrs Asher already sent payment. Quite as generous as she is beautiful.'

She was beautiful? Hugh had known so. He'd felt her beauty under his fingertips. Soon he would see for himself.

He opened the door and Wynne gave a little wave and strode off.

Hugh turned to Toller. 'I must find Mrs Asher.'

He could hardly contain his excitement. He would surprise her, take her in his arms, ask her to marry him.

Toller frowned. 'She's not here, Mr Westleigh.' He handed Hugh a folded and sealed note.

Hugh gave him a puzzled look, broke the seal and unfolded the paper. The handwriting was neat and precise with a decorative flourish to some letters, just as he would have expected her handwriting to look.

Dearest Hugh,

If you are reading this, then my heart soars for you. If not, words cannot express how very sorry I am. I am gone. I cannot explain the reason, except to tell you it is for the best. It is no use to try to find me.

There is no Mrs Asher. I am not who I said I was. The only truth about me is how dearly I came to love you. I thank you for the most glorious week of my life. I shall live the rest of my life on its memory.

Forget me and be happy.

My enduring love remains with you for ever.
Daphne

The air whooshed from Hugh's lungs, as if he'd fallen from a great height. He'd plunged, all right. From the highest joy to the deepest anguish.

She was gone?

No. Impossible.

He rubbed his eyes and read the letter again. What good was seeing now, if he must read these words? There was no mistaking it. She was gone.

He glanced over to Toller, despair creeping through his body like a venomous snake.

'Does she tell you she has left, sir?' Toller asked, distress written on his face. 'She, Mr Carter and Miss Monette left in their carriage—'

Hugh would have heard a carriage. Unless it waited for her at some distance. She'd deliberately fooled him.

Toller went on. 'She wrote letters for Mr and Mrs Pitts, for Mary and Ann and the stable boys. She left us all with pay to cover two years instead of two weeks. That is all I know, sir. We are to help you in whatever way you need. You may stay here as long as you like, because we're all paid for two years.'

How generous of her. Why so generous to them when she'd robbed him of what he'd needed most?

'Thank you, Toller,' Hugh managed, although it felt as if his insides had been eviscerated. 'I—I will let you know if I need anything.' What he needed most had left him. Vanished.

And he did not even know what she looked like.

Toller bowed and left the hall.

Hugh glanced around him, but sight was no comfort. He felt as disorientated as when he'd first woken in this house. His hand gripped her letter. He lifted it and read the words again:

The only truth about me is how dearly I came to love you. I thank you for the most glorious week of my life. I shall live the rest of my life on its memory.

Pretty words, but surely as false as the story she'd told him from the start. Was any of it true? Love. It was not love to lie, to leave with no good-bye, with no explanation.

His chest ached and he cried out, a frustrated, helpless, angry sound.

There was more than one way to be blind. She'd blinded him to the truth of her. Deliberately. She'd made a fool of him, pretending at love.

His fist crumpled the paper.

Curse her! He did not even know who she was.

Chapter Twelve

The next day was overcast with grey clouds that threatened showers, but Hugh was determined to leave. Even Wynne's warning to rest his eyes would not stop him. He unpacked his greatcoat and arranged to have his trunk shipped to his mother's house in London. He purchased the horse he'd been riding for nearly two weeks and settled generous vails on the cottage servants. Daphne, if that was her name, was not the only one who could be generous.

With one last look at the place he'd been unable to see, he bid the servants goodbye and mounted the horse. Let it rain, let the heavens pour down on him, he did not care. He wanted to be away from this place. He needed the open road. He needed the air. He needed freedom. A carriage would close him in like a coffin and trap him with his own thoughts.

London was less than a day's ride away, but he

took it slowly, not changing horses, instead sticking with his old equine friend, who had offered him such essential diversion when he'd needed it. *She* had arranged that diversion. How was he to make sense of that?

Hugh wanted the miles to strip away memories of the cottage in Thurnfield, but that was futile. The memories would never fade. The memories flooded his mind, repeating over and over, and if he stopped them, the questions rushed in. Why had she deceived him? What sort of woman would do such a thing? Had she merely been toying with him? Seduce the blind man. Make him think it is his idea and convince him he is a great lover. Then what? And why? Why do that? Why make herself a part of him, then strip herself away? Would it have made a difference if he'd not regained his sight? Had Toller been given two letters, one for each situation?

No. She'd known the whole time she would leave.

Curse the woman.

She might as well have sliced him with a sabre. The ache inside him began to burn white-hot. It was good that he could not go in search of her. His anger seethed so strongly, who knew what he would do?

Anger was preferable to the sheer despair of losing her.

* * *

His mind and his emotions had spun in circles as the horse plodded steadily forwards. By the time he neared the shores of the Thames and spied the dome of St Paul's Cathedral, he'd made some decisions. First, he would not say anything to his family about the fire or Daphne or his recuperation. There was no reason they should know any of it. He'd say he came directly from Brussels. If they noticed any burn marks on his face, he'd tell them he came too close to some flames, which was true. Second, he'd cut himself loose from the family and book passage to… somewhere. He'd continue on his original plan to travel the world and do anything he damned well pleased.

Hugh crossed the Thames and made his way to Mayfair. Riding past the familiar buildings on familiar streets gave him more comfort than he would have guessed. He rode on Piccadilly, passing near the Masquerade Club. He was half tempted to drop in to see how it was going, but his eyes were aching from the strain of riding all day. He continued on to the family stable at Brooks Mews and gave charge of the horse to the Westleigh stablemen, trying not to remember Daphne's stablemen, workers she'd had no need to hire.

He walked the short distance to Davies

Street and, finding the door locked, sounded the knocker.

Mason, the butler, opened the door. 'Why, Mr Hugh! Did we know you were to arrive today?'

Hugh suspected there would be a scramble to make certain his room was ready. 'I didn't send word, I'm afraid. But do not fuss for me.'

'Oh, your mother would want your room properly prepared.' Mason peeked out the door. 'No luggage?'

Hugh lifted the satchel he'd carried with a change of clothing. 'My trunk is being shipped.' He stepped into the hall. 'Is my mother at home?'

Mason took the satchel from Hugh's hand. 'I believe she and General Hensen are in the drawing room.'

The ever-present General Hensen, his mother's lover. 'I'll go in and let her know I'm home.'

He glanced around the hall, at the portraits that hung on the walls and thought of a smaller, wainscoted hall he'd known only by feel until yesterday. He walked to his mother's drawing room, gave a quick knock and entered the room.

His mother and the general were seated together on a sofa, looking into a kaleidoscope. Both looked up.

'Hugh!' His mother's face lit up in a smile and, to his surprise, Hugh felt uncommonly glad to see her. She might act the tyrant at times, but, to be fair to her, it was always on behalf of her children.

General Hensen helped her to her feet. 'How nice this is, eh, Honoria?'

His mother hurried over to him and waited for his kiss on the cheek. 'Mother. General. Yes, here I am, back from Brussels.'

The general shook his hand. 'It is good you are back, safe and sound.'

'I am so glad to see you, but you look a fright.' His mother touched his face. 'What happened here?' Of course she would notice the burn marks.

He shrugged away from her touch. 'Nothing of consequence. Some cinders blew in my face.'

She pursed her lips. 'You ought to be more careful, Hugh. Fire is nothing to trifle with.'

As well he knew. He'd run into an inferno after all.

The general chuckled. 'Now, Honoria. He is not two years old. Hugh is a man who has fought in war.'

Hugh wanted to dislike a man who took his mother to bed, but Hensen was a decent sort and good to her. Hugh laughed at himself. He was not unlike Hensen. He'd been bedding a widow, too.

If she'd really been a widow. She might have lied about that, too.

He stepped away from his mother and looked down at himself. His clothes were damp and mud splattered. 'You are quite right, Mama. I am not fit for company at the present moment. I merely wanted to inform you of my arrival.' *And to see you,* he thought, *because I feared I might never see you again.* 'I must change out of these clothes.'

'Yes, do,' His mother settled back in her chair.

He bowed and turned to the door.

His mother's voice followed him. 'So fortunate you have come today. We have a family dinner tonight.'

A family dinner? He'd hoped to have a day or two in relative peace, if peace and his mother could coexist in the same house.

He turned back to her. 'Who is coming?'

She beamed. 'All of them!'

Hugh washed off the dirt of the road and unpacked clean clothes to wear, but his eyes ached so much all he wanted to do was close them. Clad only in his drawers, he lay on the bed. Best he rest his eyes for a few moments. Wynne had told him not to exert himself.

Next thing he knew, Higgley, his mother's footman, knocked on the door. 'Almost dinnertime,' Higgley said. 'Your mother sent me up here to assist you.'

Hugh groaned as he sat up. 'I must have fallen asleep.' Not that it had helped his eyes. They still ached.

Higgley went straight to the clothing he'd laid out. He handed Hugh a shirt.

'Tell me what is happening in the family, Higgley.' Hugh pulled his arms through the sleeves. 'Anything I should know?'

Hugh had grown up with Higgley. They were nearly the same age and had played together as boys. Since Higgley had come to work for the Westleighs, he and Hugh had a bargain. Higgley would tell Hugh whatever family secrets he discovered and Hugh would never betray him for it. Plus he always found a way to slip Higgley a few extra coins or see he received a special privilege or two.

The footman brushed off Hugh's waistcoat. 'Nothing of consequence, to my knowledge. General Hensen is here much of the time, but I am certain that is no surprise to you.'

It was certainly no surprise.

'What about my brother and his wife? What news of them?' Hugh buttoned his breeches.

'The earl is very busy, of course, it being his first year in the Lords. The countess is finally increasing, which is a good thing, because your mother was becoming impatient. I take it the countess was none too happy that your sister and Mrs Rhysdale bore children and she hadn't.' Higgley enjoyed talking about the family.

He was like Toller in that way. Hugh thought he might miss Toller. He'd missed Higgley, he realised. He'd missed the comfort of home.

'How are your parents?' Hugh asked. Higgley's parents had also worked for the family. They'd been pensioned off some years ago and lived in a small house near the village. They would have been among the many people connected to the Westleigh estate who would have suffered if Hugh and Ned had not found a way to restore the family fortune.

'Doing very well,' Higgley answered. 'My mother thinks her flower bed the equal of any around Westleigh House and my father claims to have the best kitchen garden in the county.'

Hugh asked about other members of Higgley's family while Hugh buttoned his waistcoat and was helped into his coat. The familiarity of it soothed him. He allowed Higgley to tie his neck-cloth, although it was something he usually did for himself. After he finished dressing, Hugh ran a brush through his hair and put on his shoes.

He left his bedchamber and descended the stairs. A memory flashed of the fiery staircase at the inn, of carrying Daphne to safety. He closed his eyes and compared walking down these steps to descending the stairs at the cottage in Thurn-field.

He opened his eyes. Forget this!

The sound of laughter came from the drawing room. The family had gathered, obviously. Hugh forgot his desire to be alone and his wish to rest. He hurried to enter the room.

'Hugh!' His brother Ned saw him first and im-mediately strode over to shake his hand. Ned's brow was etched with lines and he looked weary, as if assuming the family title had automatically aged him.

Before Hugh could get out even a word of greeting to Ned, his sister, Phillipa, rushed over with a huge smile and sparkling eyes. Her scar still marked her face, but it had not been the first thing he'd noticed about her. The first thing he'd noticed had been her happiness.

'Phillipa, you look beautiful,' he exclaimed. It must be the first time he'd ever said those words to her. He kissed her cheek, the cheek with the scar, and then simply gave her a hug. 'Beautiful.'

She laughed.

Her husband, Xavier, a longtime family friend, stood behind her. 'Motherhood agrees with her, does it not?'

Yes. She was all softness and womanliness, no longer the little girl he used to ignore.

He released her and shook her husband's hand. 'Xavier. Good to see you.'

'You must call on us soon,' Xavier said. 'And meet our little girl. She is the image of your sister.' The man was nearly bursting with pride.

'I will. I will.' He could spare enough time to visit his sister before travelling.

Hugh spied his half-brother, Rhys, and his wife, Celia, holding back. The next person he must greet was Ned's wife, Adele, who happened to also be Celia's stepdaughter. Protocol demanded he greet a countess before his bastard brother. 'Adele, you look lovely, as well.'

She giggled at the compliment, her blonde curls bobbing.

To his surprise, a wave of fondness for her washed over him. He could forgive her for being a silly chit. She was young, perhaps not yet twenty. Besides, she adored his brother. Even now she gazed at Ned as if he were Zeus.

Had his week with Daphne turned him sentimental? Or had it been her abandonment that made it so comforting to be in the company of people who cared about him?

Hugh took both Adele's hands in his and stepped back to give her an approving look. 'You look different somehow. A lovely difference.' He knew the reason, thanks to Higgley.

She blushed and leaned forwards conspiratorially. 'That is because I am increasing. We are going to have a baby!'

'Is that not delightful news?' His mother's voice reached from several feet away. Stood to reason she'd heard everything. Nothing got past her.

Even that filled him with tenderness. 'Delightful, indeed.' He squeezed both Adele's hands and smiled. 'Very wonderful news. I am as happy as I can be for you.'

He meant it. Having a child would mean a great deal to Adele.

Once he'd imagined that Daphne had to give up a child—but then, he'd been mistaken in everything about her, why not that, as well?

He mentally shook himself again and kissed Adele on the cheek before releasing her to her husband. Ned put his arm around her. Their mother called the two over to where she was conversing with the general, and dutiful son Ned immediately went over to see what their mother wanted.

Hugh crossed the room to greet Rhys and Celia. 'Rhys.' He extended his hand.

Rhys shook it. 'Hugh.'

Theirs was an uneasy relationship, entirely Hugh's fault. As a boy Hugh had hated to think of his father siring a bastard son, betraying his mother like that. Hugh had taken it out on Rhys. He'd been monstrous, picking fights with Rhys every time he saw him. Now his admiration for his base-born brother was vast. As he'd told Daphne.

Blast! Why did everything remind him of her?

He turned to Rhys's wife, Celia, who had once been a baron's widow. He gave her a kiss on the cheek. 'How is my third sister faring?'

She returned a mocking look. 'I am waiting for my compliment.'

He tilted his head, not certain he'd heard her correctly.

She laughed. 'Well, Phillipa is beautiful. Adele

is lovely—both of which are true, but where is my compliment?'

He pretended to eye her from head to toe. She was not the fashion in beauty. Too tall. Too thin. But her features shone with intelligence. She was the sort of woman who became more beautiful the longer you spent with her. In fact, she'd once been the sort of woman of whom one took little notice, but no longer. Love had transformed her.

'You are peerless,' he said.

She laughed again and threaded her arm through her husband's. 'That will do nicely.'

Hugh smiled back and turned to survey all his family. His eyes pained him, his muscles felt fatigued from riding half the day and the ache inside him persisted as his emotions continued to wage war. His anger was as raw as seared flesh, such a contrast to the loving joy surrounding him, the joy he'd briefly thought within his grasp, the joy that had evaporated like a mist.

His family was faring well. That helped ease his discontent.

Conversation at dinner covered discussion of children, Parliament, the Masquerade Club, Rhys's steam-engine factories and Xavier's shops. Ned and their mother wanted to hear details of the disentangling of their father's affairs in Brussels, what Hugh had done and how much he'd needed to spend. No one asked Hugh about his own affairs. They rarely did, he suddenly realised, but this evening he was grateful. This evening he did not wish to speak of his own affairs—his brief liaison with Daphne.

Dessert was served. Baskets of cakes, bowls of fruit and, most distracting to Hugh, dishes of marzipan. Mason and Higgley poured champagne. When they were finished, General Hensen stood.

He held his glass of champagne. 'Your mother and I have an announcement.'

Conversation ceased.

He gazed down at her and reached for her hand. 'I want you all to know that your mother has made me the happiest man on earth. She has consented to marry me.'

'Ooooh.' Adele clapped her hands in delight. 'That is such happy news.'

Ned frowned. 'When do you plan to marry? A year has not yet gone by. You must not marry before waiting the full year of mourning, Mama. The family must not be subjected to more scandal.' Ned was the arbiter of everything correct in the family. In that sense he was the direct opposite of their father.

None the less, their mother tossed Ned an annoyed look. 'Of course we will wait a year. We decided to announce our betrothal now, though, so we may be seen together without talk.'

Hugh suspected there had already been plenty of talk, but why not seize happiness when it was offered? 'If this makes you happy, Mother, it is good news,' he told her.

She gave Hensen a loving look. 'It makes me very happy.'

'I propose a toast.' Hensen raised his glass. 'To your mother. May she never regret saying yes. May I succeed in making her every day happy.'

Congratulations and good wishes broke out from everyone. They'd always been united in support of their mother's happiness—unless she was telling them how to live. She'd been appalling to Phillipa in that regard. Cruel, even. Amazing that Phillipa appeared to have forgiven her.

They ate cakes and drank champagne and soon the ladies retired to the drawing room. Hensen went with them. Mason poured brandy for Hugh, Ned and Rhys. Higgley removed the baskets of cake, but left the fruit and marzipan.

Hugh took two pieces of marzipan, one shaped like a strawberry, the other like a pear, and rolled them in his fingers. The scent of the confection and of the brandy brought him back to the cottage drawing room and evenings he and Daphne had shared.

Damnation! Could he never stop thinking of her?

'I am glad we are all here.' Rhys's voice broke

Hugh's reverie. 'Because I want to discuss the Masquerade Club. I must give it up. You see, I need to spend too much time at the factories now. I've asked Xavier to take it over, but he cannot.'

'I wish I could assist you.' Xavier looked regretful. 'Time simply won't permit.' He was too busy investing in shops and employing out-of-work soldiers.

'This cannot be.' Ned's eyes darted around in panic. 'We cannot give it up now. We still need the revenue. We are not yet on firm footing. One bad crop and we'll be under again.'

Rhys shook his head. 'I cannot run the place any longer. I simply cannot. As it is now I never see Celia or the children.'

'I cannot do it.' Ned's voice grew strident. 'Not only would it be unseemly for a peer to run a gaming house, but I am already buried in estate matters and Parliament. And now with the baby coming—' He broke off and turned his gaze on Hugh. 'You must do it, Hugh.'

'Oh, no. Not me.' Hugh put up a hand. He'd already devoted the years since the war to family needs. 'I have other plans.'

'What plans?' Ned demanded. 'What could be more important than preserving the family fortune and ensuring the well-being of our people?'

Put that way, travel seemed a petty ambition.

'You must help us. There is no one else.' Ned shifted in his chair.

'You know enough about the business now,' Xavier added. 'It will not be difficult.'

'You may always consult me,' Rhys added. 'I certainly can be available to advise you on the running of the place.'

'And if Rhys is out of town, I will assist you,' Xavier added. 'I can do that much.'

'You must do it, Hugh,' Ned insisted, his legs shaking nervously. 'You are the only one of us at liberty to take it on.'

'But—' Hugh began.

Ned cut him off. 'Meet with me tomorrow and I'll show you the ledgers. We cannot abandon the club now, not when solvency remains at stake. I'll prove to you how our situation stands. Our father's latest business in Brussels managed to cost us a great deal, as you well know. It has put stress on the finances.' His voice turned despairing. 'You must do this, Hugh.'

Hugh closed his eyes and sipped his brandy, but that only brought him back to peaceful evenings in the cottage with Daphne. He blinked and scanned the three pairs of eyes anxiously staring at him.

What was the use? He would be unhappy on his travels, thinking he'd abandoned his family in their time of need. He certainly knew the pain of being abandoned. Besides, what did any of it matter? He might as well be unhappy in London.

He might as well make his family happy, even if he could not be.

He blinked again and sipped more brandy. 'Very well. I will do it.'

Chapter Thirteen

Daphne stared at the calendar and realised it had been exactly one month since she'd left Hugh. It was remarkable to think so much time had passed and she'd managed to endure it without falling into complete despair.

She thought of him much too often. Wondering where he was. On some ship bound for a distant shore? Or in a carriage on the Continent on a more tried and true course? Would he travel through the valley in Switzerland? Would he pass by the whitewashed walls of Fahr Abbey?

Wherever he was, she wished him happy. She hoped he had forgotten her.

She pulled up the sleeve of her robe and tapped her finger on the desk. Sitting in her bedchamber sipping a cup of chocolate, not yet dressed, she reviewed her list for the day. She'd begun creating lists of tasks to accomplish each day. It helped to make her busy. If she did not fill her day with several things she must accomplish, she was at the mercy of that ever-lurking despair.

'Good advice, my dear, dear abbess,' she said aloud. The abbess had often told her that busy hands were happy hands. *Happy* was too much to hope for in Daphne's case. Daphne no longer aspired to happiness.

Instead, she resolved to do good works, starting with her own property. Her husband had left her this small estate in Vadley in lieu of a dower house. When he died and his second cousin's son had inherited Faville House, she'd come here to wait out her grieving period before searching for Xavier. This estate had not been home then, but now she was determined to make it so.

The day after she arrived in Vadley, she'd sent for Mr Quigg, the estate manager, and asked him to take her on a tour. She wanted to meet all her tenants and employees and learn their names, like Hugh had said of his mother, Lady Westleigh.

To her shock, she'd found tenant cottages in need of repair, hungry children and struggling people. Her husband's financial arrangements for this estate had not accounted for the current difficult economic times. Or perhaps that had been her fault. She'd been the one responsible since her husband's death. In any event, not enough money had been allotted for the tenants and workers to live comfortably and to have enough food for their children. The bank that managed his money, now hers, had ignored the manager's request for more revenue. Had she ignored the man, as well?

Stinging with still more guilt, Daphne had immediately sent a letter to the bank, via her man of business, approving the funds.

The money was released and improvements were underway, but her man of business was travelling to Vadley to discuss the matter with her. He was expected to arrive today.

Dear Mr Everard. He'd been so devoted and she had taken such advantage of him. He'd escorted her to the Masquerade Club almost every night when she'd been in pursuit of Xavier. She dreaded his arrival. Seeing him again would remind her of how badly she'd behaved.

To think, if she'd not behaved so badly, she and Hugh might have remained together. She dropped her head into her hands.

But then they would not have met.

Trust God's plan, the abbess had told her. Many times.

There was a knock on the door and Monette entered. 'Good morning, my lady. Are you ready to dress?'

Daphne stood. 'I suppose I had better do so.'

Monette brought her a blue-madras day dress and helped her into it. When Monette stood in front of Daphne to straighten out the skirt, Daphne noticed her eyes were red. 'Monette! Have you been weeping?'

Fat tears immediately brimmed on the young woman's lids. 'Perhaps a little, my lady.'

Daphne felt her own tears, the ones that were never far from the surface, sting her eyes. 'Whatever is distressing you, Monette? You must tell me.'

Monette wiped her eyes with her apron. 'I—I am missing someone. That is all.'

The young woman had changed her whole life. Daphne could understand that it would be sometimes difficult. 'You are missing Fahr? Some of the nuns in the Abbey? I miss them, too.'

Monette shook her head. 'It is not the nuns—I mean—I do miss them, but I did not want to be there. It does not make me cry to not see them.'

'Who, then?' Had there been someone in Switzerland who'd been important to her?

'I—I am homesick for the cottage. The people there. I liked it there.' She stifled a sob.

'I liked it there, too,' Daphne said, her voice low, the ache inside her growing.

Monette gestured for Daphne to sit at the dressing table. She stood behind Daphne and combed out her hair. 'How do you endure being away from Mr Westleigh? I mean—I know— you—you—were lovers. How did you bear leaving him?'

The dagger always in Daphne's heart twisted. 'I told you that I had to leave. He could not know who I was.'

'I know, but you did not wish to leave him, did you?' Monette arranged Daphne's hair into a simple knot.

'No.' Daphne's throat tightened. 'I did not wish to leave him. I had to. It was for the best.'

Monette stuck pins in her hair.

Daphne glanced up at Monette's reflection in the mirror. 'But you are not weeping for Mr Westleigh.'

The maid coloured. 'No.' She stepped back, her head bowed. 'It is Toller I miss the most.'

'Toller?' Daphne had had no idea.

'We became friends.' Monette glanced up at her. 'Remember when we went to the village together and I asked you about women and men?'

'I remember.' She'd thought Monette, who'd grown up amongst celibate women, had been trying to figure out Daphne's relationship with Hugh.

'I was talking about Toller. I liked him very much, but in a different way than I liked Mary and Ann.'

'I see.' She understood that *different* way only too well.

'And I miss him!' Monette burst into tears.

Daphne left her chair and held the maid in her arms, like the abbess had once held her. What else did she know of comforting? 'There, there.' She felt as if Monette's pain were hers. It was all she could do to keep from weeping herself.

'I wish Toller were here!' Monette wailed.

'I could send for him.' The words were out of her mouth before she even thought of them. 'I could send a letter to Thurnfield and ask if he would like to come work for me here. Would you like that?'

Monette pulled away, a huge smile on her face. 'Oh, yes!'

Daphne walked over to her bureau and pulled out a handkerchief. She handed it to Monette. 'I will write the letter this very day.'

Daphne finished the letter to Toller, posting it in care of Mr Brill, the leasing agent in Thurnfield, who she knew would put it into the young man's hands.

She soon heard a carriage. No doubt Everard had arrived.

She stood and straightened her spine. She could face him, this man she'd so misused. If she could face the pain of leaving Hugh, she could face anything.

Carter soon announced him and Everard walked in the drawing room.

'My lady.' His voice cracked. 'It—it is a privilege to call on you.'

She extended her hand to him. 'Everard. I am delighted to see you.' It was not precisely true, but she'd not forgotten how to sound sincere.

He took her hand and merely squeezed her fingers.

Carter waited at the door.

'Would you bring some tea, Carter?' She turned to Everard. 'Or do you wish to rest from your journey?'

'I would be grateful for tea,' he replied. 'I will rest later at the inn.'

'The inn?' She signalled Carter to bring the tea. 'I will not hear of it. You must stay here. I have a room ready for you.'

'Here?' Everard looked about, as if the drawing room were where he would be sleeping. 'I do not wish to put you to any trouble on my behalf.'

'Nonsense!' she retorted. 'You will be no trouble and it will make conducting our business so much easier.'

'Very well.' He bowed. 'I do thank you.'

She asked questions about his health and he asked about hers and she wondered when he would start to scold her for lavishing so much of her capital on improvements for the tenants and the workers.

He waited until they settled down with tea. 'As you know, there was great concern about your decision to deplete your capital.'

'I hardly depleted it,' she countered.

'Forgive me.' He inclined his head. 'An unfortunate choice of words. Diminish, I meant. I fear you might not comprehend how these matters work. Once you spend the capital, you cannot get it back. It is best to leave the capital in the four per cents and other investments and live on the income.'

'I do understand, Everard.' She continued to use her charming voice. 'But a great deal of money was required, and I still have plenty in the investments, do I not? One would still call me a wealthy widow, would they not?'

'You do have plenty of capital,' he admitted. 'But it is imperative that you do not pull it out for frivolous spending.'

'For improvements to the farm buildings?' She made herself laugh. 'Is property not the best investment?' She smiled and looked directly into his eyes. 'My husband always said so.'

He blushed and noisily stirred his tea. 'You know I dislike countering your judgement in any way, my dear lady, but after your husband died, I pledged to make certain your welfare was protected in all ways.'

It was her turn to feel the heat of shame tinge her cheeks. The man was devoted to her. It was why he'd agreed to accompany her to the Masquerade Club. It had not occurred to her that he would see her purpose in any manner different than her own. She'd assumed she and Xavier should be together because they made such a pretty-looking couple. Everard must have thought her foolish and frivolous, and she had behaved shabbily by making the poor man come with her night after night. She'd never considered that he must have had to work during the day.

She lowered her gaze and dropped her charming voice. 'I am very grateful to you for it.'

He pulled at his neckcloth. 'As you can imagine, I was quite concerned about your travel to the Continent and your—your extended stay in Switzerland—'

He'd known she'd stayed in a convent. He had written concerned letters to her to return to society, as well as letters pertaining to business, of course. She'd written back, assuring him that she was doing well and trusting him to take care of matters in her absence. He'd been the only person with whom she'd corresponded.

'My stay in Switzerland was good for me,' she told him.

He looked embarrassed again. 'I have no doubt…' He quickly drank some tea.

She handed him a plate of biscuits. 'If you are up to it after our tea, I will have Mr Quigg, my estate manager, take you on a tour of the property and show you where the money is being spent, then we can discuss the matter further.'

She knew he would not refuse. Everard never refused anything she asked of him.

Daphne did not see Everard again until dinner. After the soup was served, she asked in her charming tone, 'So what did you think of how my money is being spent?'

He slurped soup from his spoon before answering, 'I cannot argue with what you have done except to say you might have been a bit extravagant.'

She lifted a disapproving brow. 'Oh?'

He sputtered. 'I mean—I confess to being surprised at your exceptional generosity to your workers and tenants. You might have confined your spending to essential repairs only, and you need not have lowered the rents and increased the salaries.'

In other words, he valued money over the comfort of those people on whom the prosperity of the estate depended. Once she might have agreed—or, rather, she would not have given the people one moment of thought.

She dipped her spoon into her soup. 'What did Mr Quigg say about it?'

He lifted his shoulders. 'He spoke with ebullience about all that you have done, saying it was a long time coming.' He frowned. 'But I must be concerned for your welfare. You must not give your fortune away.'

Why not? So far, being generous had helped her feel she'd atoned for her selfishness. She'd never experienced that sort of satisfaction purchasing jewels or clothing or any such thing. And he had never scolded her for throwing away her money at the gaming tables of the Masquerade Club.

But to argue this point with Everard would certainly distress him. Discussing the Masquerade Club would distress her.

She favoured him with one of her most amiable smiles. 'If you will but indulge me these whims from time to time, I promise you, I will trust you to warn me if I ever spend too much.'

He flushed. 'I am ever your faithful servant.'

Carter and a footman—named Finn, Daphne had learned—served the next course and she and Everard spoke in more detail about the improvements. Everard did not presume to do anything but praise the work she had approved, and the time passed more pleasantly.

When the apple tart was served and more wine poured and the conversation about the estate exhausted, Daphne groped for other topics to discuss. 'What of you, Mr Everard? Tell me how you are faring. What is happening in your life?'

'Me?' He flushed again. 'I am doing well enough. Business is tolerably good.'

'I am delighted to hear it.' She'd not thought of it before. He must have other clients to assist. She knew very little of him, she realised. 'And—and do you have family? I suddenly am aware that I do not know. I am sorry for never asking before.'

His eyes widened in surprise. 'Why should you

ask, my lady?' He sipped his wine. 'But, as a matter of fact, I have taken a wife in this last year.'

'You are married?' She loved the idea that this sweet man might have found the happiness that escaped her. 'How wonderful for you! Tell me about your wife.'

He answered in a serious tone. 'She comes from a good family. Her father is in banking and that is how we met.'

'No,' she scolded. 'Tell me about *her*! Is she pretty? Is she accomplished?' Goodness. Those were Daphne's own qualities. They might have made her a desirable wife, if not a very good person.

He lifted his gaze to her. 'She is not beautiful like you.'

Oh, dear. Certainly she did not intend to go in that direction.

She waved a dismissive hand. 'But is she pretty?'

Do you love her? Do you love her as I have loved Hugh, with every inch of your body and soul?

He glanced away. 'I think her very handsome and sensible.'

Poor Mrs Everard.

She made herself smile again. 'I am very happy for you.'

In fact, she should give him a raise in salary. If he was supporting a wife now, he could use a raise. That idea comforted her. It was another good deed she could perform.

But she feared being taken into further confidence about Everard's marriage, since he described his wife as handsome and sensible. 'Tell me news of London,' she asked instead.

To her surprise, his countenance became very serious. 'I quite understand.'

He understood she wished to change the subject? Why this intensity?

'I do not know very much, you understand, merely what I have heard people say and what has been written in the newspapers.' He drained the remainder of his wine down his throat.

Goodness. She was merely hoping for general gossip or what debates were consuming Parliament or what was being performed at the Royal Opera House.

Carter and Finn removed their dishes and put a fresh cloth on the table. Fruit and biscuits appeared and port wine was poured.

Everard continued after the food was served. 'The gentleman of whom you wish I would speak—' did he mean Xavier? No, she did not wish him to speak of Xavier '—did marry the Earl of Westleigh's daughter—'

'Yes, I knew this,' she broke in.

His brows rose. 'He no longer runs the club. Did you know that? Rhysdale returned to run it. People say your gentleman has turned into a shop owner, but I do not know the truth of that.'

She had no right to care what Xavier did. She had no right to even speak of him. 'I—I gather the Masquerade Club was repaired at my expense?'

'Oh, yes.' He chewed on a biscuit. 'It is as prosperous as ever, they say, although the masked *pianiste* does not play there anymore.'

Of course not. She was married and bore a child.

'That is excellent,' she said too brightly.

'Although I read just the other week that the new Lord Westleigh's younger brother has taken over the managing of the club. Apparently the Westleighs were partners in the enterprise all along.'

Daphne felt as if the air had been knocked out of her lungs. 'Younger brother?' she managed. Her heart beat faster.

Hugh!

He nodded and took a sip of port. 'The old Lord Westleigh, the scandalous one, died suddenly and his older son inherited. Did you know of that?'

With difficulty she kept a pleasant expression on her face. 'Yes. I heard of that.'

He prattled on. 'So when I said the new Lord Westleigh, I meant the older son. The younger son recently returned from the Continent. Their father left his affairs in a terrible mess and the younger

son was sent to settle them.' He picked up another biscuit. 'So when I said younger brother,
I meant it is Hugh Westleigh who now manages
the Masquerade Club.'

Hugh.

Her mind raced the whole evening, thinking of
him. She barely made it through tea in the drawing room after dinner and was relieved to be free
of the obligation to make conversation when she
noticed Mr Everard tiring.

'Dear Mr Everard.' She could at least hide her
swirl of emotions behind charm. 'I hope you will
forgive me. I am greatly fatigued and would beg
you excuse me for the night.'

The relief on his face was immediate. 'Yes.
Yes. I will retire, as well. I must head back to
London in the morning.' He stood and offered
his hand to help her stand.

She accepted it, but kept her distance from
him as they walked out of the drawing room into
the hall.

When he reached the stairs, she stepped back.
'I must speak with my housekeeper for a minute, so I will bid you goodnight here.' It was not
true, of course.

He looked relieved again. 'Goodnight, my
lady.' He spoke formally and bowed correctly.
That reassured her.

'Goodnight, sir.' She released a breath and

turned to the door of the servants' wing, but did not open it. Instead, she leaned against the wall and waited, listening to his footsteps recede as he mounted the stairs.

Hugh.

She was free to think of him again.

Tears stung her eyes. *Hugh, you are not blind!* He could not be blind. If he was blind, how would he be able to manage a gaming house where the job was to watch everything and everyone? *But why are you not on some exciting voyage somewhere?* What happened to change his plans?

She closed her eyes and remembered the Masquerade Club. She imagined him there walking through the rooms like Xavier had done, speaking to the patrons, watching everything. He would look magnificent in formal clothes, circulating among guests both masked and unmasked. She could not imagine his face precisely. She could only remember him bandaged.

If she saw him she would know him, though. She'd recognised him during the fire after all. But she longed to gaze at him at length, see every detail, discover the colour of his eyes, reassure herself that he was indeed as strong and robust as she remembered. If she only had a chance to memorise all of him, she'd hold that memory for the rest of her days.

Her heart started pounding. The Masquerade

Club was the one place she could see him! It was perhaps the only place she could see him.

At the Masquerade Club she could wear a mask. Nobody would know her.

It felt like her heart would burst, she was so excited. She opened the door and hurried down the servants' staircase in search of Carter.

Mr Everard would have company on the road to London.

The next morning Daphne made certain she was at breakfast with Mr Everard.

When he entered the breakfast room, set up in a sunny sitting room not far from the formal dining room, he looked pleased. 'My lady, I did not expect to see you about so early.'

She smiled at him. 'I wanted to be certain to see you first thing.'

The man blushed.

She went on. 'You see, I have decided to go to London, as well. Just for a few days. So you do not have to take the public coach. You may ride with my maid and me.'

His brows rose. 'You are travelling to London? This is sudden.'

'Indeed, it is very impulsive, I admit.' She fluttered her eyes. 'Please choose your food. I hope Cook has prepared something you will like.'

He filled his plate from the sideboard and sat in a chair across from hers. 'Please do not feel compelled to time your travel around my need. I do not mind the public coach.'

She nibbled on a piece of toasted bread and raspberry jam. 'It is no trouble to me at all.'

The footman Finn attended them and poured Everard a cup of hot tea.

He nodded his thanks and turned to Daphne again. 'If I travel ahead of you, I can make certain your house is ready to receive you.'

'It is not necessary,' she assured him. 'I have already dispatched a messenger. We will not require much on arrival.'

He frowned. 'My lady, why the urgency to visit London?'

'No urgency.' Except she could not bear to wait. She was convinced that seeing Hugh vital, fit and sighted would finally settle the unrest inside her. 'I—I merely discovered that I had a great desire to visit London after hearing you speak of it and it seemed silly to send you in a public coach when we could use my carriage.'

His gaze turned sceptical. 'My lady, may I speak with frankness?'

She was certain she did not wish to hear this, but she nodded. 'Of course.'

'Did my speaking of—of that certain gentleman in London precipitate this decision?' His voice was concerned. 'Because I must advise you not to attempt a meeting with him.'

A certain gentleman, yes. But not Xavier. 'Not

at all, Mr Everard. I have no plans to attempt a meeting with him.' In fact, if she thought he would be in attendance at the gaming house, she would hesitate to go there, even masked. He'd recognise her at once, even with a mask.

There was a knock on the door and Monette entered, looking very distressed. 'Forgive the interruption, my lady, but I cannot find the masks you wished me to pack. They were not in the drawer in your wardrobe.'

Monette's timing was unfortunate. Daphne had not intended to inform Everard of her plans to visit the Masquerade Club. 'Perhaps the masks are in a trunk. Have one of the maids show you where the trunks are stored, but do not fuss too much. We can purchase what we need in London.' Her old masks would need to be altered anyway. She wanted her whole face covered so that there was no chance anyone would recognise her.

'Yes, m'lady.' Monette curtsied and left the room again.

Mr Everard gaped at Daphne. 'You cannot mean to attend the Masquerade Club!'

'Do not fret, Everard,' she said in her charming voice. 'I wish only to make certain all the repairs were made and that the rooms are restored to their previous condition.'

'I would be honoured to perform that task for you,' he said. 'You were asked not to return to the club, if you recall.'

'I know.' How mortifying to be forbidden to return to a place because of your bad behaviour. 'That is why I plan to be well masked. I wish only to see what I would come to see.' Hugh. She would come to see Hugh.

'I cannot dissuade you?' he asked in a hopeless tone.

She returned a most pleasing smile. 'Please do not worry over me. I promise I will be on my best behaviour.'

He sighed. 'Then I will accompany you, of course.'

She did not want him there! 'You certainly will not!' Her voice turned sharp. She softened it. 'If you come with me, we are almost certain to be recognised. You must not come.'

'I cannot allow you to attend there alone,' he insisted.

She waved a hand. 'I will make other arrangements. A servant can come with me.'

Two hours later they were ready to depart. The carriage waited in front of the house, Smith at the reins and a stable boy seated at his side. Carter would ride on top of the carriage with them. Everard, Monette and Daphne would ride inside.

Monette was last to leave the house, looking as if she was bound for the gallows rather than taking what ought to be an exciting trip for her.

Daphne took a basket of food from Monette's

hand. 'Goodness, Monette. Do not worry so. We can purchase anything we forgot. One can purchase anything in London.'

'It is not that, my lady,' her maid said in mournful tones. 'It is about Toller. We won't be here if he sends a letter.'

She patted the girl's arm. 'I wrote to Toller when I wrote to the housekeeper in London. I asked him to contact us there.'

Monette looked only a little more hopeful.

Daphne leaned closer to her. 'I promise we will not leave London until we hear from Toller. Will that please you?'

The maid burst into a smile. 'Very much, my lady!'

Carter helped Daphne and Monette into the carriage. Everard entered last, and soon they were on their way. Everard took the rear-facing seat. Monette shared the other seat with Daphne. As soon as they were on the road, Daphne closed her eyes and leaned her head against the deep red velvet upholstery of the seat. The trip would take seven hours at the most. They would reach London in daylight, but she'd be exhausted by the time they arrived at the London town house her husband had left her. She must wait until tomorrow night to go to the Masquerade Club.

And then she would see Hugh.

Chapter Fourteen

Daphne stood at the door of the Masquerade Club, her heart in her throat. Carter accompanied her, and she'd arranged for Smith to pick them up in the carriage in two hours.

Two hours. Too brief a time to see Hugh again, but she dared not risk much more lest she call too much attention to herself. She'd chosen her most demure dress, in deep blue, and a black mask. She and Monette had added black satin to the mask, covering almost her whole face, just to be certain she would be unrecognisable. Carter was also masked and seemed perfectly comfortable with the idea of visiting a gaming house.

But that was something to enquire about another time.

Carter sounded the knocker and the door opened. The footman attending the door was the same man who had been there two years before. Cummings. She must remember not to call him by name.

'We have come to gamble,' she told him. 'May we come in?'

Cummings nodded and stepped aside. Carter took off his hat and gloves as if he were a proper gentleman and handed them to Cummings.

Daphne removed her cloak. 'What do we do next?'

Cummings peered at her, too closely, she felt. 'See the cashier.' He pointed to a door off the hall that was ajar.

She took Carter's arm and they walked together to the door and entered the room. The cashier was also the same man who had been there before. MacEvoy. He passed out mother-of-pearl gaming counters to a gentleman ahead of them.

The gentleman, an older man, glanced at Daphne, smiled and bowed. 'Good evening, ma'am.'

Another man she remembered.

'Sir Reginald at your service, ma'am.' The man's glance scanned her from head to toe. 'Do let me know if I may be of assistance to you.'

Daphne inclined her head. 'Thank you, sir.' She had no intention of asking anyone for assistance.

MacEvoy cleared his throat. 'Ma'am? Sir? Perhaps you have not been here before? Step up to the table and I will tell you how the house works.' He spoke quickly. 'Masked gamblers must not wager beyond the amount of counters they purchase or win. Masked gamblers are not permitted to sign vouchers. You may not incur debt to the house or to another patron unless you are unmasked and your identity verified. Each patron must know who borrowed from them and who owes them money. Is that clear to you?'

'It is.' Daphne had understood two years ago, as well.

Carter stepped forwards and purchased the counters for them. While he double-checked the number MacEvoy gave them, Daphne noticed MacEvoy staring at her.

'Are you certain you have never been here before?' he asked.

'Never,' Carter answered truthfully. 'Where is the gaming room?'

MacEvoy gestured with his hand. 'Right off the hall. Follow the sounds.'

They walked out of the room, and Daphne released a relieved breath. She'd obviously seemed familiar to Cummings and MacEvoy. She had been a frequent visitor during that summer two years ago and had made a spectacle of herself in so doing. Hugh had certainly seen her a few of those times. He and the others would have known her as Lady Faville then.

Carter handed her half the counters. 'I truly may gamble with these?' he asked, displaying his portion on his open palm.

'You may indeed,' Daphne answered. 'And

keep the winnings. Enjoy yourself, Carter. There is no need for you to stay at my side. Just be ready to leave in two hours.'

'Yes, m'lady.'

They entered the gaming room and it was as if Daphne had never left. The card tables were still arranged throughout the room, filled with four people playing whist, or two concentrating on piquet. At the back of the room and along the side of one wall were the faro, hazard and *vingt-et-un* tables. All were crowded with gamblers. Most of the men did not wear masks, but many of the women did. The hum of their combined voices filled the room, along with the shuffling of cards and tossing of dice.

Daphne scanned the room. 'Do you see him?' she asked Carter.

Carter knew she'd come to see Hugh. He also surveyed the scene. 'I do not.'

What if Hugh was not here tonight? To come all this way and not see him would be agony.

'Go and gamble, Carter.' She shooed him off. 'I'll just take a turn around the room before playing a little hazard or something.'

Carter nodded and strode off.

Daphne strolled through the tables, trying not to look as though she was searching for one certain person. As she passed, both men and women took notice of her. Once it would have pleased her for heads to turn wherever she went, but tonight she wanted to blend into the walls. Carter quickly found a card game and began expertly shuffling the cards. He looked as if he was in his element.

She wandered over to the faro table, thinking she ought to make the appearance of gambling, as well. She glanced over to the croupier, a pretty young woman, who was about to start another round.

'Place your bets, ladies and gentlemen,' the croupier called out. Daphne remembered her name was Belinda. She'd handled the hazard table before.

Daphne placed two counters on number seven, the number of days she and Hugh had so intimately shared together.

Belinda popped a card from the faro box. 'Ten.' The first card was the losing one.

All the gamblers who had placed their counters on the number ten groaned as Belinda collected them for the house.

She popped out a second card from the box. This would be the winning one. 'Seven!'

Daphne smiled. Her lucky number.

She scooped up her winnings, but left two counters on number seven. There were three more sevens in the deck of cards after all. She might win more.

She glanced up at Belinda, but riveted her gaze on the man who'd come to stand next to the croupier.

Hugh!

Her insides fluttered with excitement. A face she'd only glanced at in her past now loomed more important than anything else. His looks were not perfection, but were ruggedly handsome. The shadow of dark beard made him look rakish. She stared at his eyes. Even from across the table she could see they were brown. Large brown eyes with thick brows above them. She nearly laughed in delight as his eyes darted here and there, watching the room even as he conversed with Belinda.

He could see!

She'd known he could see, of course, but witnessing it made it all seem real. Her purpose in coming here was satisfied.

If only it were enough. She yearned to touch him. Trace his brows with her thumb. Comb back his unruly dark locks with her fingers. Cup his face in her hands, like he'd once done to hers. It was impossible. She must be content with gazing upon him.

Belinda popped another card from the faro box. 'Seven!'

Daphne won again. All eyes, including Hugh's, swung her way as she collected her winnings, but his interest in her seemed impersonal. A few gentlemen placed counters on number seven and she let her original two counters ride. It truly did not matter to her if she won. In fact, she'd prefer losing, because losing would benefit the Westleighs and thereby benefit Hugh. Besides, her debt to the family could never be completely repaid after she'd almost burnt down this building and risked so many lives.

'Luck is with you, ma'am,' a voice at her elbow said. She turned to see Lord Sanvers standing next to her. Sanvers had been in the fire at Ramsgate. He'd spoken to her that night. He'd seen her tend to Hugh.

'Yes. Luck,' she responded, her heart pounding.

He could not possibly recognise her, could he?

She waited at the faro table until she lost her two counters and was happy to move away from the attention. She wandered over to a hazard table, keeping Hugh in sight. He'd not given her another glance, but Lord Sanvers followed her.

'I have not seen you here before, have I?' he asked. 'I am Lord Sanvers. Are you alone?'

What an impertinent question. 'I am not here alone, sir. Are you?' She'd intended to sound dampening, but her voice was too accustomed to being pleasing.

He flushed with pleasure. 'I am quite alone and would be grateful for company.'

'Oh, dear.' She was eager to shed him. 'I must look for my escort. If you will excuse me, sir?'

She hurried away, sorry to give up sight of Hugh. She'd retire to the supper room for a few moments. She did want to see it before leaving,

as she'd told Everard, to make certain it had been
restored to its former beauty. She left the room
and climbed the stairs to the supper room.

As she crossed the threshold, she saw immediately that it remained very much in the style
of the Brothers Adam. Pale walls. Decorative
plasterwork. Phillipa Westleigh's pianoforte still
stood in the same place. She could half-imagine
the masked Phillipa seated on its bench, playing
and singing and totally anonymous. Daphne had
enjoyed listening to her perform.

A footman, another familiar face, approached
her, carrying a tray. 'Some wine, ma'am?'

She took a glass and walked over to the buffet. It was on a table like this that the lamp had
stood, the lamp that Daphne had thrown against
the wall in a fit of temper. She closed her eyes
and remembered the curtains aflame, spots of
fire on the carpet, her skirts aflame.

She shuddered at the memory.

'Ah, there you are.' It was Sanvers again. 'May
I help fix a plate for you?'

Hugh noticed Sanvers talking to the woman
who'd won at faro. The woman walked off and
Sanvers, the lecherous old roué, followed. Women
patrons who were masked typically were not at
the Masquerade Club for seduction, but to gamble. If this woman found the man's attentions
unwelcome, she might not return to lose money

another day. It was part of Hugh's job to see women guests were not so bothered.

Neither Sanvers nor the woman remained in the game room, and Hugh guessed the woman might have fled to the supper room. He walked up the stairs and entered the room, immediately spying the woman and Sanvers at the buffet. It was still difficult to tell if she was flattered by or objected to Sanvers' attentions.

He watched her draw away from the man, a sure sign his instincts had been correct. Hugh crossed the room to where two men and another woman also stood selecting food. Hugh approached casually, as if about to join them.

He overheard Sanvers. 'Would you do the honour of sharing my table, *madame*?'

Hugh caught a whiff of roses and froze. He closed his eyes and inhaled the scent again.

He heard her reply. 'It was kind of you to ask, sir, but no, I prefer to be alone.'

The scent. That voice.

'A lovely lady such as yourself ought not to be alone,' Sanvers persisted.

'Surely no harm will come to me here,' she retorted. 'And surely a gentleman such as yourself will respect a lady's wishes.'

There was no mistake. The one person he expected never to see was here.

Hugh opened his eyes. 'Pardon me, Sanvers.'

His limbs trembled as he stepped between Sanvers and the woman.

Her eyes widened.

Hugh seized her arm. 'I must speak with this lady.' Hugh pulled her away. 'Come with me.'

He did not even know by what name to call her. His grip was firm, but she did not attempt to pull away. Together they crossed the room and stepped into the hallway where they were alone.

It was only then she spoke. 'What is this, sir?' she demanded, using the governess voice he remembered so clearly.

He was not about to confront her there. 'Come upstairs.'

He held her arm while climbing the stairs that led to Rhys's private rooms. Hugh had moved into them when he took over the management of the house, an arrangement he preferred over living with his mother...and her lover.

He escorted her into the drawing room and shut the door.

'Who are you to treat a woman so?' she demanded.

'Come now, Daphne, or whatever your name is. You, at least, know who I am, which gives you an advantage. I demand to know what you are doing here.' He released her, but stood between her and the closed door.

'I came here to gamble. Is that not what one does at a gambling house?' She straightened her spine. 'You speak as if you think I should know you.'

Did she think he would fall for her protestation of innocence? 'Take off the mask, Daphne.' His whole body coursed with rage, but even so, his eyes ached to see her at last.

She folded her arms across her chest. 'No. I came to this club because I can wear a mask. I will not take it off for anyone. Not even you, sir.'

'Not even me?' He advanced on her and she backed away. 'So you admit knowing me?'

She retreated until he backed her against a wall. 'I admit nothing.'

He made a cage of his arms. 'What is your reason for coming here? Was it for more amusement at my expense? To watch me and believe yourself safe from my knowing who you were? Or was there some other plan? Had there always been some other plan?'

She seemed small and vulnerable next to him. Ironic that when his eyes were bandaged he'd been the one who'd depended upon his strength. He remembered holding her in his touch. He remembered exploring... to envelop him.

brief moment... again to glare down at her. For a eyes again and felt wanted to—to attend here,' she her scent... one was supposed to know.' ...med down to her, inches from her masked ...so close he felt her breath against his lips. There was much I was not supposed to know.'

'Leave it that way, Hugh,' she whispered. 'Please. Let me leave now and I promise you will never see or hear from me again.'

'Allow you to leave?' He shook his head. 'You want to walk out again without any explanation? Did what passed between us not give me the right to an explanation, at least? Or was that a lie, as well? Were you deceiving me then, when we were in bed together?'

Her gaze reached his. 'Not everything was a deception.' She glanced away. 'But it is best we leave it at that.'

Her eyes were the blue of cloudless spring day and her lips the pink of her rose scent. He longed to see all of her.

'Best for who?' he countered. 'Do not presume to know what is best for me. Take off your mask. Show me your face and tell me who you really are. You owe me that.'

She pushed against his chest. 'No. Please let me go,' she begged.

Her touch inflamed him. His arms encircled her and pressed her against him. She struggled only for a moment. 'Hugh. Hugh.'

They remained in an embrace, holding each other as if clinging to a cliff. He ground her against him and he was instantly hard for her. He longed to taste her, demanding a taste of her, a taste for his own felt starved since she'd left him. His kiss was urgent and angry and full of need.

She gasped beneath this onslaught, but met him with matched intensity. Her hands cupped his face, holding him in the kiss as urgent sounds came from deep in her throat.

He wanted no barriers between them. No secrets. No deceptions. No cloth.

He reached up and pulled off her mask.

She let out a cry and pushed him away. He stared at her, his body still throbbing with desire for her, his breath still coming fast. The ache inside him shattered like shards of glass, slicing him to pieces.

He knew her! By God, he knew her!

He spat out her name. 'Lady Faville.'

There was no mistaking her. Smooth, alabaster skin with a natural blush to her cheeks. Full mouth. Huge blue eyes fringed with long dark lashes. Hair the colour of spun gold. Tantalising curves. Anyone in London would know her. She knew he'd know her.

Could her deception be any crueller? This was a thousand times worse than being played for a fool. She'd known the connection between them from the start.

How had she dared hide her identity from him, knowing all the while it would matter to him? His mortification at her hands was complete.

Blast! Now even the memory of their time together was tainted. He could not even cling to a delusion that being with him had meant anything to her. He lost her all over again.

This time he lost the illusion of her.

Daphne felt tears sting her eyes and she ached with anguish. 'I told you. I told you it would be better to leave my mask in place.'

The mask was still in his hand. She snatched it away, but did not attempt to put it back on. What was the use now?

'All this while.' He laughed drily. 'Lady Faville.' He said her name like a curse.

She waved a hand and put more space between them. 'I comprehend. I was forbidden to come here. I will not come again.'

He continued to glare at her.

She lifted her chin. 'I assure you I will not burn this place down, if that is your fear. In fact, I will leave now so you will know I can do no harm.' She started for the door.

He seized her arm. 'You are not leaving yet. Do no harm, you say.' His face was stiff with anger. 'You have already done harm—more than enough.' He tightened his grip. 'You are not leaving until you give me an explanation.'

His grip hurt, but she'd never let that show. 'Is it not obvious, Hugh?'

'Not to me.' He released her, but his gaze

pinned her in place. 'Was this a new trick to play on my family? Some kind of revenge on Xavier?'

'Neither.' She collapsed into a nearby chair, trying to resist the impulse to cover her face. It was too late for that now. 'I have no defence, Hugh. I deceived you terribly and I should never have come here. It was just another foolish whim.'

He planted himself in front of her, looking even more imposing than when she'd been standing. 'Foolish whim? You spent two weeks pretending to be someone else, when you knew all along I would know you. You shared my bed, knowing! How am I to feel learning who you are now?'

'It was a terrible thing to do to you.' What else could she say?

Her heart was breaking. Rather, it was being slashed to shreds by the dagger that had taken up residence there. She rose from the chair, but he did not back away. He stood too close to her, assaulting her with the memory of his arms around her, his body flush against hers.

And now he despised her, as she always knew he would.

'I will go now,' she said in a low voice. 'I promise I will not return.'

She took a step, but he seized her arm again. 'You promise? Have you not proved the quality of your promises?'

She was reasonably certain that she had never

promised him anything, but what good would it do to argue that point with him? 'It does not matter if you believe me or not. Even if I desired to return, you would recognise me, obviously, so I would be foolish to attempt it, would I not?'

He leaned closer to her and whispered in her ear, 'You probably knew I would recognise you this time.'

But she hadn't. It had never occurred to her that he could tell who she was by any other means but sight.

She stepped back. 'I was fully masked. At worst someone might have guessed Lady Faville had returned, but you never saw Mrs Asher. I never imagined you would know it was me.'

His eyes bore into her; their gleam heightened her senses. 'I knew you in other ways, Daphne.' He blinked and his eyes grew hard again. 'It is Daphne, is it not, Lady Faville? Or was that a lie, too?'

She cleared her throat. 'I was Daphne Asher before I was Lady Faville.'

He smirked. 'Oh, just a little lie, then.'

Or a very childish desire to be mere Daphne Asher again. 'Yes. A little lie.'

The clock on the mantelpiece chimed twice, startling them both.

Two o'clock. 'I must leave, Hugh. My carriage is coming to pick me up.'

He stepped back. She managed to walk to

the door even though her feet felt gelatinous. She could not help but glance back for one last look at him. He stood with arms akimbo, glaring at her. She swallowed the tears that finally fell from her eyes as she reached the door and opened it. Once in the hallway, she stopped to tie the mask onto her face again. Her hair and clothing were mussed, but she did not care. For most people here, she was merely a masked lady come to gamble, and if anyone else guessed who she was, they'd never know she'd briefly been Daphne Asher again.

She descended the stairs, where Lord Sanvers lingered on the landing like a hunter waiting for his prey. Must she deal with him again?

'What the devil was that all about?' he asked, his voice amused. Likely he thought it a trifle.

To her it was like a mountain falling on top of her. 'Nothing for you to know, sir.'

She passed by without looking at him and continued to the hall.

Carter waited for her there. He did not ask her any questions. 'I will cash in your counters, m'lady.'

'Thank you, Carter.' She fished in her reticule for the counters and handed them to him.

The hall servant—Cummings—stood nearby.

'Would you please bring us our things?' she asked him.

He nodded and disappeared into the cloak-

room. Daphne stared vacantly at the door. All
she wanted was to leave this house. There would
be plenty of time for regret later. Now she could
add coming here, revealing herself to Hugh, to
her long list of regrets.

She heard Cummings come back and turned,
ready to take her cloak from his arm.

Hugh descended the stairs. She'd not expected
him to follow her.

'I'll help the lady with her cloak, Cummings,'
he said. He must wish to make certain she truly
left the premises; it was the only explanation.

Cummings handed him her cloak and he
walked over to her. She endured the bittersweet
sensation of Hugh's hands upon her shoulders as
he draped the cloak around her.

'Who escorted you?' he asked her, his voice
low enough so only she could hear. 'No other
men, indeed. Another lie, I suppose?'

She did not turn. 'It was Carter.'

He released a surprised breath.

Carter, still masked, emerged from the cashier's office and took a step back when he spied
Hugh standing next to her. Bless Carter; he did
nothing more to betray his identity. He handed
her a purse filled with coin.

'We will settle it later,' she told him.

Carter nodded.

Hugh approached him, a sceptical look on his
handsome, angry face. 'Carter?'

Carter nodded. 'Sir.'

'We must go,' Daphne said. 'The carriage…' The least she could do was spare Carter from being interrogated by Hugh as he'd interrogated her.

Cummings handed Carter his hat and gloves. He put them on and walked to the door, opening it for Daphne. To her dismay, Hugh took her arm and walked out the door with her. He stood with them on the pavement where the carriage was to pick them up. Carter stepped a few paces away, giving Daphne privacy she did not want.

'I suppose it is Smith coming to pick you up,' Hugh remarked. 'Assuming your servants were not using fictitious names, as well.'

'All of the names were real,' she retorted. 'Including mine.' She squared her shoulders. 'Why are you out here, Hugh? To make certain I leave as I said I would?'

'Perhaps I find it difficult to be certain of anything you say.'

She lifted a shoulder. 'Of course. I cannot blame you for that.' It was the consequence of not telling the truth. Trust once betrayed was difficult to earn back, if even possible to earn back.

They stood in silence for what seemed an eternity to Daphne, but must have only been a few minutes. Smith finally drove up in the carriage. He warily nodded to Hugh.

'Smith.' Hugh nodded back.

Carter hurried over to open the carriage door and let down the steps. He waited for Daphne.

'Goodnight, Hugh,' Daphne murmured.

By the rushlight of the doorway, he looked very handsome, very mysterious. Very angry. She stifled a sob. She'd wanted one more look at him. This would certainly be the last one.

Hugh walked with her to the carriage door and helped her climb inside, but said nothing. He nodded to Carter, who entered the carriage after her.

When Smith pulled away, Daphne turned around to get the very last glimpse of Hugh, still framed in the light, now no more than a silhouette.

Carter sat opposite her in the rear-facing seat, taking off his mask immediately, although he kept silent and left her to her thoughts. Dear, dear Carter. His intent was to be kind, she was certain, but at this moment, she felt too much agony to be left alone. She needed a friend, even if he was her servant.

'He recognised me, Carter,' she said. 'He heard me speak and he recognised me.'

'So I gathered, m'lady.'

'It never occurred to me that he could recognise me by my voice. I never intended to be so close to him.' She reached behind her head and untied her mask. 'He was so angry.'

'I am sorry, m'lady.' Carter sounded genuinely sympathetic.

'I should never have come.' She rubbed her forehead. 'We should have stayed in Vadley.'

'It is done now,' he said. 'Some good will come of it, you will see.'

She glanced at him in surprise. Such words might have come from the mouth of the abbess.

She smiled. 'Thank you, Carter. You comfort me.' She felt the coin purse in her lap. 'I won a little. Did you?'

The corner of his mouth turned up. 'I did all right.'

'You are no stranger to cards, are you, Carter?' She lifted the purse.

He frowned. 'I hope that does not distress you, m'lady.'

'Not at all,' she said. Perhaps someday she would ask him more about that. Might it have had something to do with finding him penniless and jobless in Fahr? 'I am glad you won.'

Perhaps that was the only good that was meant to come out of this night.

Chapter Fifteen

Hugh watched Daphne's carriage until it disappeared around the corner of St James's Street. His insides were churning with rage and confusion. Why had she come here?

She'd given him no answers. He knew little more than the day she'd left him. He knew only that she was Lady Faville and that she had pretended to be someone else. But why? Why deceive him?

He'd known Lady Faville only to nod a greeting to. He'd seen her a few times at the Masquerade Club in the days she'd been pursuing Xavier. That very pursuit had prevented Hugh from joining the ranks of her many admirers. She'd wanted Xavier and had no concern for whom she hurt in the process. He'd learned later it had been his sister who was hurt.

And that final act. Attempting to burn down the club. What would have happened to his family if she'd succeeded? The Westleighs would have drowned in the River Tick, that was what.

Hugh shook his head. He'd been staring at an empty street. She was gone and he did believe she would not be back.

But why had she come? Apparently not to speak to him. To see the Masquerade Club again? It made no sense.

He walked back to the gaming house door.

Why, she might have been in London all this time without him knowing. Had he read anything about Lady Faville being in town? He could not remember, but she might have been mentioned a hundred times. He rarely read that part of the newspaper.

Forget this. Forget *her*.

He opened the door and re-entered the hall. Cummings stood there, as if at attention. He'd been in Rhys's regiment, Hugh recalled, not that he talked of it. Cummings rarely talked at all.

Cummings's brows rose. 'Lady Faville?'

Hugh was surprised the man guessed. 'Yes.'

'Thought so,' Cummings said. 'Needed a second look.'

In his month managing the Masquerade Club, Hugh had become pretty good at guessing the identities of the masked patrons. He was nothing to Cummings and MacEvoy, though. Those two knew everyone. They also could spy a card shark within a couple of minutes.

'Well.' Hugh blew out a breath. 'She won't be back.'

Cummings's brows rose again.

Let him be sceptical. Hugh knew she would not be back.

He headed for the game room. *Forget her,* he told himself again. It was time to perform his duties.

Daphne sat at her dressing table already dressed for bed. All that waited was Monette to remove the pins from her hair and brush it smooth so she could put it in a plait. At the moment Daphne despised looking at her own reflection, but she could not expect Monette to understand that. So she sat in front of the glass as she did every night. This dressing table was her most ornate, with two side mirrors and dozens of compartments for her creams and tints and hairpins and combs. And her rosewater scent.

'Was he really very angry at you?' Monette asked as she pulled out pins.

'I knew he would be.' The pain of it shot through her again. 'I knew he would be angry to discover I was Lady Faville.'

Monette untwisted a coil of hair. 'That is why you did not tell him before, is it not?'

'Yes.' She'd been correct that he would both despise her for being Lady Faville and for not telling him who she was. There was no winning.

She'd made him pay a high price for those glorious two weeks.

Monette took out the last pin and Daphne's blonde hair tumbled to her shoulders. She glanced at Monette in the mirror. The maid's lips were pursed and her brows knitted.

'Monette, these are my troubles, not yours. Do not let it distress you.' Daphne had enough on her conscience already.

'It is not that, m'lady.' Monette brushed her hair. 'I mean. I am distressed for you. I do not want you to be unhappy, but—' She clamped her lips shut and brushed with more vigour.

'But what, Monette?' Daphne asked.

It took several strokes of the brush before Monette answered her. 'It is just that— Are we returning to Vadley now?'

Daphne understood. 'You are worried that I will order us all back to Vadley as quickly as I sent us to London.'

Monette nodded.

Daphne continued, 'And you are worried that Toller will send a letter here and that we will miss it.'

Monette stared at Daphne's image in the glass and nodded again.

There was nothing more Daphne wished to do than run back to Vadley and make herself busy again. She did not care if it took her entire fortune, she wanted to do so many good works that she would not have a moment to think about herself.

Or about Hugh.

She reached back and squeezed Monette's hand reassuringly. 'Do not worry. We will wait here for word of Toller. I promised you that you would see London. Perhaps we will take in some of the sights while we are waiting. There is much we could do here. Order new livery for the footmen, new dresses for the maids. We must think of what the house in Vadley needs and purchase it here. One can find anything in the shops of London.' She'd make herself so busy in London that she would not have time to think of him.

Monette smiled. 'I would like that, my lady. The part about Toller I would like the most.'

Daphne smiled in return. 'I know. We will wait to hear from him and, if he wishes to come, we will wait for him to arrive here.'

After her terrible behaviour with Xavier and Hugh's sister, Mr Everard had encouraged her to remove to the Continent until society forgot the whole episode. She'd stayed away two years. Was that enough time? She had no intention of attending parties or the theatre, but would she be given the cut if the *beau monde* encountered her shopping at Floris or consuming an ice at Gunter's?

She must not care about matters such as this. She must instead try to make reparation for being

vain and selfish and wicked to people who deserved none of her nonsense.

And now she needed to do something to make
up for deceiving Hugh. Not directly, though. She
must never seek to see him again.

Monette put Daphne's hair into a plait.

She bid the maid goodnight and climbed into
her bed. When Monette closed the door behind
her, Daphne extinguished her lamp and lay in the
darkness, staring at the glow from her fireplace.
How was she to sleep? She wanted to weep, but
what good would weeping do?

Instead, she closed her eyes and tried to remember Hugh's face, especially his dark brown
eyes that so burned with anger at her. How would
those eyes appear during lovemaking? She again
felt his hands exploring her body, touching her
face, joining his body to hers. She remembered
the ecstasy of her release, of sharing the blissful
moment with him.

She'd live on these memories. What other
choice did she have?

When morning came Daphne forced herself to
eat some toast and jam for breakfast. She feared
offending her London cook's efforts to please her
with kippers, veal pie and baked eggs, but toast
was all she could manage. She was sipping a cup
of tea when Carter entered, looking again like a
servant, not a masked gambler.

'Mr Everard, m'lady,' Carter announced.

'Everard? Here? So early?' It was ten in the morning, too early for callers.

'Yes, m'lady. He is eager to speak with you, he says.'

She'd hardly slept, still felt near tears and was not in the mood for callers. 'Very well. Tell him to join me here.'

A moment later he entered and immediately bowed. 'My lady.'

'Good morning, Everard.' She managed a smile and a bright voice. 'Do serve yourself some breakfast from the sideboard. I insist.' Perhaps his appetite would gratify Cook's desire to please.

'As you wish, ma'am.' He bowed again, piled food on his plate and sat down opposite her.

Daphne poured him tea. 'To what do I owe the honour of your visit?'

He had already put a forkful of food in his mouth and held up a finger to signal he would answer after he swallowed. 'I was concerned about your intention to go to the Masquerade Club last night, as you know. I simply wished to make certain nothing went amiss for you.' He speared a piece of veal from the pie. 'I hope you do not think it improper of me to be concerned.'

She did think he took too much of an interest in her affairs, but it was her own fault for manipulating him into escorting her to the Masquerade Club night after night two years ago.

'Not at all,' she said. 'But you must not be so concerned about me. You have much more important matters to tend to, I am sure.'

He placed his fork down on his plate and gave her a direct look. 'Nothing is more important than your well-being, my lady.'

She must do what she could about this devotion to her. 'Nonsense.' She took a sip of tea. 'As you can see, I am well. How is your wife? She is fortunate indeed to have a husband who concerns himself with the welfare of others.'

'My wife?' He sounded as if he'd forgotten the woman. 'She is in good health.'

'I am so glad to hear it. I should like to meet her some time.' She took a bite of toast.

'You would?' He tackled more of the food on his plate.

Did she really wish to meet Mrs Everard? It would be a nice gesture, she supposed. 'Of course I would. Why would I not?'

He devoured yet another forkful of food before asking, 'Did you find everything satisfactory at the Masquerade Club?'

Her stomach fluttered at the mention of the club, but she put on a pleased expression. 'Oh, yes. I was so happy to see it looking so unharmed. The supper room was as lovely as always.'

He took a gulp of tea. 'Then you will not go back?'

She glanced down at the table. 'I will not go back.'

He looked relieved. 'Is there any service I may render while you are in town?'

She made herself smile. 'You may pay my bills. I intend to do some shopping while we are here.' She sounded like the old Daphne, even to herself, although this time she could think of nothing she wished to buy for herself.

She wondered if there were items she could purchase for the tenants. Perhaps she ought to send a letter to Mr Quigg. The estate manager would know what they might need. Perhaps some furniture. Furniture was so expensive. The tenants might like a nice bureau or a chest or something. Who could not use a pretty chest?

'Do you know of any good furniture shops?' she asked him.

'Furniture shops?'

'Oh, not fine furniture shops, but some that might be appropriate for an ordinary household.'

He looked very puzzled. 'I cannot think offhand, but I will make enquiries, if you like.'

'That would be so good of you,' she said.

If she kept very busy, shopping for her servants and her tenants, she might not think of Hugh so often and she might not always feel this despair so acutely.

Hugh stumbled out of bed with a colossal headache. No doubt the bottle of brandy he'd consumed after closing the Masquerade Club had done the damage. He was half tempted to drink down another. Better to remain in a stupor than to remember. He walked over to the mantel clock and read the time. Ten minutes to noon. Why was he up so early?

Because even the brandy did not help him sleep. His mind whirled with thoughts of Daphne. He felt fresh rage at her for leaving him, for deceiving him, and a deep painful ache of desire for her that even his anger could not eliminate.

Daphne had returned to him for one more deception, one more trick, and was this not the biggest and best of all her tricks? She'd known him all along. She'd been the bane of his family for a time, nearly ruining his sister's happiness and almost burning down this building.

Why had she done it? Why had she deceived him from the beginning and why had she returned? Apparently she'd not planned to make herself known to him. Why?

He'd allowed her to slip through his fingers again without answering any of these questions. Well, this time she would not get away with it. Now he knew who she was, he could discover where she lived. In fact, he probably had the information in the Masquerade Club records. She would have wanted Xavier to know where she lived; she probably had provided the location of her town residence.

He rummaged through the cabinets in the

bedchamber and in the drawing room until he found another bottle of brandy. He drank enough to calm the headache, even though it burned his stomach. He poured water from the ewer into the basin and washed, shaved and dressed before going below and looking for some breakfast.

He found MacEvoy at the breakfast table, as well.

'I counted our take from last night,' MacEvoy said.

'How did we do?' Hugh asked, although the success of the Masquerade Club was not at the forefront of his mind this morning.

'Better than the previous night,' MacEvoy said, 'by about two hundred pounds.'

'Well done.' That was a very tidy sum.

When Hugh and Ned first convinced Rhys to run the club for them, Rhys took half the profits, but now that he'd given up the management, his share dropped to one quarter. Hugh would receive the other quarter, and half still went to repay the Westleigh estate. At least, if this rate continued he'd come out of this latest family task with a fortune.

'Yes, indeed,' admitted MacEvoy. 'The club is still doing well.' He sounded surprised.

Hugh supposed Cummings and MacEvoy and the croupiers did not expect him to be as successful as Rhys. Hugh figured that Rhys had built the foundation and there was not much he could do to weaken it. The idea of being able to gamble masked was still a popular one.

One of the kitchen maids brought in Hugh's breakfast and he made himself eat, knowing it would sooth his brandy-burnt stomach. There was also a welcome pot of coffee on the table.

Hugh poured himself a cup. 'I have a favour to ask.'

MacEvoy looked up warily from his plate. 'What is it?'

'See if you have Lady Faville's location in the records.'

MacEvoy nodded knowingly. 'So that was the lady, eh? I suspected as much. Why did she come back? Was she looking for Campion?' Campion was Xavier's surname.

She'd been obsessed by Xavier before; Hugh feared she still was.

'I do not know why she returned,' he answered MacEvoy. 'But I intend to find out.'

MacEvoy gave him an approving look. 'Good idea. Make certain she keeps to her bargain and never returns here.' He turned thoughtful. 'Although with Campion busy with his shops, there's really no reason for her to come back.'

Somehow that did not appease Hugh.

After breakfast, MacEvoy checked the records and found the location of Daphne's town house. Hugh immediately set off to call upon her.

She resided in Mayfair, but where else would Lady Faville reside? Her house was on Hereford Street, a few streets from Grosvenor Square and near the corner of Hyde Park that bordered Oxford Street. From the Masquerade Club near St James's Street, it was a little over a mile. Hugh welcomed the walk. He'd been spending too much time in darkness, watching people play cards and dice. Even though the nightlife suited his recent gloom, the sun and fresh spring air made him feel more alive than he had felt in over a month.

Or was it the prospect of seeing Daphne again that roused him?

Perhaps anger was a step up from gloom. He refused to believe that anything but anger prompted him to make this visit. He wanted answers, answers she'd cleverly avoided giving him. This time he would not leave until he knew precisely why she had returned to the Masquerade Club. If Lady Faville planned more mischief for his family, he would nip it in the bud right now.

While he'd tossed and turned in his bed that morning, one thought had consumed him, and it was not the notion that she'd come to the Masquerade Club looking for him. It was that she'd come looking for Xavier.

Apparently she'd held her obsession with him for ten years. What made him think it was over now? Or had been over even when she'd been with him in the cottage? What other reason than Xavier would have made her come back? She might not have known Xavier was rarely at the club now that Hugh had taken over its management.

If she was really pining for his brother-in-law, what had been her meaning in making love to him?

He passed Berkeley Square and walked down Mount Street to Park Lane, which bordered the park. He needed to smell trees thick with new leaves, spring grass and flowers. Scent had become so much more important to him, a vestige of his two weeks of blindness.

He turned onto Hereford and found the house easily. With no hesitation, he strode up to the door and sounded the knocker.

A footman opened the door and broke out into a smile of recognition before composing his face again. 'Mr Westleigh.'

'Carter?' This was Hugh's first glimpse of Carter's face. The man had been masked at the Masquerade Club. Hugh returned the man's smile. 'Believe me when I tell you it is good to see you.'

Carter grinned again. 'I am delighted you can tell me so, sir.' He stepped aside to allow Hugh to enter. 'Have you come to see—?' The man shut his mouth and looked perplexed, probably not knowing which name his mistress wished him to use.

'I have come to see Lady Faville.'

Carter bowed. 'Allow me to see if she is receiving callers.' Carter's voice was comfortingly familiar.

He escorted Hugh to the drawing room and, leaving the door open, left him there to find Daphne.

The room was dominated by a full-length portrait of Daphne—or rather, Lady Faville—her expression too cool and remote to be the Daphne he thought he'd known. Hugh closed his eyes and remembered the cottage drawing room, which he'd learned to navigate without sight. He turned away before opening his eyes again. This room was larger, more formal and feminine than the cottage's furniture had turned out to be. This room was decorated in fine brocades and velvets in shades of ivory and blue, no doubt to reflect the blue of her eyes. There was no pianoforte in this room, which somehow made it seem cooler, more impersonal, not warm and comfortable like the cottage had been.

Perhaps this room suited the cool beauty of the portrait, whose appearance was always calculated to turn heads. At least, that had been his impression of Lady Faville. That was not the same woman he'd known in the cottage. He closed his eyes and remembered her, the sound of her voice, her scent, the warmth of her skin. That Daphne had not been real, but a fabrication based on her lies and his need. To know her as Lady Faville could only make it easier to forget the illusion she'd been.

He heard a swish of skirts behind him and her voice. 'Hugh?'

Daphne stood in the doorway. Or rather, Lady Faville stood there. Her gleaming blonde hair was pulled away from her face into a simple knot and the rose-coloured dress she wore accented her flawless skin and matched the pink of her full lips. This paragon of beauty, so cool and flawless, was, indeed, not the Daphne he'd known.

'Why have you come here, Hugh?' She'd not moved from the doorway, as if she was afraid to enter the room.

'We have unfinished business, you and I.' He stared her in the eye. 'I would speak with you.'

She blinked and glanced behind her. Looking for an escape? But she closed the door and took a step closer to him. 'I have apologised for coming to the Masquerade Club. I will not come there again.'

'As you said.' His voice sounded bitter. 'But that is not why I have come.'

'What more can be said?' She lifted her chin regally.

There was no reason to mince words. 'I want to know why you came in the first place.'

She clasped her hands together. 'I—I wanted to see the place.'

'See the place?' He gave a dry laugh. 'Do not play me for a fool. Again.'

Her eyes flashed. 'Then why did you think I came there?'

He glared at her. 'To find Xavier.'

'Xavier?' She acted surprised.

'Xavier,' he repeated. 'You remember him. Xavier Campion? My sister's husband? The man you lusted after for weeks—years. You planned to break up his marriage, if you recall.'

She lowered her gaze to the floor. 'That was a long time ago.' She raised her eyes again and her expression was like ice. 'Surely you have not come here simply to point out my past failings. I assure you I am well acquainted with them.'

'I want to know if you came to the Masquerade Club to see Xavier.'

She stepped towards one of the chairs and placed her hands, delicate and long fingered, on the back of it. 'You took the trouble to call upon me merely to ask me that?' Her voice rose in pitch. 'You want only to know that I will not further trouble your family?'

That was not the only reason. He wanted to know how deep her deception had been in those two weeks he'd been blind. He wanted to know if she was still as obsessed by Xavier as she'd been before. If so, what had he, Hugh, meant to her?

He moved closer, standing behind her, close enough for her scent to reach his nostrils. Her scent matched the rose of her dress.

'I will cause no more trouble, Hugh,' she said, her voice weary.

That did not answer his question. 'I am to believe you? You made other promises and broke them. You've told other lies.'

'Yes,' she admitted. 'But whether you believe me or not, I will trouble you and your family no further.'

He scoffed. 'Maybe you cannot return to the Masquerade Club, because now you know even a mask cannot disguise you from me, but how do I know you are not plotting some other mischief?'

'You cannot know.' She shook her head. 'I mean, I ask only that you believe me this time.'

Believe her? 'I am to believe you do not have some other mischief to wreak upon my family?'

'Yes, because I do not.' Her voice turned very quiet. 'I mean none of you any harm at all.'

He strode up to her and held her by her shoulders. 'Then tell me why you came. If not to start that business with my sister's husband again, then why?'

It was a mistake to come so close to her, to touch her. His body was drawn to her like a magnet to metal.

She made no effort to pull away. Instead, she

looked up into his face. 'Would you believe me if I told you I came to see you?'

His senses heightened at her words and her nearness. It hurt to look at her; she was that beautiful.

'I would not believe it,' he managed.

She took a breath and it felt as if she'd robbed him of air. 'Well, I did come to see you. I wanted to look at you without bandages, to see for myself that you were not blind. When I left the cottage, I did not know if you would be blind or not.'

'If you'd cared so much, Daphne—' he released her '—you never would have left.'

She stepped away from him. 'If I'd stayed, you would have discovered who I was.'

His voice dipped low. 'I would have discovered how seriously you deceived me, you mean.'

'Yes,' she agreed again. 'That is what I mean.'

Had he meant that much to her that she needed to see him healed? Wait. He must not fall for more deception. 'How did you even know I was at the Masquerade Club?'

She paused before answering, 'Mr Everard, my man of business, told me.'

Her man of business? Hugh knew that Lady Faville's man of business had met with Rhys and Xavier to arrange the compensation for the damage to the Masquerade Club.

'Your man of business told you I was at the club and that was why you came there?'

She nodded.

He could not believe her. If he'd been that important to her, she would not have deceived him. She would not have left him. 'You came to assure yourself that I was not blind and not to see Xavier?'

She turned her head away. 'Yes.'

Was she jesting? 'Your man of business would have mentioned a blind gambling-club manager. There cannot be so many of those in London. When he spoke of me, surely you knew then I was not blind. Why come to see it?'

Her shoulders slumped and she retreated to the fireplace. 'It does no good to banter back and forth. You cannot believe me and I cannot convince you. Suffice to say I will not bother you again, Hugh. I do promise that.' Her voice cracked. 'Please leave me now.'

He crossed the room and turned her around to face him. 'Not before you tell me why you lied to me! Why did you not tell me you were Lady Faville? Why did you let me think—think you were someone else? That our time together meant something else?'

Her eyes glittered with unspent tears and she trembled beneath his touch. Instead of pulling away and slapping him across the face as he deserved for such roughshod behaviour, she reached up and touched his cheek.

'I am so sorry, Hugh,' she whispered.

Her voice was like her whispers in bed. He could resist no more. He crushed his lips against hers. Closing his eyes, he brought back the Daphne he loved, warm and soft and real.

Daphne threw her arms around him and kissed him back, starved for his touch, the feel of his lips. He tasted wonderful, so familiar, so masculine. She held him in the kiss by burying her fingers in his hair, savouring the feel of his thick, dark, unruly hair no longer covered by bandages. The heat of his body inflamed her and she could think of nothing but joining with him again.

In the month they'd been apart it was if she'd been torn in two. She needed him to be whole again, to give her life some kind of meaning. She clutched at him with a desperation that matched his own. He backed her to a *chaise longue* near the fireplace, and her need was too great to wait upon removing clothes. She undid the buttons of his trousers while he pulled up her skirts. Suddenly she was beneath him, pulling him to her, opening herself to him. It was madness, but a glorious derangement, this urgent need to make love to him, to again share the ecstasy of a passionate release.

They freed themselves of enough clothing, and

he thrust into her, his power so exhilarating that she thought she would weep for the pleasure of it. She rose to meet him in a frenzied, desperate rush that was unlike any of their past lovemaking. Never had her need for him risen so quickly, become so violently intense.

She clutched at him, fearful something would yank him away, like a sailor swept from his ship in a storm. This storm was of their own making, Daphne thought, but she felt as helpless as if it had come from the wind.

She felt the sensations inside her grow more intense, building with each rhythmic thrust. Did he realise what his body did to her? Did his need drive him higher and higher, harder and harder? Suddenly she reached the precipice and his seed exploded inside her. She cried out as her own release came and she quivered beneath him in waves and waves of supreme pleasure.

A moment later, it was over. They plummeted quickly from the highest peak straight to the deepest reality.

He lay atop her only briefly before standing, looking alarmed. She made an attempt at covering herself with her skirts when he fumbled through his pockets and handed her his handkerchief. It was a kindness she didn't expect after such an animalistic coupling. He glanced at her, but quickly turned away to button his trousers and straighten the rest of his clothes.

'Did I hurt you, Daphne?' He faced her again.

She shook her head, but felt a tear escape her eyes and run down her cheek.

He leaned down and gently wiped it away with his thumb. 'I am sorry for that.'

Her brows knitted. 'Sorry?' Had he regretted this?

'I should not have treated you so. It was not well done of me at all.'

Was he ashamed? 'Then why—?' She could not get the words out.

'Why?' He blew out a breath. 'I honestly do not know why. Your beauty—?'

Her beauty.

The dagger inside Daphne's heart twisted.

Of course. Acclaimed beauty, Lady Faville. What man did not want her?

Besides her husband, she'd allowed no man in her bed. Except Hugh. Even though he despised her for causing trouble for his family and lying to him, he'd made love to her beauty.

And she'd allowed it.

She'd wanted it. She'd wanted nothing more.

Except perhaps that he make love to Daphne, a woman he couldn't see.

She glanced around the room. The curtains were open and sunlight streamed in. Anyone walking by might have seen them on the *chaise*. Her cheeks burned at the thought.

'I must go,' he said.

She managed to stand and to smooth her skirts. 'Yes. Go.' He'd walk out the door, out of her life, and she feared all the shopping and good works in the world would not be enough to take away the pain of that.

He nodded and crossed the room to the door. She could not take her eyes off him. Tears still stung, but she refused to let him see her cry. There was plenty of time for weeping in the middle of the night.

He reached the door and opened it. Her breathing quickened. This was the end.

He turned around. 'Daphne?'

Her heart pounded. 'Yes?'

He waved a hand, erasing whatever it was he'd been about to say. He crossed the threshold and walked out.

She watched until he disappeared in the hall. He said a word or two to Carter and the front door opened and closed. She hurried over to one of the windows and watched him step onto the pavement.

As he passed by the window, he turned and saw her there. Their gazes caught for a moment before he continued walking and was soon out of sight.

She looked down at her hand. She still clutched his handkerchief, all that she had left of him. Hurrying out of the room, she climbed the

Chapter Sixteen

After one last glance at Daphne through the window, Hugh turned away and strode quickly down the pavement. The sight of her disconcerted him. It wasn't that he'd formed a clear vision of her when his eyes were bandaged. It was seeing her as Lady Faville that sparked a whole set of disparate emotions.

The Daphne of his imagination had never been Lady Faville.

Hugh chose the bustle of Oxford Street rather than retrace his steps through Mayfair. He walked at a brisk pace, needing to put as much distance between himself and Lady Faville as possible.

No matter who she was in reality, he'd behaved appallingly towards her, coupling with her in such a lustful frenzy. Where had been his control? His gentlemanly respect? Never before had he moved with such desire for a woman.

One look at her revealed how he'd upset her.

How could he have taken her with such swift need? It was just that, for a moment, that brief moment of lovemaking, he'd thought he'd found her again.

He turned onto Bond Street and pushed past the street vendors, crossing sweepers and other pedestrians. He passed a jewellery shop and almost collided with a gentleman coming out the door.

'Hugh!' It was his brother Ned.

Hugh, in no mood to speak to anyone, mumbled a greeting.

'I've not seen you in over a fortnight. I keep meaning to stop in the club...' Ned looked apologetic.

'All is well there,' Hugh assured him.

'Where are you headed?' Ned did not wait for Hugh to answer. 'Have you time? Come with me to White's. We'll have a drink.' His eyes pleaded for Hugh to say yes.

How could Hugh refuse?

Ned began talking right away. 'I had no idea what work it would be to sit in the Lords, about the complexity of decisions to be made. The Poor Relief Bill. Usury laws. Timber duties. Not to mention the budget and preparing for the coronation.' He took a breath. 'I do not see how Father did it.'

'I suspect he shirked his Parliamentary duties as he did all the rest,' Hugh responded.

'I suspect you are correct,' Ned admitted. 'But to me, it all seems too important to neglect.'

Ned was the best sort of man to own a title. He strove always to do his duty, to do what was good and right. He was the opposite of their father, as a matter of fact. To an annoying degree, sometimes.

Ned talked of the various bills on which he had to vote, seeking Hugh's approval of his decisions all the way to White's. He continued talking as they sat down and ordered glasses of claret. Hugh noticed several members in the gaming room, deep in their cards. He recognised some of the gentlemen and expected to see them at the Masquerade Club that night. Did they not take Parliamentary duties as seriously as Ned, or were they working on gaining support for their various positions? There was more than one way to achieve a result.

'How is your wife?' Hugh asked when Ned stopped talking long enough to take a sip of his wine.

'Adele?' Ned's expression softened. 'She fares very well, except in the morning. She cannot keep food down in the morning. It is common amongst women when they are increasing, she assures me.'

Hugh thought of Daphne, never having children. He'd been certain it had made her sad. Had it made Lady Faville sad? He could not stop thinking of them as two separate people.

He could not stop thinking of her at all, not even under the deluge of Ned's words.

He asked Ned about the rest of the family. Their mother. Phillipa. Rhys.

Ned asked about the Masquerade Club, detailed questions about its profits, the expenditures Hugh had incurred. They debated the necessities of new dice and new packs of cards, items that Hugh insisted upon. Rhys had instilled in him the importance of assuring the patrons that the games were honest. New dice, new cards were a part of that.

By the time the clock struck the hour for the second time, Ned jumped to his feet. 'Gads. I must be off. Adele is expecting me.'

Hugh rose more slowly, but followed Ned back out to the street.

Ned shook his hand, clasping his arm at the same time. 'So good to see you, Hugh. I promise to stop by the Masquerade Club the first chance I get. In the meantime, if you need me for anything, you have but to ask.'

Hugh had no doubt that Ned would drop everything and come if Hugh needed him, although he was self-absorbed enough to neglect enquiring about anything of Hugh's life besides the Masquerade Club. Nothing besides the task assigned to him.

Would he have told Ned about Daphne if Ned had asked? He doubted it.

Hugh watched his brother hurry down the street and disappear in the crowd of pedestrians. With nothing better to do, he turned to walk the short distance back to the Masquerade Club.

That night Rhys and Xavier visited the Masquerade Club. After greeting the workers and the patrons who frequented the club, they sat down with Hugh in a corner of the supper room. In front of them were plates laden with food and bottles of wine. Hugh poured them each a glass.

Rhys tasted the food and nodded appreciatively. 'I see Cook is still up to her old standards. I'd forgotten how good the food could be.'

Hugh also appreciated her and made certain she knew it. She was the widow of one of the men in Rhys and Xavier's regiment and was intensely loyal to both men.

'I've had no problems to speak of,' Hugh told them. 'Do you see any?'

Xavier's gaze wandered to the pianoforte. He grinned. 'You are missing the masked *pianiste*.' His wife, Phillipa, the woman so wronged by Daphne, had increased the crowds at the club the few weeks she'd performed.

Hugh made himself smile back. 'Perhaps she will return? Are her nights free?'

Xavier's expression turned sly. 'Her nights are very occupied, I am afraid.'

Hugh regarded the man discreetly. Xavier was

indeed very handsome. The gazes of women in the supper room often turned his way. With his thick, dark, poetically unruly hair, manly features and startling blue eyes, it was no wonder Daphne had been enamoured of him. They would have made a very handsome couple.

Hugh shook that thought away.

At least Xavier was a decent man. In fact, Hugh suspected his appearance meant nothing to him. The opinion of others meant nothing to him. He'd defied society's expectations of the son of an aristocrat and invested his money in shops. If he stank of trade, as the saying went, then the women in the room liked the smell.

Hugh asked about Phillipa and the baby and went on to ask about the shops.

'I have ten of them now.' Xavier straightened. 'The furniture shop is doing the best. There's a good market for good furniture at moderate prices. I prefer enterprises that require manufacture. We can employ more workers that way. I added a pianoforte maker recently.'

'A former soldier knew how to make pianofortes?' Rhys asked.

Xavier mainly hired out-of-work former soldiers.

'No.' Xavier sipped his wine. 'The man who made Phillipa's pianoforte was in danger of going out of business. He agreed to train some former soldiers in the trade.'

Xavier's benevolence reminded Hugh of Daphne's generous overpayment of the cottage servants.

He shook himself. He needed to change this subject. 'Rhys, how are your interests faring?'

Rhys was heavily invested in the manufacture of steam engines. 'We are seeking to improve designs all the time, but some of our machines have started selling to factories and mines. You know there is a steam locomotive operating between Stockton and Darlington. I am certain there will be more in the future.'

Hugh shrugged. 'This is another form of gambling, is it not?'

Their father had disowned his bastard son, Rhys, after his mother died. He'd been a mere lad who learned to survive by gambling.

Rhys nodded. 'It is indeed, but more exciting than the turn of a card. More useful, too.'

Xavier saw one of his brothers enter the supper room and excused himself to go and speak to him.

After he'd left the table, Hugh asked Rhys, 'Have you found a life that suits you, then?' Hugh might have been hateful to Rhys when they were boys, but now all he wanted was for Rhys to do well.

Rhys glanced away and back, his eyes warm and intense. 'I have more than I could ever have dreamed of possessing.' He took a bite of food. 'And I do not mean money.'

Hugh met his gaze. 'You have a wife and children.'

'A family,' Rhys said, his voice low.

'We are your family as well, Rhys,' Hugh added in the same tone. 'We Westleighs. I know I did not always think that way, but my mind has changed.'

Rhys maintained the mood. 'People can change. I certainly have.'

Could they? Could people truly change? Or were their characters forged at birth? Did circumstances foster certain traits to come to the fore and others to be hidden? He and Rhys had hated each other since boyhood, until Hugh saw him for the decent, strong, compassionate man he was. Had always been, Hugh suspected. Perhaps as a boy, Hugh had only seen Rhys's facade, a tough ruffian always up for a fight.

Was Lady Faville the facade or was Daphne? He knew he must find out.

When Xavier returned to his seat, Hugh asked him, 'Where is this pianoforte shop of yours?'

'Why?' Xavier asked.

Hugh pierced a piece of cold beef with his fork. 'I may be wishing to purchase one.'

Xavier gestured to the instrument sitting idle in the supper room. 'You have a pianoforte right here. Or do you mean this for someone else?'

'Yes. Someone else.' He was not ready to say who, but they had spent many a pleasant hour seated together on the bench of the pianoforte in the cottage. Maybe the gift would at least convey his gratitude to her for tending to his care those two weeks. And his apology for ill using her this day.

Maybe it would give him an excuse to see her again.

It was no difficulty for Daphne to rise early the next morning. She had hardly slept at all. It seemed as if only in the privacy of her bedroom, late at night, could she free the grief that wreaked havoc inside her during the day. The darkness took away all reminders of who and where she was. What remained were her emotions, which she dared not release during the day.

The previous day had not been at all busy enough to distract her, although she'd done her best. Monette needed distracting, as well. The girl fretted that they would not have a reply from Toller or that he would decide to remain in Thurnfield.

For want of anything better to do, Daphne and Monette had gone through several trunks stored in the attic. She'd packed away so many clothes, so many pairs of shoes, gloves, hats, cloaks. How shameful of her to pack away items that might make others happy or be of good use to them.

What Monette did not want, Daphne offered to
the maids and the kitchen staff. When they were
all through sorting and selecting, what remained
they could sell on Petticoat Lane.

But digging through memories had not been
the easiest way to endure the day. Over and over
Daphne had been compelled to face the woman
she'd been, the woman she feared she could never
escape.

But this morning dawned a new day and
she had a new resolve. Today she would show
Monette London's shops. Give the young woman
some pleasure, some adventure. Oh, perhaps not
adventure like Hugh had once talked about, but
certainly sights Monette had never seen. Nothing could compare to the vast array of London's
shops.

She was nearly through breakfast when Carter
entered the room. 'Mr Everard calls again, my
lady.'

'Everard?' He'd just called the day before. She
feared he was forming an attachment that would
simply hurt everyone. 'I suppose you must tell
him I'll see him here.'

A moment later he appeared in the doorway.
'Good morning, my lady.' He bowed.

'Good morning, sir.' She tried not to sound
too curt, but also not too inviting. 'You are back
to see me so soon. I do hope nothing is amiss.'

'Not at all. Not at all.' He remained in the doorway.

She sighed inwardly. 'Do come in and have something to eat, if you'd like. I confess I do not have a great deal of time as I am going out very soon, but tell me why you have come.'

'Some tea, perhaps,' he said as he sat.

She poured him some tea.

He took a grateful sip. 'I come only to inform you that I have done what you wished of me.'

What had she asked of him? She could recall nothing.

She waited and eventually he continued, 'You asked me for recommendations for furniture shops.'

'Oh, yes.' But a note bearing the names of the shops would have sufficed.

'I am not well versed in such matters, but I have arranged for someone who is quite knowledgeable to call upon you.' He looked quite pleased with himself.

Daphne did not want callers, although she supposed she could not hide from all society for ever. Who would Everard send? 'Who is it who will call upon me?'

'My wife.'

His wife? The poor creature. What was Daphne to do with a visit from his wife?

She caught herself. It would be a kindness to

receive his wife. She would be kind to the young woman.

She made herself smile. 'How lovely.'

'She purchased most of the items in our residence and has a good eye for quality at a fair price. I could think of no better person to advise you.' He paused. 'And you did say you wished to meet her.'

'I did, did I not?' She took a bite of toast. 'I suppose she could call on me this afternoon. I will certainly be at home after two o'clock.'

He stood. 'I shall make certain she knows this. She will not fail you, my lady.' He bowed. 'I fear I must take my leave. With your permission, of course.'

'Of course,' she said somewhat gratefully. 'Good day to you, sir.'

Shortly after Mr Everard left, Daphne set out with Monette to show her the shops and distract her from the fact that they had not yet heard from Toller. They started on Oxford Street, it being so close, and visited linen draper after linen draper. In one, Monette found a blue muslin that was just a shade deeper than Daphne's eyes. She begged Daphne to purchase it and allow her to make a gown for Daphne from it, in repayment for Daphne's generosity to her.

It was a hard decision to make. She did not need a new gown. Had she not the day before given away countless gowns? But she was forced this time to admit that accepting Monette's gift was the most generous act she could make at the moment.

They explored hat shops, glove shops and jewellery shops. Daphne had several pieces of fine jewellery locked away, expensive gifts from her late husband, which she'd not worn since leaving London for the Continent two years ago. She certainly had not needed jewels in the abbey. It surprised her how little she had missed them.

They stopped in a clock shop. On the shelf, among grander pieces, was a clock in a porcelain case that might have been a twin to the one she'd placed in Hugh's bedchamber in the cottage. Swallowing tears, she purchased it and arranged for it to be sent to her town house.

They bought Dutch biscuits from a street vendor and savoured the sweet and spicy taste. As they finished the last crumbs, they passed a sheet-music shop.

'I want to look in here.' Daphne opened the door and entered the shop.

Monette followed her.

The proprietor approached. 'May I be of assistance, ma'am?' His look of admiration was familiar.

'I hope you may assist, sir,' she responded. 'I am looking for music for the pianoforte written by a lady.'

'A lady?' His brows rose. 'Do you know the name of the lady or of the piece?'

She smiled. 'I do not. I suspect she has written the music anonymously.'

He tapped his finger against his lips. 'I have an idea.'

He let her to a file of music sheets and riffled through them, pulling out one. 'Perhaps this one?'

She took it from his hand and read that it was a sonatina by Lady Songstress. Her heart beat faster. Lady Songstress had been the name she'd given to Phillipa Westleigh when she'd known her only as the masked *pianiste* at the Masquerade Club.

Daphne's throat tightened. Had she been a better person, Lady Songstress might have been a friend.

'Yes,' she told the proprietor. 'This is it exactly. Are there other compositions by Lady Songstress?'

He found three others, one quite new. A lullaby.

'I will buy them all.' It was at least something she could do for Phillipa. It would honour her music.

'My lady?' Monette touched her sleeve. 'You do not have a pianoforte here. What will you do with this music?'

Daphne had not thought about playing the music, but would that not be the best way to respect Phillipa's talent?

She turned to the store proprietor. 'Is there a pianoforte shop you might recommend?'

'Indeed there is,' he responded. 'Near here on Duke Street.'

She made her purchases and she and Monette left.

'Are you going to buy a pianoforte?' Monette asked.

Daphne smiled. 'I believe I will.' Playing music would be another way to pass the time.

And to remember when she and Hugh played music together.

They found the pianoforte shop and entered. The shop had several instruments on display. The clerk was busy talking to three gentlemen, so Daphne and Monette walked around, looking at simple pianofortes, ornate ones, even a small one that could be carried from place to place. The clerk broke away from his conversation and approached Daphne.

He flushed when he looked upon her face. 'Are you interested in a pianoforte, my lady?'

'I am indeed,' she said.

When she spoke, the three gentlemen turned and Daphne felt the air leave her lungs.

It was the new Lord Westleigh, Xavier—and Hugh.

Hugh felt both his brother Ned and Xavier stiffen when they saw her. She looked equally as shocked, but more than that, she looked vulnerable. How would Ned and Xavier react? Even in front of the pianoforte clerk and her maid, a cut would wound her.

He stepped towards her and bowed. 'Good morning, ma'am. Daphne.' He could not help calling her by name. 'You are planning to purchase a pianoforte?'

She darted a glance at Xavier and Ned before answering. 'Yes. I—I do not have one and I am lately interested in playing again.' She held out a large envelope. 'I purchased some music.'

'Did you?' He extended his hand. 'May I see?'

She turned paler, hesitating before handing over the packet. He glanced inside. His head snapped up, catching her gaze, when he saw what she had purchased. Phillipa's music.

'I—I was interested in this composer. I wanted to give my support,' she explained.

What was he to make of the fact that she'd purchased his sister's compositions? He glanced back at Xavier. Had it been because of Xavier?

Ned gazed at her as if she was a pariah. Xavier looked on guard. Both reactions annoyed him. Was there a need to be cruel to her? 'Xavier, Lady Faville has come to purchase one of your pianofortes. Ned, you remember Lady Faville, do you not?'

Ned inclined his head to her, but did not speak.

Xavier stepped forwards. 'Did you know this was one of my shops?' His words might have sounded polite to the clerk and Monette, but Hugh suspected both Ned and Daphne sensed the sharp edge to them.

Daphne looked genuinely surprised. 'I had no idea of it.'

Monette edged closer to her.

Hugh nodded to the young maid. 'How are you, Monette?'

'Very well, sir,' she replied shyly, her eyes wandering to Xavier. 'We—we just learned of this place at the music shop.'

Brave girl to defend her mistress in front of an earl and son of an earl. Although she would not know that.

He handed the envelope back to Daphne and their fingers touched. She flushed. 'I did not know,' she said just loud enough for Hugh to hear.

He nodded slightly and turned to the clerk. 'Do you have a recommendation for the lady? Which do you feel would suit her best?'

The man snapped back from gazing upon her. 'You might try them for sound. All are manufactured to the highest standards, but their sound will differ slightly.' He pressed the keys of the nearest instruments.

Hugh could hear a difference.

The clerk cleared his throat and continued. 'Or perhaps the decor of the cabinets will matter more to you.' He walked over to one that was painted with pink roses, its corners edged in gilt. 'This would be a fine addition to any room.'

'I—I prefer one that is less flamboyant.' She turned to one that was plainly styled. It was quite like the one at the cottage, although obviously of higher quality. 'This one. You may prepare the bill of sale and have the instrument sent to my residence.' She gave him the direction to her town house.

The clerk looked to Xavier.

'Yes, Mr Ball. You may do that for Lady Faville,' Xavier said.

'Yes, sir.' He walked over to the counter and pulled out a book to prepare the bill of sale.

Xavier turned to Daphne. 'I did not know you were in town.'

She darted a glance at him, but did not sustain it. 'Yes. We have come to do shopping.'

Monette spoke up again. 'My lady is showing me all the shops.'

Ned broke in with a sarcastic tone. 'The shops?'

Daphne turned to him. 'That is all. I have no other plans. Although we might visit some of the special sights. The Tower. Westminster Abbey. The Egyptian Hall…' Her voice faded as if she feared she'd said too much.

She glanced at Xavier again.

What was she thinking at seeing Xavier again? Hugh wondered. Had she really not known this was his shop? It seemed too coincidental.

Although how could she have known Xavier would be at the shop? Investors did not spend a great deal of time in their shops. Did Lord George Cavendish patrol the Burlington Arcade like one of his beadles? Indeed not. How would she even have known Xavier owned such shops? From Mr Everard, perhaps, if there was some way that man might have known of it.

It made more sense that she would want to show Monette London. She'd brought the girl from Switzerland and treated her more like a younger sister than a lady's maid.

The clerk returned with the bill of sale.

'You will be paid promptly after the instrument is delivered,' Daphne told him. She turned to Ned and Xavier. 'Good day, gentlemen.' She gave Hugh a direct gaze. 'Hugh.'

He walked with her to the door and opened it for her. 'Enjoy your music, Daphne. Monette.'

When he closed the door again the clerk excused himself and went to the back of the shop.

Ned turned on Hugh. 'What was that all about, Hugh? You acted as if Lady Faville was an old friend of yours.' Ned shot daggers at him. 'Let me remind you that she nearly ruined us.'

'I did not know she was in London,' Xavier said, as if he talking only to himself. 'God knows I want no more trouble with her. I won't have Phillipa hurt again.'

'Trouble.' Ned laughed drily. 'That is what

she is. You know that, Hugh. Have you lost your senses?'

He had lost his senses with her, but it would be no use trying to explain why to his brother. 'No more than you, Ned,' Hugh shot back. 'There is certainly no reason to discuss this with you.'

Ned glared at him. 'I think there is every reason to discuss her with me.'

'I am acquainted with Lady Faville,' Hugh admitted. 'But she is hardly the terror you make her out to be.'

'I suppose you met her in Brussels,' Ned scoffed. 'It was said she ran off to the Continent. Were you one of her conquests over there? You stayed a long time. Perhaps not all your time was spent tending to our father's affairs.'

'You know nothing of it, Ned.' Hugh raised his voice, his anger reaching boiling point. 'If you did not trust me to take care of things in Brussels, maybe you should have gone yourself. Cleaned up the mess yourself.'

'You cannot speak to me in that fashion!' Ned countered, his face red.

'Why? Because you own the title? Remember, I'm your brother. I've seen you without your Parliamentary robes. And it has been a long time since you could best me in at fisticuffs.' He wished Ned would challenge him right now. He'd relish punching him in his aristocratic nose.

Xavier stepped between the two of them.

'Enough. You don't have to scrap like a couple of schoolboys. Lady Faville is my problem, if she is anyone's.' He faced Hugh. 'Are you going to buy a pianoforte?'

Hugh shook his head. 'Not today. I've changed my mind.'

'Very well,' Xavier said. 'I'm leaving. I need to tell Phillipa about Lady Faville being in London.'

'Do not tell her,' Ned protested. 'It will upset her.'

'Not as much as keeping it a secret from her.' He called to Mr Ball that he was leaving, gave Ned and Hugh one more annoyed look and left the shop.

Hugh started for the door, as well.

Ned was at his heels. 'Promise me you will have nothing more to do with Lady Faville.'

'Promise you?' Hugh laughed as he walked out of the shop. 'Why not simply trust me to do the right thing?'

He strode away from his brother and did not look back. At the moment he was too angry at Ned to deal with him a moment longer.

Chapter Seventeen

Daphne walked so briskly, Monette had difficulty keeping up with her. She stopped and waited. 'I am sorry, Monette. I simply must return home.'

'Yes, *madame*,' Monette said, out of breath. 'It upset you to see Mr Westleigh. I am sorry for you.'

'It—it surprised me, is all. I did not expect it.' She had not expected to ever see him again.

He'd been civil to her, even kind. That made the pain greater. Had he been as rude as his brother, her anger might have blocked out the ache of losing him all over again.

'Who were the other gentlemen? They were so angry at you, I think,' Monette asked. 'One man was very handsome. I have never seen a man so—so handsome.'

Another surprise. Seeing Hugh had so completely overshadowed the sight of Xavier that she'd no emotion to spare for him. It simply had not mattered to her to see Xavier again. She'd never truly known him, merely the superficial fantasy of him she'd created herself.

She'd known Hugh, though. Intimately. She knew his character, his determination, his strength.

She answered Monette, 'The handsome man is married to Mr Westleigh's sister and the other man is Mr Westleigh's brother, Lord Westleigh.'

Monette's eyes widened. '*Lord* Westleigh?'

'He is an earl.'

'*Mon Dieu,*' Monette murmured.

They retraced their steps on Oxford Street and returned to the town house. When they walked in the door, Daphne said, 'I will be quite myself again, Monette. I simply need some solitude for a little while.'

Monette nodded.

Daphne forced herself to climb the steps at a normal pace. When she entered her bedchamber, she realised she was still clutching the envelope containing the music sheets. She dropped it on a table, pulled off her gloves and hat and pressed her hands against her temple.

Calm yourself, she scolded. It is very unlikely she would see Hugh again, even if she went out. It was merely a terrible coincidence this time. She hurried over to her bureau drawer and pulled out his handkerchief, all clean and folded.

She held it in her hands and flopped into a

rocking chair. She gazed out the window while she rocked, but she did not see the blue sky or the green trees. She was consumed by the memory of his fingers brushing against hers, by the kind look in his eyes. Of course, he'd appeared puzzled when he'd seen what music she'd purchased. Why had she done such a thing? She could have purchased any music. What was he to think of her selecting Phillipa's music?

She could barely remember what Xavier had said. There was not even a vestige of her former infatuation.

Hugh's brother's anger had been very evident. She'd expected such a reaction from a Westleigh. She deserved it. The surprise had been Hugh's defence of her. At least it felt like he'd defended her, practically forcing his brother to be civil. Why had he done such a thing?

Her mind whirled in circles for the next hour and always wound up in the same bleak place.

There was a knock on the door and Monette peeked into the room. 'Mrs Everard has come to call.'

Daphne had completely forgotten about Mrs Everard.

She rose wearily. 'I must see her.'

'Wait.' Monette touched her gown. 'Do you not wish me to help you change? One of your morning gowns is ready for you.'

Daphne looked down at herself. She supposed

her skirts were a bit soiled from the street. 'Might we simply brush off the dirt? I hate to keep her waiting long.' Truly she wanted to be done with this interview, regretting she'd ever said anything to put Mrs Everard in this position of having to call upon her social superior.

Monette quickly brushed the hem of her skirt. 'You must let me dress your hair,' she said when finished.

Daphne glanced in her mirror. Her hair was coming loose of its pins, strands escaping from the knot atop her head.

She sat at her dressing table and allowed Monette to make her hair presentable, although it might have done just as well to cover it with a cap.

Daphne was certainly not looking forward to this interview, but poor Mrs Everard was in a worse position. Daphne could not greet her with this gloomy mood. The woman would likely think her presence to be the cause.

She'd make herself friendly and cheerful. She'd been trained to do so no matter how she felt inside. For so many years she'd performed the task so well, she'd forgotten how to feel.

No longer.

Monette tied Daphne's hair with a ribbon, and her curls fell around her face as if it all had been carefully arranged.

Daphne stood and straightened her spine.

'Thank you, Monette,' she remembered to say. 'I do look a great deal neater.'

She left her room and descended the stairs, placing a smile on her face and stuffing all other emotions deep inside. With her social facade erected, she entered the drawing room, where Mrs Everard stood staring at Daphne's portrait so prominently displayed.

She really ought to have it replaced by some nice landscape.

'Mrs Everard?'

The woman turned and quickly composed her unhappy face into an expression of politeness. She curtsied.

Daphne approached her with hand extended. 'I am Lady Faville.' She glanced at her portrait. 'As you have undoubtedly guessed.' She shook the woman's hand. 'I am so sorry to have kept you waiting. Especially when it was so kind of you to come.'

Mrs Everard's handshake was very tentative. 'Ma'am' was all she said.

Daphne took her arm and led her to a set of chairs near the fireplace. 'Do sit.' She gave Mrs Everard a chair that did not face her portrait. One Lady Faville was enough for the woman to deal with.

Daphne had always known she was prettier than most women. Her mother certainly had told her so from the time she was in leading strings.

It had been the abbess who helped her understand how much a barrier her beauty could be. She'd realised, though, that the biggest barrier had been one she created herself. She'd been the one who'd not looked beyond a person's physical appearance.

She smiled at her guest. 'I've ordered tea. It should be here any minute.'

Mrs Everard's gaze did not quite meet Daphne's. 'You ought not to have gone to so much trouble for me,'

Mrs Everard was young, perhaps no more than twenty. She was pleasant looking, but plain, although with a little effort she might actually be pretty. Her hair was a nondescript brown, pulled away from her face and covered by her bonnet. Her dress was well cut and well sewn, but it was an unadorned grey, the colour of a dreary day. Her eyes were an identical shade of grey, but Daphne suspected they would brighten with colour if she chose to wear rich greens or blues. Daphne could think of three gowns in her wardrobe that would look lovely on the young woman. Would Mrs Everard accept them? she wondered.

Daphne exclaimed, 'Gracious! It is no trouble to serve tea. And it will make our visit more cosy, will it not?'

The young woman's eyes flashed. 'As you wish.'

Mrs Everard was angry about the visit! Daphne

had not seen it at first, thinking her merely un-comfortable, but Mrs Everard resented being here, Daphne would wager.

The tea arrived, carried in by one of the London footmen. Daphne resolved to learn his name.

'Thank you,' she said as he placed the tray on the table between the two ladies.

He left the room.

Daphne lifted a tea cup. 'How do you take it?'

Mrs Everard removed her gloves and placed them in her lap. 'A little milk will do.'

It stood to reason she would not want sugar. There was no sweetness in her manner at all, but the unguarded expression of her face suggested her acerbity was meant entirely for Daphne. Such a reaction, to dislike her for her looks, was as familiar to Daphne as being liked for them.

She poured the tea and handed the cup to Mrs Everard. The silence between them stretched until Daphne was considering making the weather a topic of conversation.

'My husband talks of you a great deal,' her guest finally said.

Ah, jealousy. Daphne lifted her cup to her lips. 'Does he?'

Mrs Everard nodded. 'He has talked of noth-ing else, I believe, since your letter arrived that you were returning to England.'

Daphne knew how dangerous jealousy could

be. It had nearly caused her to burn down a building. 'He takes his duties very seriously.'

'Too seriously, some might say.' Mrs Everard lifted her cup, but did not take a sip. 'I believe he frets more over your finances than he does over our own.'

Daphne laughed a little, trying to make light of it. 'I cannot see why he should.'

The woman's eyes flashed again. 'Can you not?'

Oh, dear. She must tread very carefully. She took another sip and took on a thoughtful expression. 'Perhaps your husband has more trust in your management of money than he does mine. He spoke in such a complimentary manner of that very thing when he called this morning.'

Mrs Everard's gaze shot back to Daphne's. 'He called on you this morning?'

Oh, dear. 'Very briefly,' Daphne quickly assured her. 'Merely to make certain I would be home to receive your call, so you did not exert yourself for no purpose.'

The young woman's brows knitted as if she had not considered that possibility. Of course, Daphne feared the visit from Everard had been mostly to indulge his infatuation. How could she convince him that an infatuation was nothing but fantasy?

Daphne went on. 'I asked your husband for the name of a good cabinet maker and he spoke of you as the expert in that area. I understand from him that you have very nicely decorated your home at the most reasonable cost.'

Mrs Everard swept a gaze over the room. 'What need have you of furniture, especially furniture of modest cost?'

Maybe if she pretended to take Mrs Everard into her confidence, the young woman would become more at ease. She'd tried such a tactic with Phillipa Westleigh once upon a time, when she'd pretended to herself they'd been friends.

It would be so nice to have a woman friend. Not this woman, though. Mrs Everard hated her without knowing her, hated her by sight alone.

Daphne leaned towards her. 'I will tell you why I wish to buy furniture, but you must promise to say nothing to your husband.'

Mrs Everard returned a wary look. 'I am not in the habit of keeping secrets from my husband.'

Spoken like a newly married woman, indeed. Daphne waved a dismissive hand. 'Oh, but this is a matter only of importance to me. You see, I recently authorised the repair of my tenants' cottages and I thought it would be a nice gift to all of them if I would buy them each a piece of furniture.' She took a sip of tea. 'What do you think? I thought perhaps a bureau for each family would be best. And some nice wooden chests for the farm and stable workers.'

Mrs Everard spilled some of her tea into the

saucer. 'You are purchasing furniture for your tenants?'

'And the workers,' Daphne added. 'So I need good sturdy furniture, but I want it to be well made and pleasant to look at, too.' She gave Mrs Everard another thoughtful look. 'I do think everyone enjoys pretty things no matter what their circumstances.'

'I see.' Mrs Everard took her first sip of tea. 'Why would you do such a thing?'

To atone for never giving such people any thought her whole life, she could say. 'Call it a whim,' she said instead.

'Well.' Mrs Everard placed her tea cup back on the table and opened the strings of her reticule. She took out a piece of paper and handed it to Daphne. 'Here is the name of a cabinet maker in Cheapside.'

Daphne read from the paper. 'Jeffers Cabinetry.' She smiled. 'Thank you so much for this! I am so greatly indebted to you.'

Mrs Everard picked up a glove and put it on. 'If you would forgive me, I must leave. I have taken up too much of your time already.'

Daphne stood. 'Nonsense. It has been delightful to meet you.'

Mrs Everard rose, putting on her second glove. She started to walk away, but stopped and turned to Daphne. 'One thing more.' She looked Daphne directly in the eye. 'My husband is unnaturally attached to you.' She glanced from Daphne to her portrait and back. 'A woman like you must—must exert an undue influence on men. I would ask that you release my husband from your clutches.' Her eyes flickered with pain. 'He is all that I have.'

She turned to leave, but Daphne put a hand on her arm. 'I am fond of your husband, but he is my man of business. Nothing more. I wish you both happiness in your marriage.'

Mrs Everard moved out of Daphne's grasp. 'You outshine me. He cannot even see me when you are near.'

Daphne wanted to tell her she would not be around for long. Toller should be in touch any day now. If there was one thing today had taught her, it was that she should not come to town. Here she only made people unhappy.

She walked Mrs Everard to the door. The footman, whose name she did not know, stood in the doorway about to knock.

'Another caller, my lady,' he said. 'Mr Westleigh.'

Hugh?

Her heart flew into her throat.

Mrs Everard's head cocked in recognition, but she could not know of Hugh. More likely she knew of Phillipa Westleigh. Perhaps even her foolish husband had told that whole story.

No wonder the poor woman feared she would steal her husband.

'Mr Westleigh may come in,' Daphne said to the footman. To Mrs Everard she said, 'Thank you so much for coming and for bringing me such an excellent recommendation. Please do not worry over the rest.'

Mrs Everard avoided looking at her and simply followed the footman back to the hall.

The woman in grey glanced at Hugh as she passed him in the hall. She did not seem the sort who would call upon Lady Faville.

'Lady Faville will see you in the drawing room, sir,' the footman said, gesturing to the doorway to the room where Hugh had been the day before, where he had made love to Daphne.

He nodded politely to the woman in grey and crossed the hall to the drawing room.

Daphne stood waiting for him. 'Hugh, come in.'

He inclined his head in the direction of the hall. 'Did I interrupt?'

She shook her head. 'She was just leaving.' Her brow knitted. 'Is—is this about the pianoforte shop? I give you my word I did not know anything of Xavier's connection to the shop. If I had known, I would have gone to a different place.'

She wore the same green-and-white-striped walking dress she'd worn earlier, only her hair was a loose cascade of blonde curls tied with a ribbon high on her head. Her expression was not the cool perfection of her portrait, but seemed wounded and sad.

He remembered their frenzied lovemaking in this room. Was she still reeling from that assault or was encountering Xavier responsible?

Or the lady in grey?

In any event, she was on the defensive.

And he with her. 'Why did you purchase my sister's music?' he said, forgoing niceties.

She flinched at his words. 'I felt I owed it to her. It was the least I could do.'

Owed it to her?

She went on, 'I also enjoyed her music when she performed.'

'And you bought a pianoforte so you could play her music?' Was that not a bit much?

She glanced away. 'I purchased the pianoforte because I do not have one here. As you know, it helps one pass the time.'

'Do you need help passing time in London during the Season?' Usually a lady received more invitations than she could accept.

Her lashes fluttered before she gazed at him again. 'I am not attending social events.' She brushed a curl off her forehead. 'Not that I expect any invitations.'

He frowned. 'No invitations?' Had her scandal with Xavier and the Masquerade Club damaged her reputation to that extent? Surely someone would want such a beautiful creature in their ballroom.

'I did not announce my arrival in town.'

Then why had she come?

She stepped away from him and faced the window, the same window through which he'd glimpsed her the previous day when he'd had no intention of seeing her again. 'I am only staying a few days, but I promise you, any encounter with you or—or your family will be a happenstance, like today. I say again, I do not wish to trouble your family.'

But she troubled him. He closed his eyes and caught her scent of roses. His hands itched to hold her again. His body yearned to join with hers. The anger that had once burned as hot as the inn's fire now merely smouldered in a corner, nearly forgotten. Much hotter had been his need to protect her from his brother's rudeness to her in the pianoforte shop.

'You are in town only for a few days?' He tried to make his voice sound as if this did not greatly disappoint him. 'May I call upon you while you are here?'

She whirled around. 'Call upon me!'

'Start over. Become acquainted. You with the new manager of a gambling club, me, with Daphne, Lady Faville, a woman I do not believe I know.'

'I—I do not know what to say.' Her voice was little more than a whisper.

'Say you will walk with me in the park. Right now.' Why not? They'd enjoyed walks together when he'd been blind.

She stared at him.

He averted his gaze. 'I promise to be a gentleman. I will not repeat yesterday's appalling behaviour.'

He looked back at her and could read only puzzlement in her expression. 'A walk? Like old times?' he pressed. 'It is early. The park should not be crowded yet.'

It was not yet three o'clock. The fashionable hour for being seen in the park came at four o'clock.

He lowered his voice. 'Daphne?'

She swept a curl off her forehead. 'Just give me a moment to get my hat and gloves.'

Daphne rushed up to her bedchamber, her heart racing with pleasure. He'd said he wanted to spend time with her. To take a walk with her.

Perhaps it would feel a little like the walks they'd taken at the cottage, only this time he could see. She could take his arm and he could lead her, not the other way around. And she could see his whole face, all his expressions, nothing blocked by bandages.

Even if it lasted only the few days she was here in London, it was more than she'd ever dreamed.

Monette was in her room, folding her laundered undergarments. She looked up, all bright eyes, when Daphne entered the room. 'My lady, there is a letter for you!'

'A letter? But I am in a hurry.' She rushed up to Monette and clasped her hands. 'Mr Westleigh has called and invited me for a walk!'

Monette seemed to force a smile. 'Oh, that is so nice for you.'

Daphne peered closer at her. 'Something is troubling you. Tell me what it is.'

Monette turned away. 'Oh, it is nothing that cannot wait. You must hurry.' Her tone was flat.

Daphne persisted. 'What is it?'

Monette glanced towards the table near the door. 'The letter.'

'Oh.' Understanding dawned. 'Is it from Toller?'

Monette cheered. 'I believe so. Would—would you please open it? See what he says?'

Daphne strode over to the table and picked up the letter. 'It is from Thurnfield!' She broke the seal, unfolded the paper and read aloud, '"Dear Lady Faville."' She had explained to Toller her true identity. '"I most gratefully accept your offer of employment. I will travel to London in four days' time and will anticipate returning to your employ with great pleasure. Yours respect-fully, Toller.'"

She looked up.

Monette beamed. 'He writes a pretty letter.'

'He does indeed,' Daphne agreed.

'He will be here in four days' time!' Her voice rose in excitement.

'In three days' time, Monette,' Daphne said. 'The letter is dated yesterday.'

Monette flung herself into Daphne's arms and hugged her tightly. 'Oh, thank you, *madame*. Thank you!'

Daphne's spirits soared. She'd done something good.

Monette released her. 'But you must hurry! Mr Westleigh is waiting for you.' She ran to a drawer and pulled out a fresh pair of gloves. Her expression turned worried. 'He is not angry at you, is he?'

Daphne grinned. 'No, he is not angry. So I am happy, too.'

She reached for the hat she'd worn earlier, but Monette stopped her. 'No. No. Wear a prettier one.' She went into the closet and brought out a bonnet trimmed in silk flowers with a thick satin ribbon to tie under her chin. Monette put the bon-net on Daphne's head and fussed with the bow. She helped her into the spencer that matched her walking dress. 'There, you look very pretty now.'

Daphne gave her a quick hug. 'Thank you, Monette!'

She rushed out of the room and down the stairs.

Hugh stood at the foot of the stairs, waiting for her, his hat in his hands. She'd seen similar admiring looks on countless men's faces, but seeing it on Hugh was an entirely new thrill. It mattered to her that he admired her. She wanted his admiration for her character, as well.

It was something for which she would strive. Even if she never saw him again, it could be like a little test—*would Hugh think well of me for this?*

He put his hat on his head and offered her his arm. 'Shall we go?'

She nodded, liking him all the better for not prosing on about her beauty.

The footman opened the door and they left the town house.

They had only to cross Park Lane to reach the Cumberland Gate to Hyde Park. They chose a path that led to the Serpentine. It might not have been the fashionable hour, but there were other people in the park. Governesses with children in tow. Clerks and shop girls taking a quick respite. A few gentlemen with fancy-dressed women who were likely not their wives.

'It is not as quiet as the cottage in Thurnfield, is it?' Daphne remarked.

'It was not quiet there,' Hugh said. 'Although I might not have heard all the noises, had my eyes not been bandaged.'

She held his arm tighter. 'Those must have been difficult days.'

'Difficult,' he agreed. He stopped and lifted her chin up with a finger. 'Difficult, but happy. I do not regret a moment of it.'

'Truly?' She was surprised.

He started walking again. 'Only the end,' he murmured. 'When you were gone.'

She lowered her head. 'I made so many mistakes. I should have told you who I was that first day.'

'Why didn't you?' he asked.

'I was cowardly.'

'Cowardly?' He sounded surprised.

She'd promised she would be honest with him. 'I knew you would hate me. I did not want to face that. Oh, I did not want you to be forced to accept care from someone who had been such a torment to your family, but mostly I did not want to face being disliked.'

He squeezed her hand. 'Instead, you wound up being nursemaid and costing yourself a lot of money.'

'Not a lot of money,' she said. 'At first I thought it would only be for a day or two. It didn't seem like such a bad thing to pretend I was not Lady Faville for a day or two. But then—'

He interrupted. 'But then I refused to have my family contacted and you were stuck with me.'

'But you also became my friend,' she added. 'I did not want to spoil having a friend.'

She glanced up into his face. His expression was puzzled, but full of sympathy. How rare, to be looked upon with sympathy.

Likely she did not deserve it. 'A wise woman once told me that even little lies grow big. That is why one should not lie. I knew that and still I did it.'

They came upon a patch of spring flowers and discussed the variety of each. She was no better than he at naming flowers. Perhaps she would add gardening to the list of activities to pursue when she returned to the country.

'I should tell you that Toller is coming to work for me,' she said later. 'He is coming in a few days.'

'Toller?' His brows rose. 'I am surprised. He seemed so very attached to Thurnfield.'

She smiled. 'I think he is rather attached to a Swiss lady's maid.'

'Ah.' He laughed. 'I take it you do not really need another footman, but you hired him anyway.'

She felt her face turn red. 'One can always use another footman.'

Hugh glanced down at the woman walking beside him, blushing at his suggestion that she'd hire a footman to please her lady's maid. Was this the same woman who'd pursued Xavier so relentlessly? Xavier said it had been because she thought they would have made a handsome couple.

And so they would, a contrast of dark and light, the handsome man and beautiful woman.

He walked in silence for a while, unable to forget her past and unable to reconcile her with the woman she seemed to be now.

He finally spoke. 'What was it like for you to see Xavier again? I assume the pianoforte shop was the first time you'd seen him.'

She did not answer right away. 'I felt I deserved his anger and suspicion.'

That was not the answer he sought. 'You were unrelenting in your pursuit of him two years ago. Was that all you felt?'

'I felt sorry he had to encounter me. I am certain he would have preferred never seeing me again.' She said this without any tone of resentment.

He stopped and made her face him. 'Daphne, what I want to know is, do you still want him? Did that attraction you had for him return?'

She turned away while he spoke, but slowly lifted her gaze to his. 'No. That left me a long time ago. After the fire. The fire I caused, I mean.'

He believed her. He was unsure how long it

would last, but at this moment he was entirely certain she spoke the truth.

'Daphne,' he whispered, wanting more than anything to touch his lips to hers and feel their warmth, their singular taste.

She glanced around and stepped away. They were in plain view and there were people who would see.

He smiled and leaned down to her ear. 'Perhaps later.'

The colour rose in her face again, making her even more beautiful than she'd been a minute before.

'We should walk,' she said.

They continued on the path and were halfway to the Serpentine when Hugh spotted another couple walking in their direction.

'Blast.'

'What is it?' she asked.

'My mother and General Hensen.' Of all the luck. His mother would be walking in the park at this same moment.

'General Hensen? I remember him from the Masquerade Club.'

They were still some distance away, but close enough to recognise faces. His mother had seen him, he was certain. He was equally certain she had noticed Daphne.

'We do not wish to encounter my mother, however,' he said. Ned had been rude enough to Daphne. There was no telling how his mother would behave. 'Let's turn here and leave by the Grosvenor Gate.'

They could do so without looking as if they were fleeing. Which they were.

'I understand,' Daphne said. 'You do not wish to be seen with me.'

She was correct. He did not wish to explain something he did not understand himself, and his mother would demand an explanation of why he was strolling through Hyde Park with Lady Faville.

Their camaraderie disappeared. After spying his mother, it seemed to Daphne that all Hugh wanted was to take her home and be rid of her.

The dagger twisted in her heart again, but she understood. His mother would hate her. What other choice would a mother have?

If only Daphne could shut out her past and its consequences. If only she could truly emerge as Daphne Asher and start anew, then perhaps she would have a chance to be with Hugh.

He walked her to her door.

She offered her hand to shake. 'Goodbye, Hugh.' It seemed she was always saying goodbye to him.

He took her hand, but pulled her into an embrace. 'I am sorry our walk was cut short,' he said. 'May I call upon you tomorrow?'

Her eyes widened. 'Call upon me?' She would
see him again? 'Yes. Yes. Of course.'

He leaned down and lightly kissed her on
the lips.

Chapter Eighteen

By the time Hugh returned to the Masquerade Club, the message was waiting for him. From his mother. Summoning him to dinner.

He was not fooled. She'd seen him with Daphne.

He might skip dinner, send his regrets, spend these next few days with Daphne and leave the family out of it, but that seemed a cowardly thing to do. He'd face his mother and explain.

If he could.

He arrived at the appointed hour and was ushered in to the drawing room. To his surprise, Ned and Adele were there, with Xavier and Phillipa. So this was to be a family meeting? Family pressure.

He glanced from one to the other. 'What? No Rhys and Celia? Or are they not family enough?' More likely they would inject some sanity into the situation to which his mother would object.

'Rhys had to leave town,' Xavier said. 'What is this about, Hugh? None of us knows.'

Hugh crossed the room and poured himself a glass of claret from a crystal carafe on the side table. 'I expect we will find out soon enough.'

A short time later, his mother entered the room on the arm of General Hensen. 'So good of all of you to come.' She glanced at Adele. 'Are you feeling well, my dear?'

'Mostly,' Adele responded. 'Well enough to attend the opera with you and the general, I am sure.' The opera was the big entertainment of the evening, after which the Masquerade Club would flood with more patrons.

His mother smiled. 'Excellent.' Her gaze rested on Hugh for a moment, but she addressed them all. 'I am so glad you could come, because this seems to be a family matter we should discuss together.'

'What is it, Mother?' Ned asked.

She turned to Hugh. 'Tell them, Hugh.'

He did not waver. 'Tell them what, Mother?' He knew precisely what she meant.

She lowered herself into a wing-back chair, as regal as a queen on her throne. 'Do not play coy with me, Hugh,' she scolded. 'Tell them who you were with in the park today.'

He took a sip of his wine. 'You tell them, Mother. I expect you will imbue the story with more drama than I.'

She narrowed her eyes at him and turned to the others. 'The general and I saw Hugh walking in the park with Lady Faville.'

'Lady Faville?' Adele piped up. 'Isn't she the one who tried to burn down the Masquerade Club?'

'It was not quite like that, Adele,' Phillipa said.

'Hugh!' Ned turned on him. 'You sought out her company when you knew I wanted you to have nothing to do with her?'

'It was not for you to tell me what to do,' Hugh shot back.

Ned straightened in outrage. 'As head of this family, I dare say it was my concern.'

His mother gave Ned an approving look, but her expression turned stern when she addressed Hugh again. 'Why you were with that woman, Hugh?'

He glared at her. 'What if I told you I was courting her?'

'Courting her?' his mother cried.

'Are you mad?' Ned took an angry step towards him.

'I did not realise you knew her,' his sister said, her voice tight, but absent of Ned's and their mother's outrage. She, over all of them, was entitled to be outraged.

He had no wish to hurt her. 'I became acquainted with her before returning to London,' he responded.

He was still not ready to share the whole story. In fact, he much preferred his family's typical un-interest in his affairs.

'Oh, yes, Xavier said she had been on the Continent.' Phillipa glanced at her husband. 'He also said you saw her at one of his shops today.'

Ned pointed to Xavier. 'She has come back to try to ruin our sister's marriage, you mark my words.'

Xavier raised both hands. 'I want nothing to do with her.'

'She is dangerous!' Ned insisted.

What right had he to judge her?

His mother broke in. 'She is not the sort of woman we would desire to be a part of our family, so courting her is out of the question.'

Hugh had forgotten. Ned had inherited his priggish behaviour from their mother.

She went on. 'I presume you were merely taunting us with the idea of courting her, but Ned is correct. She is dangerous. We managed to keep the whole affair of the fire out of the newspapers, but there is no telling what new scandal she might bring upon the family. If she is currying your favour, Hugh, undoubtedly it is so she can contrive to be near Xavier.'

'Are you certain, Honoria?' the general asked. Brave man. 'She seemed a charming woman to me when I met her years ago.'

His mother gave him a quelling look.

'Remember, she nearly destroyed the Masquerade Club,' Ned told him. 'Where would the family be if she had succeeded?'

'I absolutely forbid you to see that woman!' his mother said. 'Think of what talk there would be. Think of how dangerous it would be to give her such access to Xavier. It will ruin Phillipa's happiness.'

Hugh turned to Phillipa. 'Do you think she seeks access to Xavier?'

She shrugged. 'I do not know what to think, but I certainly believe it is possible that is her motive—'

Xavier broke in. 'No matter what, she will not ruin Phillipa's happiness, because I will not allow that to happen.' He took Phillipa's hand in his. 'I caution you, Hugh. Daphne has a way of using her charm to get what she wants. She can play a role quite convincingly.'

'See?' Ned broke in. 'She is duplicitous.'

His family's worries were ones that hid deep inside him, Hugh had to admit. At the same time, he yearned for the Daphne he'd known at the cottage, the Daphne who had looked so vulnerable at the piano shop and who had walked with him in the park this afternoon. The more his family spoke against that Daphne and told him what he must do, the more Hugh chafed at their words.

He put down his glass. 'Was there any other

reason for summoning me here?' he asked his mother.

'This is enough of a reason.' His mother sniffed.

Mason, the butler, who undoubtedly had been listening to the whole exchange, knocked on the door. 'Dinner is served, my lady.'

His mother rose. 'Thank you, Mason.'

The butler bowed and was about to leave.

Hugh stopped him. 'Mason, would you get my hat and gloves? I am not staying.'

'Not staying?' His mother's eyes flashed.

He walked over to her and grasped her hand. 'I know you mean well, Mother, but you must not dictate our lives.' He turned to his brother. 'You neither, Ned. I cannot stay.'

He strode to the door.

Ned reached it first and spoke quietly so only he could hear. 'I don't mean to dictate, Hugh. I—I do not wish to see you or the family hurt. Is—is that not my role?'

Hugh had forgotten that Ned was still learning to be the Earl of Westleigh, but too many emotions warred inside him to be charitable to his brother at the moment.

His voice softened, though. 'Say no more, Ned.'

He left the room. Mason waited in the hall with his hat and gloves. He took them and walked out the door.

He was two houses away when he heard a voice behind him. 'Hugh!'

It was Phillipa.

She caught up with him. 'Are you all right?'

He nodded. 'We did worse to you when Mother tried to force you to do what she wanted and Ned and I did not protect you.' He looked into her eyes. 'I am sorry for it.'

She waved her hand. 'That is all past.'

He expected her to press him about Daphne, but she did not.

He put an arm around her. 'It is chilly out here. You should go back.' He walked with her, but paused at the door. 'She bought your music, Phillipa. Before she went to the pianoforte shop.'

Her brows rose. 'My music?'

'She said she owed it to you.'

'That seems odd.' She peered at him. 'I feel I must say something, but I do not wish to influence you one way or the other.'

He stiffened.

'Back at the Masquerade Club, when I was masked and she called me Lady Songstress, I sometimes thought she truly wanted to be friends, but it was so hard to tell, because she tended to be whatever people expected her to be. And she expected people to be whatever she wanted them to be. Xavier never gave her the least encouragement, but she truly believed he would be hers, because she was beautiful and she wanted it. When she discovered he loved me, a scarred woman, it shocked her.'

'And she started the fire,' he added.

'She set herself on fire, too,' she told him. 'Did you know that? Her skirts caught fire and she was so terribly frightened. It was far worse for her than for Xavier and me.'

Poor Daphne. No wonder she'd been terrified when the inn caught fire.

She patted his cheek. 'I cannot forgive her, I'm afraid, but, for what it is worth, my dear brother, I sometimes felt sorry for her.'

'Sorry for her?' His brows rose.

She shrugged. 'She seemed pitiful to me, sometimes.'

He leaned forwards and kissed the scar that ran from the corner of her eye almost to the edge of her lips. 'Thank you, my dear sister.'

She went back inside and he set off again, walking the short few streets to the Masquerade Club off St James's Street. When he entered the club, the delicious odour of Cook's fare for the night reached his nostrils. Cummings, Mac-Evoy and some of the croupiers were all busy setting up. They would open at eleven, but the place would only fill after society's events were over and people with more money than sense came to seek the excitement of the gaming tables.

He thought of walking in the park that day in the fresh air, with the scent of green grass, spring flowers and leaf-filled trees wafting around him. To remain in the closed, lamp-lit rooms of the gaming house seemed akin to the prison of his former blindness.

MacEvoy approached him. 'Everything is ready, Mr Westleigh, or almost so. We've replaced the faro box with a new one that does not stick. The cards come out one at a time. We tested it.' He went on detailing a dozen other matters that he and the others had seen to, matters that now seemed inconsequential to Hugh.

That itch to be free returned with great intensity. 'MacEvoy, tell me, can you run the house without me tonight?'

MacEvoy nodded. 'Certainly. We've done so before on occasion. I'll walk the floor and one of the croupiers can act as clerk.' He indeed acted as if the request was nothing.

'Good.' He put his hat back on his head. 'I will be off, then. Likely I will see you tomorrow.'

MacEvoy did not even seem concerned where Hugh might spend the night. 'Right. See you tomorrow. All will be taken care of here.'

Where was Hugh to spend the night? At the moment, he cared for nothing but being free to walk wherever he pleased. No obligations. No dictates. No destinations.

He stepped back out into the evening air. In moments it would be dark, but he did not care. He wanted only to empty his mind, to set aside his family's voices and his own doubts. He wanted to shut his eyes to visions of Daphne—warm, loving Daphne and cool, conniving Daphne. He walked up Bond Street where shops remained open and the pavements were nearly as crowded as daytime. When he crossed onto Oxford Street, though, he knew where he was heading.

To Daphne's house.

He wanted to be with her in spite of his family's warnings, his own doubts. When he was with her, none of that mattered.

He reached her door and knocked.

Carter answered. 'Mr Westleigh!'

'I know it is unforgivably late, Carter, but would you ask if Lady Faville will see me?'

'She is in the drawing room awaiting dinner,' he said. 'One moment, please.'

Hugh stopped him. 'Wait, Carter. Might I go in unannounced?'

The footman thought a moment. 'I suppose you might.'

Hugh did not give him a chance to change his mind. He gave him his hat and gloves and crossed the hall to the drawing room. When he opened the door, her back was turned. Probably thinking it was Carter, she did not turn around right away.

'Daphne?'

She whirled around. 'Hugh!'

He could not find words to speak.

'What is wrong?' she asked.

'I come from my mother's house. She gathered the family to tell me not to see you again.'

She flinched, as if stung. 'Then you should not be here, should you?'

Why had he put that burden on her? It was cruel. He closed the distance between them and wrapped his arms around her and spoke the truth. 'I realised there was nowhere else I wanted to be.'

He lowered his lips to hers and kissed her as though he'd been starved of her kiss for too long. She flung her arms around his neck and gave herself to the kiss, melting against him.

When he finally took a breath he said, 'May I stay with you?'

'For dinner?' she responded. 'Of course you may.'

'Not for dinner,' he murmured, his lips still on hers. 'For tonight.'

Hugh woke to Daphne's warm body nestled against him, her golden hair splayed across his chest. He swept it back so he could see her face. In dawn's first glimmer she appeared like a Raphael Madonna, heavenly in her beauty.

What a change to gaze upon her now. He could hardly remember seeing the despised Lady Faville when he'd first unmasked her. Now she was Daphne, warm and giving and kind, words he would never have used to describe her when she'd glided through the Masquerade Club trying to make Xavier desire her.

She stirred and opened her eyes. Her eyes, gazing into his, reflected wonder and yearning.

The yearning he understood. His body flared with need for her, need to join her in lovemaking once more, this time in daylight, this time when he could see her as well as touch her, hear her, taste her lips, be enveloped by her rose scent.

He pulled the bed linens aside and rose above her, gazing at her smooth creamy skin, her full breasts, her narrow waist. Her hair fell upon her shoulders and on the pillow like a golden halo. He gazed upon her face that now resembled his Daphne, the woman with whom he made love in a cottage in Thurnfield.

His eyes were open now, in more ways than one. He loved her no matter who she'd once been. He loved the woman she was at this moment, a woman ready to give herself to him. He covered her with his body and kissed her, joining his tongue with hers, mingling their tastes. Breaking from the kiss, he entered her. The sensation of her body closing around him increased his arousal, and he wanted to savour the moment for as long as he could.

He moved in slow, languid strokes, relishing the quickening of her breathing, the rise of her hips to meet him. He could increase her pleasure by moving slowly, letting their passion build

like smouldering ash can build into a raging fire.
They'd originally come together in fire—let this
be a blaze to meld them together for ever. He
never wanted to lose this.

Daphne was the answer to his wanderlust. It
was not travel he needed, but a place like this,
with her, where every moment was an adventure.

His joy fanned the flames and he moved faster,
revelling in the heat they created, letting it burn
away all thought, leaving only emotion and sensation. Building. Building. Building.

To release.

He let out a primal sound and she cried out,
her own climax joining with his. This was what
he wanted. To be hers. To be forged together by
the heat of their passion.

Hugh's muscles relaxed and he lay beside
Daphne again. 'I should get dressed. Your maid
will be in to tend the fire in a moment. Perhaps
I should not be here.'

She held on to him. 'I do not want you to leave.'

He pulled her into another kiss. 'I do not want
to leave you. Ever.' He sat up and gazed down at
her, excitement invigorating him again. 'Travel
with me, Daphne. Let us go somewhere else in
the world, just you and me—and whomever of
the servants you want to bring along. We could
travel to Paris. Or Rome. Or Venice. We could
sail to America. Or India. Wherever you wish.'

She rose as well, and wrapped the linens

around her. 'What about your family? The Masquerade Club?'

'I have devoted enough of my life to my family's needs.' He took her face in his hands. 'Tell me you will come with me. Tell me you will marry me.'

Her eyes widened. 'Marry you?'

He released her. 'Yes. Marry.'

She leaned towards him. 'Hugh, I cannot marry you. Your family despises me, and rightfully so.'

'They do not know you as I do.' His high spirits fell more sensibly to earth. 'But give them no thought. I cannot live my life merely to please them.' He moved around her and embraced her from behind. 'I want to be with you, Daphne. Say you will marry me.'

Her muscles were taut and she was silent for several tortuous seconds. Finally she said, 'I want to, Hugh.' She sighed and gave herself to his embrace. 'Very well. I will marry you, because I cannot bear not to.'

He twisted around and kissed her again, a joyous kiss that threatened to arouse him all over again. Instead, he released her and bounded from the bed. 'I'll dress and be off for now. Let me see what I can do about covering the Masquerade Club. It is still my family's livelihood.'

She stiffened again. 'And if you do not find a way to deal with the Masquerade Club?'

He leaned down and brushed a kiss on her lips. 'I will.'

He put on his clothes, hoping they did not appear too wrinkled from lying in a heap on the floor all night. Daphne rose from the bed and tied his neckcloth into a quite decent knot.

With one more kiss he said goodbye. 'I'll be back this evening or I will get word to you, never fear.'

Chapter Nineteen

Daphne felt as if she were floating on clouds as Monette helped her dress and arranged her hair.

Monette smiled at her. 'You do not need to tell me why you are so happy, my lady. We know that Mr Westleigh shared your bed last night.'

Daphne grinned. 'I am not saying he did.'

'There is not much about a house a servant does not know.'

Daphne gave her an amused glance. 'You sound as if you have been in service your whole life, Monette, instead of a few short months.'

The girl sobered. 'The abbey was not much different than a house in that way. We always knew the secrets.' She nodded decisively. 'I prefer being a lady's maid, though, because soon I will have a man, too, when Toller comes.'

Daphne stilled her hand. 'Monette, you must not bed Toller, not unless he marries you. It is different for me. I was a married lady, but you are a maiden and you must guard your maidenhood until a man marries you.'

Monette's brow furrowed. 'But I can have kisses, can I not?'

The role of duenna was new to Daphne. 'You may have kisses, but you must be very careful that there is nothing more.' A thought struck her. 'Monette, do you know what takes place between a man and woman? A man and wife, I mean.'

'I know, *madame*,' Monette assured her. 'The novices talked about it all the time. And we watched the animals, you know.'

'It is a little different than what animals do.' Daphne's heart filled with fondness—and anxiety—for the maid. Was this how it felt to be a mother? She felt very protective. In fact, she must have a good talk with Toller when he came. She would not see Monette misused or hurt, not by anyone.

When Daphne walked down to breakfast, Mr Everard was waiting in the hall and Carter stood at the foot of the stairs.

'Mr Everard wishes to speak with you, m'lady,' Carter said with a barely detectable disapproving glance at the man.

She nodded her agreement and turned to Everard. 'Come in to breakfast and tell me why you are here again.'

'I do apologise, my lady.' He bowed. 'I will take up very little of your time.'

He followed her in to the breakfast room. She went directly to the sideboard and selected a slice of ham and some cheese.

'Do help yourself,' she told him.

'I will not stay so long.' He did not choose food this time, but rather paced the room. 'I fear my effort to assist you by sending my wife with her recommendations for cabinet makers has had unforeseen consequences.'

Something so dire? She sat and poured herself some tea. 'What consequences?'

'My wife believes I have—have an attachment to you that is beyond—beyond what a man of my position ought to have.' His wife was obviously more astute than he, if he did not see what was readily apparent. 'She thought it a contrivance that I sent her here and not a true need on your part.'

'Mr Everard, I did not ask you to call or to send your wife. That was your doing. You cannot blame her for finding it a strange matter.'

He rubbed his forehead. 'Yes. Yes. I know. It was a grave error.'

'I hope you apologised to her.'

He paced again. 'I did. Many times, but she thinks I see her as plain and dull in comparison to you....' He paused and shook his head. 'Of course, there is no comparison to you. I mean, I do not compare you with my wife—'

And Daphne would wager he didn't tell his wife she was beautiful or skilled or valued in any way.

He looked thoughtful. 'Perhaps I have talked of you too much. Of—of your affairs. Your financial affairs, I mean.' He seemed to reconsider that. 'Not that I divulge details, for that matter. I merely talk of my work, you see.'

How much had he told his wife about her? Had he told her of her time at the Masquerade Club? Did his wife know her as a woman who had tried to break up marriages? If so, no wonder the poor woman worried.

'Mr Everard, if your wife is concerned about your attachment to me, you should not call upon me so frequently, but only if there is a matter of great importance.'

'This is of great importance,' he wailed. 'I cannot have a wife who threatens to leave me.'

'I do not have the power to influence your wife.' His wife was clearly among the many people who despised her.

'But I beg you will do me one service.' She feared he would go down on his knees. 'It will not be difficult and you will benefit as well, I promise.'

Her egg was getting cold. 'What can I possibly do?'

He leaned towards her, his hands folded as if in supplication. 'Write her a letter. Implore her to meet you at the cabinet-maker's shop. Say you need her to advise you what to buy.'

What could it hurt? Perhaps Mrs Everard would know better what furniture would suit her tenants. Besides, she'd used Everard shamelessly two years before. She could at least humour him in this way. She had no illusions, though, that writing this letter and forcing this meeting would suddenly make Mrs Everard cease to despise and be jealous of her.

'Very well,' she said. 'I will do it, but you must do something for me and you must promise.'

His face turned worshipful. 'I will do anything you ask, my lady. I always have.'

She spoke to him as if he were a child using what Hugh called her governess voice. 'You must never talk about me to your wife. You must tell her once a day that she is beautiful. You must thank her every day for the kindnesses she does for you, even if you think them ordinary, like planning meals, seeing to your laundry or the cleaning of the house.'

His brows knitted. 'That is what you wish?'

She nodded emphatically. 'And you must encourage her to purchase pretty gowns and pretty hats, and if she has a pretty dress made for herself, you must tell her she looks lovely in it.'

These were all things her husband had done,

she realised, things that had flattered her vanity, but she'd learned later that she'd needed other things more.

'And talk with her,' she went on. 'Ask her opinion. Ask what is important to her.' Until the abbess—and Hugh—no one had ever asked what was important to Daphne.

Everard looked very sceptical.

'Promise me or I will not write your letter or meet your wife at the cabinet maker.' She spoke this like a stern governess.

'I will do it,' Everard said in a desperate voice. Unfortunate that he could not hear the wisdom in what she said, but perhaps he'd realise when he experienced the results.

'Ask Carter for pen and ink and I will write your letter.'

He rushed out to do her bidding.

When the time came she would order the carriage and ask Smith to drive her and Carter to Cheapside, to Jeffers Cabinetry Shop. She hoped she would not miss Hugh if he called while she was away. She must leave word for him to wait for her.

That afternoon, Hugh sat in the gaming room with MacEvoy, Cummings and some of the croupiers, seeking their opinion about running the gaming house without him. No one saw any difficulties. A monthly visit from a member of the family would be sufficient, MacEvoy thought, to ensure the place was being run in a manner that suited them. Perhaps they could find a gentleman to stand in for him, someone like Sir Reginald, who was a frequent visitor to the club, but who could use some additional funds.

Hugh could not wait to present the plan to the family. They would have to accept it, because he was declaring himself free of the obligation.

The door to the gaming room opened and Xavier stepped in.

'Xavier! Come in.' Hugh waved his arm. 'I want you to hear what we've been discussing.'

Xavier nodded to everyone. 'Good to see you all.' He frowned at Hugh. 'May I speak with you alone first, Hugh? Out in the hall?'

Hugh stood. 'Of course.'

Something was wrong. Was it to do with a member of the family?

To his surprise, Phillipa waited in the hall. They stepped away from the gaming room door.

'What is it?' Hugh asked, his alarm growing. 'Is someone ill? Injured?'

'Nothing like that,' Phillipa assured him.

Xavier pulled a paper from his pocket. 'I received this a little while ago. We thought you should see it.'

Hugh took the paper from his hand and immediately recognised the handwriting. He'd been handed a similar note at the cottage and had read it enough times to be familiar with the script.

> Would you be so good as to join me at Jeffers Cabinetry Shop at three o'clock this afternoon? After our meeting yesterday, I realised that I greatly need you and no one else to settle my plan.
>   Please set aside any misunderstandings and do me the honour of keeping this appointment.
>
> Yours, etc,
> Daphne, Lady Faville

Hugh crushed the note in his hand.

'A boy delivered it to me a short time ago,' Xavier explained. 'He told us a lady paid him to do it.'

Phillipa touched Hugh's arm. 'I am so sorry, Hugh.'

Hugh's throat grew tight. 'No.'

Daphne set up a meeting with Xavier? What had happened? Had she started thinking of Xavier after Hugh had left her that morning? Or had she already planned a meeting with Xavier even before he proposed marriage to her? Ned might have been right all along. Maybe Hugh had fallen into a trap intended only to allow her to be close to Xavier. Was that the *plan* she wished to *settle* with him?

A sabre's thrust could not be more painful than this betrayal. Hugh had been fooled by her once, when she'd played Mrs Asher, now he'd been fooled again.

'What time is it?' he asked.

Xavier pulled out a pocket watch. 'It is twenty past three.'

He quickly gathered his hat and gloves. 'She may still be there. I am going to meet her.'

Daphne was not surprised that Everard's wife did not show up at the furniture shop. In fact, she was relieved. She could happily select her tenants' gifts without any unpleasantness to intrude. On this day that Hugh had asked her to marry him, she wanted only happiness.

She loved the cabinetry shop. She sensed it was a happy place with happy workers. The pieces they made were skilfully done, using good timber. Mr Jeffers, the proprietor, a rather frightening-looking man with a scar on his face, was friendly and obviously very proud of his shop's work. He was more than delighted when she ordered ten oak-banded bureaus for her tenants and a dozen pine coffers for the stable and farm workers.

She and Mr Jeffers had just finished the transaction when the shop door opened.

Daphne looked over and broke into a surprised smile. 'Hugh!'

But the look he returned to her was like a knife. 'Surprised to see me, Daphne?'

Behind him walked in Xavier and his wife.

'Mr Campion!' Jeffers started towards him.

Xavier gestured for him to stay back, and Jeffers disappeared behind the curtain that separated the workroom from the store.

Daphne's heart pounded with anxiety. Something was amiss, something terrible. Carter must have sensed it, too, because he moved from where he waited in the background to Daphne's side.

She glanced from Hugh to Xavier to Phillipa. 'I do not understand.'

Hugh looked at her as if she were an infestation. He handed her a crumpled paper.

She glanced at it. 'But this is— How did you get this?'

'From Xavier, obviously,' Hugh said, his voice rough.

'How did Xavier—?' She handed the letter back to Hugh. 'I did not send this!'

He came closer to her, his eyes burning like fire. 'It is your handwriting, Daphne.'

'I do not know how to explain it,' she said. She'd sent the note to Mrs Everard.

Hugh huffed. 'Do not make an attempt to explain. I will not believe you.'

Daphne's legs weakened. She clutched Carter's arm, needing to steady herself. 'I did not send this to Xavier!' She glanced at Xavier. 'I do not know where you live.'

'You knew of my shop,' Xavier countered. 'You could learn of my residence, as well.'

'Your shop?' He owned this shop as well as a pianoforte shop?

It felt as if the walls were falling in on her, like the walls of the inn had fallen in from the fire. Hugh would never believe she'd not known this was Xavier's shop.

Everard's wife must have known. But would it not be even more unbelievable to say that the wife of her man of business must have set this up? It was no use. He would never believe her.

No one would ever believe the beautiful Lady Faville would ever change. She'd once made a fool of herself over the incredibly handsome Xavier Campion, and no one would ever think that she no longer cared for him. Xavier was not the man who mattered to her.

Hugh mattered.

She gripped Carter's arm. 'It is no use,' she whispered to herself, but she made herself look Hugh in the eye. 'I misled you once. I made you think I was someone I wasn't, but I never lied to you then and I will not lie to you now. I did not arrange a meeting with Xavier. I am nothing but ashamed of that time. I spent two years trying to change, and I have changed.' She summoned all her remaining strength and rose to her full height.

'What I cannot change is what other people think of me.' She took a breath. 'I cannot change your mind, Hugh.'

He blinked and lost the red rage that had tinged his face.

She turned to Carter. 'Let us take our leave, Carter.'

'Yes, m'lady,' he responded, giving her something solid to hold on to while her world shattered into little pieces.

Carter escorted her outside to where Smith waited with the carriage and helped her inside. Before he closed the door and climbed onto his seat on the outside, he touched her hand. 'Some things we've done never go away, m'lady, but we move on anyway, do we not?'

He sounded as if he knew firsthand of what he spoke.

She tried to smile. 'We move on.'

The coach pulled away and Daphne tried to stitch herself back together. She needed to move on. There never had been a chance that she and Hugh could be together. Her past would always separate them. No more trying. He was a beautiful memory. Proof she could truly love a man. Proof she could feel real emotions, real joy, real despair.

By the time the coach reached her town house, she'd regained a modicum of composure. She could stand. She could walk. She could speak.

She could move on.

As soon as they entered the hall, Monette ran up to her. 'My lady! My lady! Look who is here! Toller has come a day early.'

Toller stepped forwards. 'M'lady. I hope you approve of my coming early. I was able to settle my affairs in Thurnfield more quickly than I'd anticipated.'

Daphne put on a smile. She would not ruin Monette's happiness with her grief. 'I am so happy to see you, Toller. You have arrived at the perfect time. Now we can leave for Vadley tomorrow.' She turned to Carter. 'Will you arrange it, Carter? Toller can help you.'

'We are leaving London so soon?' Monette sounded disappointed.

Daphne felt a twinge of guilt. 'We'll come back again later, but I need to return to Vadley.'

'What of Mr Westleigh?' Monette asked.

'He knows.' Daphne's voice lowered. 'He knows.'

Hugh knew she would be gone.

Chapter Twenty

He'd recovered nicely, Hugh thought. He'd thrown himself into his duties at the Masquerade Club, abandoning the idea of leaving it. After the club closed at night, what did it matter that he consumed too much brandy in order to get to sleep?

He ignored the nearly daily summons from his mother. He saw no one outside of the club. In fact, he rarely went outside. The Season flourished without him. The preparations for the king's coronation created extra excitement, but what had that to do with him?

A good week went by. Daphne, he was certain, had returned to her country house, wherever that was located. He'd never bothered to discover where she lived and now it was of no importance. No importance at all.

This evening he opened the door to the supper room and walked in to make certain all was ready for the night ahead. He'd taken to checking things two or three times—to help the days go by more quickly. This evening he stared at the pianoforte, idle since his sister had stopped performing. Having a performer in this room had been a good idea. Phillipa had drawn more people to the gaming house simply to hear her. Surely there was another songstress who could be hired to play?

He sat down at the bench and closed his eyes. As he had done once before, he picked out the notes of 'The Last Post'.

He turned away and rose from the bench. He strode from the room and wondered if there was any brandy left in the bottle he'd left in the drawing room.

Before he could climb the stairs, Cummings approached him. 'Captain Rhysdale to see you.' Rhys was always Captain to Cummings.

'Where?' Hugh asked.

'Hall,' Cummings said.

If Hugh had heard Rhys was back in town, he'd forgotten. He'd had notes from Ned and Phillipa as well as their mother, but he'd paid them little heed.

When he reached the hall, he saw Rhys was still wearing his hat and gloves.

Before Hugh could say anything, Cummings handed him his own hat and gloves.

'Come with me, Hugh,' Rhys ordered.

Hugh held up his hands. 'I cannot, Rhys. I need to get ready for tonight.'

'No, you do not,' Rhys said. 'MacEvoy and Cummings will see to it. We have been summoned by your mother and I am charged with making certain you answer her call this time.'

'I am not going.'

'Yes, you are.' Rhys placed the hat on Hugh's head. 'Do not make me fight you.'

Hugh grimaced. 'I'd rather like to fight someone.'

Rhys pulled him out the door. 'I can still beat you.'

'*I* can still beat *you*,' Hugh countered, but it wasn't worth the effort. He had to face his family eventually, so why not now?

At least Rhys did not ask any questions as they made the short walk to the Westleigh town house. Xavier must have told Rhys about Daphne and the note. Hugh suspected all the family knew the whole story.

Not the whole story. None of them knew he'd shared her bed. None of them knew she'd nursed him through blindness. He held those memories for himself alone.

When he and Rhys reached the town house and walked into his mother's drawing room, the rest of the family was there. His mother. The general. Ned and Adele, who was thickening around the waist. Xavier and Phillipa, looking sympathetic. Celia, alert and not about to miss a thing. His mother had obviously issued an edict that they were not to talk to him about Daphne, because they hardly talked to him at all. They asked him nothing he couldn't answer in one or two syllables.

Through dinner, he had more appetite for the wine than the food. The conversation washed over him, and a second after, he could not recall what was said. He watched his family as if they were exotic animals on display at the Tower, an entirely different species. He'd felt that way once before when they'd tried to convince him that Daphne was not to be trusted.

Of course, they'd been right.

Although how did the passionate nights he and Daphne shared fit into the picture they created of her? That was like a piece to an entirely different puzzle.

After dinner, they retired to the drawing room, where Hugh sat with a glass of brandy, which he refilled each time he emptied it.

Hugh's mother pulled out a letter. 'Adele, dear, I received a letter from your grandmother. I entirely forgot to tell you. Shall I read it?'

'Oh, please do!' Adele cried with an enthusiasm that made Hugh wince.

His mother lifted up the letter, making a big show of it. 'It begins "Dear Honoria"—I do not know why she becomes so familiar, using my given name like that. Imagine. "Dear Honoria."'

Hugh sat up straight. *Dear Honoria...*

Something he'd not considered before this moment struck him like a hammer to anvil.

'A salutation.' His voice came out louder than he'd intended and everyone gawked at him. He turned to Xavier. 'It did not have a salutation, did it?'

Xavier looked at him as if he'd gone mad. 'What did not have a salutation?'

His mother pursed her lips. 'Really, Hugh. You do not say a word all evening, then you interrupt with nonsense.'

'It is not nonsense.' He rose from the chair and walked over to where Xavier stood. 'The letter you received from Daphne. It did not have a salutation.'

Xavier looked puzzled, but said, 'I do not believe it did.'

Phillipa broke in. 'I know it did not have a salutation. I remember thinking it odd at the time, but what does that matter?'

Hugh felt as if a fog in his brain had suddenly cleared. 'It means the letter might not have been for Xavier.' He tapped his lips with his fingers. 'Tell me, did that note two years ago have a salutation?'

Xavier obviously knew precisely which note he meant—the one Daphne sent asking him to meet her in the supper room at the Masquerade Club. Xavier shook his head. 'I do not recall.'

'I remember,' Phillipa broke in. 'I remember every word of it. It began "My dear Xavier..."'

Hugh stabbed the air with his finger. 'So why would she not start this letter the same way?'

What a fool he'd been. He'd seen what he was led to expect. That she'd wanted a liaison with Xavier. But what if the letter had not been intended for Xavier at all?

'She wrote the letter to someone else, someone who cut off the salutation.' Hugh was sure of this. The pieces fit perfectly now.

'Hugh.' Ned threw up his arms. 'You have taken leave of your senses again. That woman was after Xavier.'

'I agree with Ned,' Adele piped up, as if Adele's opinion carried any weight with Hugh.

Ned went on. 'You know what the woman was like.'

'*Was* like,' Hugh emphasised. '*Was* like. She changed. She is not the woman she was then.'

'Utter nonsense!' his mother cried.

The general wisely remained silent.

Hugh turned back to Xavier, as if his mother had never spoken. 'It was a note she sent to someone else.'

Xavier looked unconvinced. 'It seems like such an elaborate hoax, then, for her to send someone the note, for them to cut out the salutation and then know to send it to me. Why would a person do such a thing?'

'I do not know why,' Hugh admitted. 'I only know they did it.'

Xavier shook his head again. 'The only sensible explanation is that it was sent by her.'

Rhys joined the conversation. 'Hugh's version is possible, though.'

'There is one way to find out,' Celia said. 'Go to her. Ask her. Hear what she has to say.'

Things he had never done.

'You are right, Celia,' Hugh admitted, though his spirits dropped. 'There is only one problem.'

'And that is?' Celia asked.

Hugh met her eyes. 'She is gone.'

Hugh rode the horse he'd purchased in Thurnfield, the horse Daphne had arranged for him to ride while there, the one he'd ridden when he made his solitary way back to London after Daphne left him. This time, however, Hugh rode towards her.

It had been an easy matter to find where she'd gone. He simply tracked down Everard, her man of business. To Hugh's surprise, finding Everard also solved the mystery of the note. Daphne had written the note to Everard's wife, who knew from her husband of Daphne's past infatuation with Xavier. Mrs Everard had cut off the salutation and sent the note to Xavier, hoping to make trouble for Daphne. Mrs Everard had done so out of jealousy, which made perfect sense to Hugh.

At least Everard did not seem to know of Hugh's relationship with Daphne, and Hugh did not enlighten him. He offered no explanation of why he needed to contact Daphne, but Everard told him her country house was in Vadley, near Basingstoke, a long day's ride from London.

It was late afternoon by the time Hugh reached the village. He stopped at the public room of the inn for some refreshment and to ask directions to the house.

The publican took a fancy to him and chatted a great deal about Lady Faville.

'She was not a favourite here when she first came, let me tell you,' the man said. 'I do not care how beautiful she was, she thought nothing of making her servants' lives difficult with her demands, but no more. Now they say she's made improvements in the cottages and she's raised all the wages.' He went on to detail her other good deeds and poured another tankard of ale for Hugh. 'Are you a friend of hers?'

'I am,' Hugh replied. He intended to be a faithful friend from now on.

Armed with directions and the publican's good wishes, Hugh rode to Daphne's house, reached its gates and made his way down its tree-lined private drive to the large brownstone Jacobean house that stood at its end. When he reached the front entrance, he dismounted and sounded the knocker.

Toller opened the door. 'Mr Westleigh!'

Hugh smiled. 'Toller. I am surprised, but pleased to see you here.'

Toller grinned. 'Mrs Asher—Lady Faville, I mean—offered me a position.'

Another good deed. 'Is she in?' he asked. 'Would you see if she will receive me?'

Toller shook his head. 'She is out visiting the tenants, I think. You could wait for her in the drawing room.'

He could not bear waiting. 'Might I catch up to her where she is?'

'Surprise her? That would be a treat, wouldn't it?' Toller directed him to where the tenants' cottages would be found.

Hugh was soon back on his horse and hopeful it would not take long to find her.

He spied her from a distance, at first unsure if it was indeed her. She wore a dress so simple it could have belonged to one of the tenants. It was covered by a white apron and she carried a large basket. Her face was shaded by a wide-brimmed straw hat. He approached slowly and saw the moment she recognised him.

He dismounted. 'Do you see what horse this is?'

'Yes.' She stroked the animal's head.

The soft light of late afternoon illuminated her face and tinged it with colour. The blue of her eyes rivalled the sky's hue. He did not think he'd ever seen her more beautiful.

Her expression, though, was guarded. 'Why did you come here, Hugh?'

He realised she'd had to ask him that question several times before when it seemed they had parted, but he'd come back to her. 'This time, to apologise.'

She started walking again. 'To apologise.'

He fell in step with her, leading his horse. 'For not listening to you. Not believing you. I was wrong.'

'It does not matter,' she said without emotion.

'What do you mean, it does not matter?' He was filled with emotion. Joy at seeing her. Regret for his behaviour. Fear that she would not forgive him.

'I mean, it does not change things.' She sounded sad.

'I have come back to you, Daphne.' Had he missed his chance? His heart pounded. 'To ask your forgiveness. I have held on to the past. Listened to my family. Let both blind me. But I see clearly now. I want to start over. I want to be with you.'

She stopped and looked up at him, her eyes filled with pain. 'I am reconciled with this. The past is always with me, always there to come between us.' She reached up as if to touch him, but withdrew her hand. 'We've tried, but the past always comes back. I cannot change what I've done. I can never change it and it will always come between us.'

An ache grew deep within him. 'But you have changed. Even the publican at the inn knows this.'

She started walking again. 'Yes, I have changed, and I do not wish to ever be the woman I was. But that woman is still part of me. What she did, I still must pay for.' She glanced at him. 'Your family will never forgive me, nor should they.'

'Blast it, Daphne. If your behaviour was unforgivable, then mine must be, too.' He walked a few steps before halting. 'I do not care about your past and I intend never to repeat mine.' She tried to walk away, but he took hold of her arm. 'I want to be with you. I asked you to marry me once and you said yes. I renew that proposal. Marry me and let us live together. Forget the rest of it.'

Daphne searched his face, his dear face. She looked into his eyes, gazing so intently at her, and rejoiced again that he could see, remembering how it had been for him to be bandaged and blind, groping tentatively with a cane.

She wanted to be with him more than anything, but they'd come this far before and everything had shattered. Could she bear it another time?

'What of your family, Hugh? Will they not disown you?' She had no family. How much worse might it be to have family and have them not acknowledge you?

He held her firmly by the shoulders. 'They may. Or they may change, as well. That is up to them. I only know that it feels like agony to have lost you, and I am not willing to choose my family over you.'

She glanced away. 'I do not know.'

He forced her to look at him again. 'I love you, Daphne. If you need time, I understand. But let me court you. I'll take rooms nearby. Give me a chance to prove to you that I've changed, that I believe in you. Completely.'

She gazed back at him. 'But I do not want to travel, Hugh. I want to stay here. There is so much to do here. With a little effort, I could really help the people who work for me. I could make their lives so much easier.'

He grinned. 'I think you are saying yes.' He picked her up and whirled her around. The horse caught wind of the excitement and whinnied. When he set her down again, he still held her. 'No travel.' He kissed her. 'We'll stay wherever you wish to be. I have found what I was searching for in you.'

He leaned down and placed his lips on hers.

She flung her arms around him and held him in the kiss. He wanted it never to end. What a marvel. What a miracle. She loved him.

And he loved her back will all his heart and soul.

Epilogue

They arranged for the banns to be read right away in the parish church in Vadley and St George's in Hanover Square. Daphne did not make Hugh take rooms nearby, but rather welcomed him into her home and her bed for a blissful wait until they could speak their vows before God and witnesses.

Hugh had written to his family as soon as he knew the exact day of their wedding ceremony. It pained him that none of them responded to the invitation, because he wanted to share his happiness with them. He refused to let them diminish his joy, though. He'd not been happier than during these four weeks and only expected his happiness to grow.

He could no longer see the cool, perfect beauty that Daphne had once been. Now he noticed only her warmth and kindness. It made her more beautiful in his eyes.

Their wedding day was becoming a bigger celebration than he thought it could ever be, because the whole village seemed to want to celebrate the day with her. It made him happy that others could see in her what he now saw.

He laughed aloud. He was no longer blind.

The wedding day arrived and he was banished from her bedchamber while she dressed in a new gown. He walked to the church with Mr Quigg, her estate manager, a man who had nothing but good things to say about her. Quigg had agreed to stand up with him at the wedding, for want of anyone else to do it. People had already gathered, and he greeted those he'd met before and was introduced to those he hadn't. He and Quigg entered the church and the vicar strode up to speak with them.

While they were speaking, the arrival of carriages sounded from outside and Hugh assumed Daphne had arrived. The doors from the vestibule opened, but it was not Daphne, nor anyone from the house.

Down the aisle strode Hugh's mother and the general, followed by Ned and Adele, Phillipa and Xavier, Rhys and Celia. His family. They had all come.

He bounded down to them, kissing his mother, Phillipa and the wives, hugging his brothers and shaking hands with Xavier. Moved more than he could ever remember, he stepped back. 'You've come.'

'Of course we've come,' his mother retorted. She did not sound precisely happy, but she was here. 'We are family.'

He quickly introduced them to the vicar, who made certain they were seated in an honoured place at the front.

Hugh turned to Quigg. 'Do you mind? I want my brothers to stand up with me, now that they are here.'

'I do not mind at all,' the man said, smiling.

'Will you, Ned? Rhys?' Hugh asked.

Ned's smile looked forced, but he nodded. 'I will, if you wish it.'

Rhys peered at Hugh. 'Are you certain you want me, as well?'

Hugh smiled. 'I want both my brothers.'

They were all sorted out when another carriage was heard, as well as cheering and clapping. A man stepped in. 'The bride has arrived.'

More of the villagers and Daphne's servants and workers came in and took seats. The organ started to play, and Hugh saw Phillipa take Xavier's arm and place her cheek against his shoulder. The doors opened again and Monette walked up the aisle to take her place by the altar.

What would his mother think of that? Hugh wondered. Daphne's lady's maid was to be her witness and Carter, now her butler, would give her away.

Then Daphne appeared in the doorway and Hugh forgot about anything but her.

She wore a simple blue dress with tiers of blue lace at the hem and sleeves and a matching hat and veil covering her face. The dress, which might not compare with one made by a mantua maker in Mayfair, had been lovingly designed and sewn by Monette. It allowed Daphne's happiness and beauty to shine through.

She stopped when she saw Ned and Rhys standing beside Hugh. He smiled and gestured to where his mother and the others were sitting.

Daphne broke away from Carter and walked over to them, grasping their hands. 'I am honoured and grateful you have come,' she said. She paused in front of Xavier and Phillipa. 'I—I have no words.'

Phillipa, looking pale, accepted her hand. 'Best wishes.'

Xavier nodded stiffly.

Daphne glanced towards Hugh.

She returned to Carter, but before coming to Hugh's side at the altar, she greeted Ned and Rhys, thanking them, as well.

Finally, she came to Hugh, and the vicar began, 'Dearly beloved…'

Later, at the hastily organised wedding breakfast with the family, Daphne sat next to Hugh, too happy to eat. Somewhere in the house, governesses and nannies were seeing that Rhys and Phillipa's children were fed and entertained. Outside, the villagers were celebrating with food and wine. The family conversed together as if this was a family dinner. Or at least how Daphne imagined a meal with a large family might be.

She reached for Hugh's hand under the table.

He grasped it and squeezed. 'What do you think, Daphne?'

She gazed up towards the ceiling. 'I think somewhere in heaven there is an abbess who is smiling down at me and saying, "Did I not tell you so?"'

He looked puzzled, but leaned forwards and kissed her anyway.

Daphne laughed for the joy of it.

* * * * *

A sneaky peek at next month...

HISTORICAL

AWAKEN THE ROMANCE OF THE PAST...

My wish list for next month's titles...

In stores from 1st August 2014:

☐ Beguiled by Her Betrayer – Louise Allen

☐ The Rake's Ruined Lady – Mary Brendan

☐ The Viscount's Frozen Heart – Elizabeth Beacon

☐ Mary and the Marquis – Janice Preston

☐ Templar Knight, Forbidden Bride – Lynna Banning

☐ Salvation in the Rancher's Arms – Kelly Boyce

Available at WHSmith, Tesco, Asda, Eason, Amazon and Apple

Just can't wait?

0714/04

Special Offers

Every month we put together collections and longer reads written by your favourite authors.

Here are some of next month's highlights— and don't miss our fabulous discount online!

On sale 18th July   On sale 18th July   On sale 18th July

Aa a war blazes across Europe, three couples find a love
that is powerful enough to overcome all the odds.
Travel with the characters on their journey of
passion and drama during World War I.

**Three wonderful books in one from top
historical author Marguerite Kaye.**

Get your copy today at:
www.millsandboon.co.uk